JUDGE DREDD
CURSED EARTH ASYLUM

D1638194

CURSED EARTH ASYLUM

David Bishop

Virgin

First published in 1993 by
Virgin Books
an imprint of Virgin Publishing Ltd
332 Ladbroke Grove
London W10 5AH

Typeset by CentraCet Limited, Cambridge

Printed and bound in Great Britain by
Cox & Wyman Ltd, Reading, Berkshire

ISBN 0 352 32893 2

This story owes a lot to what has gone before in the pages of *2000 AD* and *Judge Dredd The Megazine*. Without the following stories and their creators, this novel would have been almost impossible to write:

Thanks, then, to Alan Grant and David Roach, for creating Hope in **Engram**.

To Pat Mills, Mike McMahon, Brian Bolland, John Wagner and many others for **The Cursed Earth**.

To Gordon Rennie and Frank Quitely for **The Missionary Man**, Si Spencer and Dean Ormston for **Harke & Burr**, and Garth Ennis and Nick Percival for **Sleeze 'n' Ryder** – sweet cameos are made of these.

This one is for my family and friends in
New Zealand –
I'll be home for Christmas, guys!

And for Paddy Ryan,
who first taught me to think.

And for Alison (again!),
she knows why.

PROLOGUE I

Twenty Years Ago

Tonight, I will die. But the evil I helped to create lives on. We've tried to kill it, Grud knows we've tried, but the creature, the monster we thought we could control is instead controlling us. The escape I seek is the only way out now. I only pray that the others will have the strength to finish this task, this nightmare.

It began with an idea, not new by any means, but one previously denied by morals and ethics. The events of the so-called 'Atomic War' proved morality to be in short supply among those who wield real power around the world. Millions of lives were ruthlessly exchanged for unstable victories and personal vanities. But worse was to follow, with germ warfare and fall-out creating monsters among the population. I'm sure that's where abberations of nature like the gila-munja came from – nothing so brutal or vicious could be the product of nature itself.

So the Judges took control, sentencing the President of the United States of America to a hundred years in suspended animation. No more wars, they promised, no more using the people as dispensable pawns in the global game. But the Judges lied!

(It's a pity no one else will read these words, for

1

they could shatter many an illusion about the true nature of the regime that guards our city. But my words must die with me, lest the mistakes of my work are repeated again.)

The idea was simple. The Judges had been using cloning to improve the genetic stock of their number, using DNA samples from the greatest among them to create replicas when the original died. But the process was erratic, little advanced since it was successfully pioneered thirty years before. Just because a Judge was formed from the same genetic material as a great lawkeeper of the past, it did not guarantee the replica would behave as his or her predecessor had done.

A classic example of this problem is the case of Judges Rico and Joe Dredd, clone brothers. Both were created from the DNA traces of the great Judge Fargo, the 'Father of Justice'. While Joe Dredd grew to become Mega-City One's finest Judge, his clone brother became a corrupt Judge, eventually being turned in by Joe and sentenced to twenty years on the penal colony on Titan for Judges turned bad. A classic example of the triumph of environment over origins, I suppose.

So a select group of Med-Judges from the cloning division were brought together to investigate some of these problems. Could the clones be improved, made better than the great Judges upon which they were based? Could the qualities for a great lawkeeper be instilled in a clone while it was still an embryo, with the human traits which might conflict with the clone's ability – such as doubt, fear, even compassion or guilt – removed? Quite simply, the group was told to play at being Grud – and I was the group leader.

We had great success at first and became proud to

call ourselves the eugenics division. I shudder now at our arrogance. Recently I read a book about a man who carried out experiments not dissimilar to some of our work, more than 150 years ago. His name was Doctor Mengele, and he came to be despised by all right-thinking people around the world. Shall I be so remembered?

We isolated several flaws in the cloning process, making it more efficient and accurate in its recreation of the past's great Judges. But could we improve on the past, not just eliminating flaws and physical deficiencies? What about designing the mind, the psyche, the soul?

The team began a new series of experiments, aimed at creating or enhancing Psi talents in clone embryos. If we could create great Psis, with the discipline and physical gifts of great lawkeepers of the past, the Judges would be invincible, the ultimate crime deterrent!

Of course, there were objections within the Justice Department once it was discovered what we were doing. In particular, I remember the vociferous objections of Psi-Judge Barbara Jong, who said only evil could come from our tamperings with nature.

Officially, we were rapped over the knuckles and the programme discontinued. Unofficially, secret new testing laboratories were built for us and every encouragement given. This was the way forward for the Justice Department, my superior told me. But if anything should go wrong . . . well, the threat was obvious, but I was oblivious. Too wrapped up in our work to realise the dangers.

Finally, after months of experimentation with different techniques on research animals, we were ready to begin using what we had learned on human embryos. Of course, we used clone embryos – my fellow Med-Judges and I were quite happy to run our tests on clones; after all, if something went wrong, you just flushed the result and knocked off another batch of clones. They didn't seem like real human beings, more like tri-D copies, duplicates. At that stage, we would never have dreamed of experimenting on natural human embryos – somehow that seemed just a little too close to home.

I supervised the first embryo experiments myself, keen to be involved at every stage of the process. Everything seemed to go well initially, but when the altered enbryo was placed into the gestation accelerator . . . it was horrible. We had created a monster, an abomination of humanity. But even then, the warped foetus hardly seemed human, just another laboratory experiment gone wrong. We tried again, and again the product of our labours had to be aborted. Every time the 'enhanced' embryo (as we liked to call it) was accelerated, something went wrong. It was as if the foetus would be driven instantly insane by the improvements we had made as soon as it achieved any level of sentience, this insanity warping its physical form as it grew.

Month after month of failures left us feeling depressed and argumentative, as if the disorder of the artificial offspring was spreading amongst us. Finally, Med-Judge Diana Thinnes came up with the answer – instead of gestating the enhanced embryos artificially, do it naturally in the womb. This was the answer to our birthing problem, but it also proved to be a major turning point in our experiments.

Before, the whole process had seemed artificial – the use of the clone embryos and the artificial gestation accelerator had put the whole issue of ethics and morality at arm's length. Now we were planning to use real women to carry our creations to full term. It brought home the reality of what we were trying to do. Several members resigned from the team, but I rallied the others to my side. This was the future of science, perhaps the future of humanity itself, I told them. Could we turn our backs on the future?

So the experiments continued, though on a smaller scale. The selection of suitable birthing mothers was difficult. Who should become the vessels for our embryos? Obviously we could not call for volunteers, because of the secret nature of the work. Instead we selected candidates from among the mentally defective and criminals without relatives, society's rejects, people that Mega-City One would never miss if something should go wrong. And it did.

Twelve women were chosen, implanted with the enhanced embryos and then monitored through the long months of their pregnancies. Some of the mentally defective mothers were at first distressed by what was happening to their bodies, but most of them grew to enjoy their situation, the care and attention they were receiving. Six of the mothers were taken from the city's toughest iso-blocks, all convicted killers or worse. They responded less well to the situation, being bitter about the placing of foreign foetuses in their bodies. Understandable, especially considering what followed.

The first woman died after ten weeks, smashing her head into a bloody pulp trying to numb the foetus's screaming inside her head. Two more went in similar circumstances within days. Another bled to death after trying to force the foetus from her body by inducing a miscarriage. A fifth died in her sleep for no visible reason – the autopsy showed that her foetus had two heads, two brains joined together.

After these initial problems we increased monitoring and two Psi-Judges were co-opted to the team to keep a mental watch on the mothers and foetuses. Everything settled down for several months and we began to congratulate ourselves again – could this be the breakthrough?

Finally came the time for our enhanced experiments to be born. This proved to be messy and traumatic, with one of the children stillborn (Thinnes almost convinced me the baby had killed itself by wrapping the umbilical cord around its neck, but I dismissed her claims as overly emotional) and all the others causing severe problems. Each foetus was removed by Caesarean section and three of the mothers died during the operation. Among the others, two were driven irretrievably insane.

The last to give birth was Doris 'Driller Killer' Davison, believed to be responsible for the death of thirty-two citizens. The Judges had never been able to prove her guilt on these charges, but had put together enough evidence to keep her off the streets for life on lesser offences. As the screaming offspring was removed from her womb, she spat at me, a mixture of blood and phlegm.

'May you rot in hell for what you've done. That little bastard will be nothing but evil – what a legacy you've created for the future!' were her final words. She swallowed her own tongue before she could speak again. For a moment I almost thought I saw a smile flicker on the face of her offspring, but put it down to overwork and exhaustion on my part.

The children were monstrosities, aberrations of the flesh. Their limbs were twisted, bodies distorted at grotesque angles, heads bulging and misshapen. They were all quite horrible to look at, except for one – Doris Davison's child. It had a mesmerising, almost charismatic quality about its face. Perhaps this came from the eyes of emerald green, but we soon learned it came from within. This child's body was perfect, pristine and utterly hairless. The only oddity was the face, which seemed to twist sideways at the nose. The strangest part of all was the mouth – the child didn't have one! Instead, the area between its nose and chin was just blank, taut skin stretched over bone.

We immediately began monitoring the children for signs of Psi abilities, to match the enhancements we had given them. Our Psi-Judges probed their minds, searching for special abilities or abnormalities. The mothers were forgotten, the survivors sent back to their places of origin. It was the children that excited us, and how excited we were!

Among the six surviving children, none showed any immediate evidence of our enhancements, beyond the disfiguring of their bodies. But soon evidence was abundant – mysterious fires in the laboratories proved to be the first flashes of pyrokenesis from one of the children. Another started propelling objects around the room, while a third communed with the feelings of anyone within ten feet, sometimes forcing them to take part in its childish pleasures. After a fire almost burned the face off one of the team members and two more were forced to defecate against their wills, we began damping down the children's abilities with special treatments from the Med-Judges assigned to Psi

Division. All the children exhibited a range of talents under controlled experiments; except Doris Davison's mouthless boy. We had decided not to use surgery to give him a mouth, and instead fed him intraveneously.

On the children's fifth birthday, we hosted a demonstration of their abilities for the top brass from the Council of Five who had been threatening to withdraw our funding. Permission to begin a new series of enhancements had been withheld since the second series of tests had produced no viable foetuses. Eight mothers had died during pregnancy, while the other four had had emergency abortions.

Most of the councillors seemed happy with the Psi abilities achieved but some expressed horror at the physical deformities. Funding was approved to continue monitoring the children but no more enhancements were to be authorised. I went ahead secretly with more experiments, but we could not replicate our success with the first group of children.

On their sixth birthday, the mouthless boy finally exhibited his first Psi ability – telepathy. He began to speak into our minds, only one word, but the same word, over and over again: 'soon'. It quickly became his name. We didn't realise it was a warning.

On his seventh birthday, Soon showed us the true nature of his abilities, of his power. It was nearly a year ago, but it seems like only yesterday, like only moments ago. I can still see it all happening before me, more clearly than I see my hand writing these words.

Thinnes, myself and the four other remaining members of the team held a miniature celebration for the children, who were taken off their drugs, at least partially, so they could enjoy the occasion.

Soon seemed especially alert, watching all around him with an awareness that seemed almost disquieting in a child of his age. But Soon had always been a leader among the children despite his wordlessness.

Thinnes was just cutting the children slices of mock-choc cake when a Psi Judge came into the room, with a message for me from the Council of Five. They had reviewed our work again and were withdrawing funding. Everything was to be closed down. I was furious, began shouting at the messenger. Suddenly blood began to gush against my face and neck.

I turned to see that Thinnes had sliced herself across the wrist with the laser-blade. Blood jetted into the air, warm and pungent, almost sickly sweet. Thinnes put the knife up to her own throat, her head shaking in disbelief the whole time, her voice crying out denial, and cut her own throat. I was bathed in the gushing claret of life as around me chaos took hold.

The Psi Judge exploded in a ball of flame, charring the ceiling panels and doorway. I could feel my eyebrows and eyelashes singeing as the heat flushed my face. Suddenly the air was alive with flying objects; chairs, tables, wall panels all turned into a deadly maelstrom. I flung myself to the floor and looked up to see if the children were all right.

In the centre of it all sat Soon, his eyes grinning with all the evil in the world. The other team members were struck down one by one, objects hurtling into their cowering bodies. Slowly, a gentle stream of blood began pooling on the floor beside me. When the sobbing of the others had died out, snuffed out like their lives, the hail of objects clattered to the floor and lay still.

I reached into my pocket and discovered a miracle – a hypo-syringe full of Psi-tranq, unbroken and full. I looked up to find Soon standing over me, as I desperately strained to mask my thoughts.

'Goodbye, Doctor Swale,' spoke the boy into my brain. 'Thank you for creating me, but now I must make a new world where more like me can be created.'

'Never!' I shouted with all my will and plunged the hypo-syringe through the child's neck, injecting the Psi-tranq directly into his bloodstream. In moments the boy's eyes clouded over and he slumped to the ground. It was only then I realised both my legs were broken, every bone in them smashed to pieces by the evil boy's will.

At the official inquiry afterwards, I was blamed for much of what had happened and happily accepted that blame. But the fools did not believe my testimony that a seven-year-old boy was responsible for the carnage committed by Soon within the space of sixty seconds. They had found some evidence of low-level Psi abilities when the boy was deep-scanned but nothing more. Of course, they rejected my plea for the child to be executed immediately. They don't realise he's just fooling them, even now.

It's been a year since the inquiry now and tonight, I shall die. I discovered today what has happened to Soon. He has been sent here, to Erebus, the Justice Department's secret asylum in the centre of the Cursed Earth. I am an inmate of Erebus, sent here rather than the penal colony of Titan because of my 'lunatic' ravings, as they were described at the end of the inquiry. Officially, the department does not even admit the asylum exists, using it as a dumping ground for the undesirable and the dangerous and the unexplainable. I fit in perfectly here with the glass towers and the radiation shield dome and the madmen.

Today I discovered that Soon and the other children are all being held inside Erebus. All on Psi-tranq, I'm sure, just in case I was telling the truth. But entrusting that monster to a squad of robo-docs and Judge-warders is like lighting the fuse on a stick of hi-ex. Sooner or later it's going to blow up in your face.

Soon is the most evil, dangerous and twisted creature on the face of this planet. I should know. I created him.

This is my last will and testament, my suicide note, my final report. Being of sound mind and body, I can safely say that death can only be a relief after spending the past twelve months in this hell-hole, reliving those terrible moments over and over again. Death will be a release, it's got to be – I couldn't stand another day like this.

So why do I feel that the evil I have unleashed will come back to haunt me, even when I am beyond the grave?

(Extracts from a handwritten note found in the 'Erebus' file; note believed to date circa 2095 AD; author thought to be Doctor Joseph Swale, born 2050.)

PROLOGUE II

Two Years Ago

Three old women, stinking of decay and despair, stood chanting on the mountainside.

'The child. Tell us about the child.'

'A sign . . . the child . . . give us a sign!'

They were mutants, their warped faces and skulls marking them out as genetic victims of the nuclear conflict two generations before. Cloaked in darkness, the old crones pleaded to the sky, their voices cracking with weariness.

Suddenly the air around them began to crackle with electricity of the mind and slowly, faintly, an image began to form from the air. An infant, hovering above the ground, almost beatific in aspect.

'The child . . . then it is true!' cried out one of the old women. 'But how will we find her?'

A bolt of lightning shot down from the sky, scattering the harridans and scorching the ground. Looking up, the eldsters could see a storm brewing in the sky away to the east. They glanced around at each other, then spoke with one mind.

'We follow the storm!'

They turned and stumped away, into the heart of the storm. Towards the east, towards the towering walls surrounding the city. Towards Mega-City One . . .

* * *

Cassandra Anderson was not impressed.

'She did what?'

'Escaped from Iso-Block 17 and stole a cube transportation pod. Evaded the gun emplacements along the West Wall and headed out into the Cursed Earth,' explained the head of Psi Division, Judge Shenker. He ran a gauntlet-clad hand over his bald pate, as if trying to smooth away the embarrassment this assignment was obviously causing him. 'But the pod only had a limited fuel supply, so she can't have got more than fifty klicks outside the wall.'

'Terrif. And why am I going after her?' asked Anderson huffily. She was one of Mega-City One's top Psi Judges and she knew it – rounding up escaped prisoners was not her normal line of work.

'Verona Rom is a grade-C pyrokinetic, a fire-starter. She's too dangerous to be allowed to roam free around that radioactive wasteland, especially as she's also a triple murderer,' explained Shenker.

This one just gets better and better, Anderson thought to herself ruefully, but didn't comment further. Psi Judges were given extra leeway for the personal quirks and eccentricities that came with being a psychic, but that leeway could only be pushed so far.

'Here's a termination warrant for Rom. Bring her back or execute her,' finished Shenker, watching Anderson carefully for any reaction.

'Uh-huh,' replied Cassandra nonchalantly, scooped up the warrant and strode from the office. Once she had gone, another Judge in Psi Division uniform emerged from the shadows at the end of Shenker's office.

'How did she respond to the termination warrant?' he asked, stepping close to Shenker's desk.

'Hard to tell. She masks her true feelings well, always has from me,' said the head of Psi Division. 'But after what happened on that assignment to East-Meg, and being temporarily crippled during the Necropolis incident, well . . .'

'I suggest we monitor her closely. Anderson's a good Psi, we need to make sure she's made a full recovery. We don't need another incident like Corey.'

Anderson gunned the throttle on her Lawmaster motorcycle and roared out through Gate 13 into the wasteland known as the Cursed Earth. As she accelerated away towards the mountains in the distance, she could see the gates closing automatically behind her in a rear-vision mirror. The clang as the huge slabs of metal slammed together had a chilling finality.

After the atomic wars of the twenty-first century human civilisation had retreated into massive conurbations, the mega-cities. Most of the United States of America was wiped out during the wars, with three mega-cities coalescing from the ruins of the old structure. Down the eastern seaboard stood Mega-City One; on the opposite side of the nation, its counterpart, Mega-City Two. In the south, the Lone Star state of Texas renamed itself Texas City, refusing to bow to pressure to become Mega-City Three.

Between all three lay the Cursed Earth, an aptly named wasteland, home to mutants, monsters, exiles, lawbreakers and scattered settlements of norms, trying to scratch out an existence from the radioactive desert.

Not the most hospitable of environments, mused

Psi Judge Anderson, as she approached a range of low mountains. A glance at her bike computer revealed she was reaching the edges of the cube pod's estimated fuel capacity for possible distance travelled. Above her storm clouds were gathered, black and pendulous in the sky. Tongues of lightning lashed down into the hillsides ahead of her. What'd I ever do to deserve having my name top of the Cursed Earth roster, Anderson wondered for the fifth time that day.

Round the next rockfall she found the wreckage of the cube pod, crashed into a hillside. Leaving her helmet on the Lawmaster, Cassandra moved closer to see if her quarry was trapped inside the pod, her Lawgiver already drawn.

A quick search determined that Verona Rom had survived the crash, her footsteps still evident in the damp yellow dirt around the base of the pod, leading away up into the hills.

'Heading for high ground,' said Anderson quietly, not even realising she was speaking aloud. Psis spent so much time with their thoughts, the border between thinking and speaking aloud was frequently blurred. 'Hope to Grud I catch her before the storm breaks.'

At that moment stinging rain began to pour down from the sky, battering the Psi Judge. Before leaving the city she had taken a standard dose of anti-rad, giving her up to forty-eight hours exposure to Cursed Earth levels of ambient radiation without permanent ill-effects. But a coating of acid rain, no matter how gentle, was never welcome.

'Thanks for nothing, ' muttered Anderson grimly, looking heavenwards in supplication.

At that moment Verona Rom launched herself at

her hunter, clawing at Cassandra's face with nails, pummelling the Psi Judge with blow after blow. The pair collapsed to the ground and began to roll over and over, each desperately trying to gain the upper hand in their conflict. Rom managed to throw Anderson clear and the Psi Judge found herself tumbled over the edge of a precipice, hands clawing at thin air . . .

Then some roots came into her hand and she grasped them, holding on for dear life. Below her a twenty-foot drop onto solid rock loomed. Anderson turned back to the roots protruding from the side of the cliff and began to pull herself upwards, hand over hand. A rush of heat from above made her look up.

Verona Rom stood on the edge of the cliff, glaring down at Anderson, heat burning from her eyes towards the roots the Psi Judge was clutching to.

'One way or another, honey – you're gonna drop dead!' gloated the murderous fugitive.

Anderson released one hand and reached it down to her left boot, pulling a viciously sharp knife from a holster embedded in the side of the boot. With just a moment to aim, the Psi Judge flung the knife upwards, embedding it deep in Verona Rom's chest. The killer fell backwards clutching at her wound, but she was already dead. In moments she lay still forever.

The flames on the roots did not die out with their creator. Seconds later they burnt through and Anderson tumbled to the stony ground below, her skull cracking against the rocks. Then there was only blackness.

* * *

16

According to the official report Psi Judge Cassandra Anderson submitted on her return to Mega-City One, she regained consciousness about three hours later, the time elapsed calculated from her bike's log recordings. She verified Rom was dead, bound the corpse to her Lawmaster and returned directly to the city. Anderson certified this was a true and accurate record of what took place during these hours.

She didn't realise she was lying.

As Anderson lay unconscious, the thunderstorm continued to rage above her. Slowly, in small groups walking in single file, black-garbed mutants began to gather in a nearby canyon, many passing the Psi Judge's body to reach the meeting place. A massive, ominous rumble of thunder brought Anderson from her stupor to find a steady stream of figures walking past her. She cried out, but was ignored by the bulbous-headed mutants as they moved on.

'What the drokk?' Cassandra stammered, wondering if concussion was the true source of these visions. Unable to get a response from the gathering mutants, she clambered back up onto the ledge from which she had recently fallen. The body of Verona Rom lay still, slowly stiffening.

Looks like another customer for Resyk, thought Anderson, before circling around to get a better view of events in the nearby canyon. Eventually she found a vantage point, looking down into the stone amphitheatre. She couldn't help gasping at what she saw.

Thousands of mutants had gathered in the canyon, all crowding around a vintage transporter, plainly disabled by its lack of wheels or hover-conversion. At one end of the vehicle a black curtain had been drawn across the interior and two old crones stood before it, as if guarding the contents.

What in the name of Grud was all this, wondered Anderson, a freak-show convention or something more sinister. Could the muties be preparing for another of their periodic assaults on the walls of Mega-City One, which forbade their presence within on grounds of genetic impurity. Before the Psi Judge could ponder any further, a murmur from the crowd grew into a groundswell and finally a clamour, a cacophony of voices calling out: 'The child! The child!'

The voices fell silent as a third old woman emerged from the curtains and thrust aloft an infant, as if brandishing a mighty weapon or a religious artefact. Suddenly Anderson was overwhelmed with the power of the child's mind, surging outwards like waves, coursing through Cassandra's mind like clear fresh water over an old wound.

Grud on a greenie!, thought the Psi Judge, as the cleansing power of the infant touched every corner of her mind, of her soul. She found herself smiling, like the smile of an innocent child, filled with a joy she had not felt for years, not since she was how old? She couldn't remember and didn't care. For a moment, all her cares and pain were soothed away . . .

Elsewhere in the Cursed Earth, someone was screaming, blood flowing down their face in a deluge. The victim was tearing at her own flesh, trying to pull her own face apart, anything, anything to push the voices from her head. Maybe if she could be reborn, clean and glistening, no skin, just flesh, the voices would go away . . .

In the next cell, the twenty-six-year-old opened his eyes, a twinkle playing about their edges. If he'd had a mouth, the smile would have spread from ear to ear.

Soon was experimenting, enjoying his newly redis-covered abilities to twist the minds of those around him. Over the past five years, his self-awareness had slowly returned, like someone who has emerged from a thousand-mile tunnel into the light: blinding, dazzling, almost impossible to absorb. But slowly the genius with the twisted face had come to a realisation – he was becoming immune to Psi-tranq.

By his own estimates, Soon had been held captive here for nearly eighteen years – a lifetime in some backward places. The robo-docs had kept him pass-ive with massive daily doses of the mind-damping Psi-tranq. But slowly, ever so gradually, his system had built up an immunity to its numbing effects until the dosage was only effective for a few hours after being administered. It couldn't be long before it had no discernible effect on him at all.

As his awareness had slowly returned, so had Soon's memories. The special dormitories, the experimental sessions with the Med-Judges, the look on that bitch's face as he forced her to take her own life, the fear in the old fool Swale's eyes as Soon had prepared to deliver the killing blow. Then, nothing –

– until becoming slowly aware again, captive in this glasshouse of horrors. Whoever decided to construct an asylum of glasseen deserved a medal for sheer vindictiveness, Soon had decided. It made testing his rediscovered talents on neighbouring inmates so much more gratifying. But the young mutant had been careful not to overplay his hand, lest the robo-docs realise the resistance he was building up against their drugs.

As a child Soon had only possessed limited Psi abilities, able to twist the minds of others only if they were in the same room as him. Even though his mind was still dulled by the effects of Psi-tranq, he could feel the potential for much more nagging inside him, like an inner energy just waiting for an outlet. Sometimes he almost expected lightning to pour from his fingertips, such were the pent-up frustrations of his incarceration and nearly two decades of lost life.

By Soon's own estimate, he would be totally resistant to Psi-tranq within three years, perhaps sooner. Having waited so long for his revenge on his captors, he was willing to wait until then to get his own back. The Judges would regret not killing him when they'd had the chance . . .

In the meantime, the twisted genius stretched out his mind, probing the intellects of the other inmates to learn as much about the asylum as possible. Careful observation of the robo-docs' routines was another valuable source of information. When it came time for vengeance, Soon wanted to know everything about his surroundings. He would use that information to make his captors suffer.

Erebus was constructed in 2072, to house the shell-shocked troops recovering from the so-called 'Second American Civil War'. More than one hundred thousand Judges died in the Cursed Earth fighting the presidential guard of President Robert L. Booth, the man who had started the Atomic Wars which had devastated much of America, Europe and the Soviet republics two years before. The death toll was appalling, but the pain and misery etched into the minds of the survivors were more terrible than any soldier had encountered before. The chemical warfare used in the conflict left thousands of soldiers' minds in tatters; walking, soulless husks.

So Erebus was built, a series of glasseen cylindrical towers, reaching up into the orange-tinged sky like fingers. Each tower was joined to the others by glass bridges. Seen from above, they formed a massive latticework of intersected circles. Over it all, a transparent dome kept out the massive radiation which soaked the region. The asylum was built on the site where the biggest bomb of the Atomic Wars had fallen. The architects reasoned that the area's incredibly high levels of radiation, the worst in all of the Cursed Earth, would dissuade unwelcome visitors. Later, when the asylum's purpose changed, it also became a way of making sure no one could escape.

Within ten years of its construction, the original patients were nearly all dead and the human staff were replaced with robo-docs as Erebus's designation was altered. Instead of being a place of caring and curing, it became a dumping gound for the unwanted, the unloved, the 'mistakes'. Judges who went crazy from the strain of patrolling the streets of Mega-City One, citizens stricken with rare and highly contagious disorders like Jigsaw Disease and Biter's Disease and other oddities were sent there. Then, when the experiments into improving cloning and the first attempts at eugenics began, the failures (at least, those who lived) were sent to Erebus.

The last new inmates to arrive at Erebus were Doctor Swale's 'enhanced embryo' children in 2095. The incident in which several Med-Judges on his team died in mysterious circumstances led to the final shut-down of the enhancement programme of experiments. Official enquiries could determine little truth about what really happened that day, and after months of being shuttled from one holding block to another, the children were finally sent to Erebus. The last words written on the transfer request haunted Soon when he discovered them, plucked from the memory circuits of an adminstrative droid in the asylum: 'To remain there for the rest of their natural lives. No release ever to be sanctioned, by order of the Chief Judge.'

The fates of Erebus and its inmates were sealed by a diplomatic incident later that year, when a squad of Texas City Judges blundered into the area and discovered the asylum. Hostilities broke out between Mega-City One and Texas City, and in the war of words it was agreed the asylum would be closed down. The last human security guards were removed, all systems were turned over to automatic control and robo-docs put in full charge. Erebus was purged from Justice Department files and the asylum was slowly forgotten.

The Judges of Mega-City One shall rue the day they forgot about me, pledged Soon to himself, and turned his attention back to the unfortunate woman in the next cell. A single vein pulsed across Soon's bald head as he concentrated on forcing her into involuntary facial disfigurement. If he couldn't be beautiful, then neither would anyone else.

* * *

Across the Cursed Earth, the old woman held aloft the infant and a pulse of power surged outwards from the child's mind.

Suddenly Soon's warped soul was exploding, as if a grenade had detonated deep within him, tearing great shards of darkness away from inside. For a moment, light and love and kindness flooded in through the gaps, and the boy/man felt a happiness he had never known before.

Then all the hatred of the world flooded back into him like water into a hole. I am a black hole and all hate flows into me, realised Soon. I am despair!

But what was this power that could pierce even his black heart, could force its joy and hope into the cancerous crevices of his psyche? Was there a new mind, like his but in reverse, a power for good, a shedder of light against his darkness? Soon's mind raced like a boy running, crazy and headlong, without care or comfort.

Then came the pain again. All his life, Soon had felt pain. The 'enhancements' had been a disaster. In improving Soon's mind, Swale had created a monster. But he had also built a progressive degeneracy into the embryo's DNA, so that from birth, Soon's body had felt an urge to reinvent itself. For no reason bones would break or warp, knitting themselves into new, more terrifying shapes.

And through it all was the pain, from a body that was always breaking itself to mend itself. For a moment, when Soon felt the first thought of the infant, the pain was gone. For the first time, Soon could move without agony. It was as if gravity had been removed for a moment.

When the pain returned, the misery was all the

more crushing. As it poured back into him again Soon wished more than anything he had a mouth through which to scream.

After Cassandra Anderson returned to Mega-City One from her trip to the Cursed Earth, her world, her mind began falling apart. She was haunted by images of a shadowy figure and found herself lashing out at other Judges. It was as if her very psyche were attacking her.

The vivid hallucinations continued, becoming more and more violent. An intensive Psi-probe failed to locate the root of the trauma, but it did reveal deep-seated psychological blocks. The psychosis deepened and Anderson put two Judges into med-bays before she could be subdued. Finally, she was cubed, a danger to herself and everyone else.

(Extract from psychfile on Psi Judge Cassandra Anderson, by Chief Psi Judge Shenker, dated December, 2113.)

Deep within her own psyche, Anderson found the cause of her psychosis. As a child, she had been abused by her father. Her first conscious psi act was to lash at the 'monster' that was hurting her, killing her father. Instead of counselling, the young girl was inducted into the Psi Academy, all memories about her father hidden behind deep psychological blocks placed in her mind by the Justice Department. Anderson confronted the truth and came to terms with it. Then she returned to the Cursed Earth.

She could feel the child's power like a beacon when she was still five miles away. When her presence was detected, the beacons shut off like a naked flame

24

doused in the night, but Anderson continued onwards. As she reached the hills where she had witnessed the mutants' ritual, the Psi Judge abandoned her Lawmaster, leaving her weapons, utility belt and gauntlets behind her.

Soon she was surrounded by mutants, clothed in black robes, faces serious and angry.

'I mean you no harm. I only want to see the child,' explained Cassandra. Slowly she was escorted to the three old crones, hidden high away in the hills in a series of rooms carved from the rocks and stone.

'The She-Judge! You remembered – but how?'

Anderson explained it all, how the memory block placed on her by the child had unleashed other, far more horrifying fragments of her past from their captivity deep within her psyche. 'Can I see her?'

Reluctantly, grudgingly, the old women parted to reveal the infant behind them. 'She is the pure child, born to the unclean. She shows us what might be,' they chimed. 'We call her Hope.'

Cassandra reached out and touched the child and knew a peace and happiness unfelt since she herself was an infant, before the monster came to hurt her, before her innocence was stolen by a man thinking of nothing but himself.

Images of how the world could be flooded her mind – clear skies, fresh air, crystal water, green life. Love. Respect. A little dignity . . .

Psi Judge Anderson pulled away, feeling purified, almost cleansed of all the unhappiness in her life. Then she remembered the city she had to return to, the life of killing and hostility and pain which waited, just fifty miles away. She looked at the old women, her face serious again, almost pleading.

'If you stay here, they'll find you. Her power's too

strong. One day they'll come and take her – or kill her.'

'What should we do?'

'Go deeper into the Cursed Earth. Care for her, bring her up right, teach her how to control her power. Above all, never let her forget how important a gift like hers is,' said Cassandra, then remembered the final words her best friend, Empath Corey, had written on her suicide note. The Psi Judge repeated them to the trio of mutant guardians: 'People with beautiful gifts should never do ugly things.'

It took several hours, but the mutants were ready to move on. Anderson waved goodbye as they slowly trudged away into the west, heading deeper into the Cursed Earth, bearing their precious cargo.

Cassandra waited until the caravan had disappeared over the horizon before returning to the dusty soil of the Cursed Earth plains to recover her equipment and weapons. With a final glance over her shoulder she gunned the engine of her Lawmaster and zoomed away towards Mega-City One.

Even in his semi-drugged state, Soon could feel the power moving nearer, like a flaming torch approaching through darkness. It was getting close, very close now, almost within reach of the grasping tendrils of his mind.

Suddenly the power shut out. Soon probed and searched, his head flicking backwards and forwards and sideways, trying to get a fix on its source again. But it was shielded from him now, he was sure of it. Still, it was close, very close.

One day, when he was free of these shackles of drugs and metal, he would search for that power again, send out emissaries, speaking words of welcome and friendship but carrying daggers of hatred within them. He would have that power as his own, twist it like his own twisted visage. That day was coming, coming soon . . .

Part One: Two weeks ago

CHAPTER ONE

'Judge Dredd – you're a dead man!'

The juve flung himself in the path of Dredd's Lawmaster just in time to have his left foot run over by the front tyre. Dredd braked and swung his bike through a hundred and eighty degrees, turning to face his attacker. The hapless teen bounced up and down on one leg, clutching his crushed foot and howling in pain.

'Dredd to Control.'

In the Halls of Justice, headquarters for Mega-City One's Justice Department, a despatcher picked up the Street Judge's transmission and responded: 'Receiving you.'

'Gonna need a catch-wagon on Sked 77. Got another of these Killer Kamikaze clowns on my case.'

'Roj that – need any back-up?'

'Hmph! Out,' responded Dredd sourly.

The Killer Kamikaze Klutz Kult (or KKKK, as they preferred to be known) had sprung up a week before, following the publication of an illegal vid-slug, *Suicide For Fun And Pleasure*. Mega-City One's population of four hundred million people was almost universally unemployed and bored. As a result, new fads and crazes would sweep through the city like wildfire, until a newer and even more bizarre craze replaced it. Mostly the fads were harmless but occasionally the Judges had to step in and take action if events got out of hand.

A suicide craze was nothing new. The vid-slug that created the latest wave of stupidity was a sequel to the hugely popular *Rough Guide To Suicide* which had caused similar mayhem. But the KKKK had taken their lead from one moment in the vid-slug, which suggested that instead of just killing yourself, it was much hipper to take as many other people with you as possible.

The late leader and founder of the KKKK, Dumb Dave Klutzovitch, decided to take this one step further. To become a member of the KKKK, you had to kill yourself in a particularly stupid way, and kill a Judge at the same time. Of course, this built in a degree of obsolescence to the cult, as anyone who met the membership criteria met their death at the same time. Dumb Dave Klutzovitch was the first prospect to achieve full membership, when he managed to crush himself and a Judge from the accounts division with a sixty-foot high replica of a cash register.

Since then only eight people had achieved full membership, but more than six thousand had tried their luck. Fortunately for the Justice Department, the criteria for becoming a successful KKKK member almost precluded success and most attempts were easily avoided. Of the 6,204 people to attempt membership status, more than half had succeeded in only killing themselves, and the rest were serving long sentences in the iso-cubes on charges of attempted murder and gross stupidity in a built-up area.

Dredd looked at the latest KKKK membership candidate. After a moment's contemplation, the Judge stood down his bike's weapons systems and dismounted. He started walking towards the hopping juve, beckoning for the teen to attack him.

'Come on, boy, let's see how stupid you really are!'

With unemployment endemic, entertainment was the most popular way to pass the hours in Mega-City One. The most popular medium of entertainment was tri-D, three-dimensional television, with an estimated number of channels approaching a hundred thousand, legal and pirate stations included.

Virtually all channels broadcasted round the clock, requiring millions of hours of programming to fill their schedules. One of the most popular ways to achieve this was to use teams of roving reporters with automated hovering camera-globes, which followed the reporters and broadcast events live to air. Among the rising stars of this challenging new art-form was Whiti Vitaliev, a Maori/Russian comedian who had emigrated to Mega-City One from East-Meg Two three years before. His quirky outlook and quick wits made him a natural at commenting on day-to-day life in the world's mightiest mega-city.

When Whiti stumbled upon the conflict between Dredd and the KKKK prospect, he immediately recognised it as a ratings winner. Sadly, he did not recognise his own danger until it was too late to avoid it.

* * *

'My Grud, this is amazing stuff! Split screen close-up on me to the left, the fight on the right – do it!' hissed the roving reporter. Whiti couldn't believe his luck: the first televised cult suicide attempt, and he was getting it! Gathering himself, Vitaliev turned to the camera.

'Today, viewers, we have an exclusive. Here, live and exclusive on tri-23, we present a prospect for the Killer Kamikaze Klutz Kult trying to earn his membership by killing himself and Judge Dredd – reputedly the toughest Judge in all of Mega-City One – in a particularly stupid fashion! Don't switch channels, this is not an exercise – this is the real thing!'

The camera zoomed in as Dredd loomed over the footsore juve, who had now slumped to the skedway, nursing his crushed toes. Fortunately he was sitting on a Judges-only sidesked, or else the unfortunate juve would have been long spread out in one long stain by passing traffic. Still, there was plenty of time in which to die that day.

Dredd noted the presence of the tri-D camera before speaking to the juve again. 'See that camera? The whole city's watching – so try your luck, punk!'

Back at Control, the monitor Judges had picked up the transmission from tri-D 23. A supervising Judge was called over.

'What does Dredd think he's doing?' asked the monitor who had first locked into the signal.

'Making an example out of the creep!' replied the supervisor, a smile of satisfaction spreading over her face. She liked to see justice in action.

'But what if he loses?' said the monitor anxiously.

'Hmph!' was the only reply.

* * *

'Watch this, boy,' grunted Dredd, as he removed his belt, gauntlets, Lawgiver and boot knife and locked them into the ammunition and stores pod on the back of his Lawmaster. 'Just you and me now – man to man. Give me your best shot, boy.'

'Stop calling me "boy" – I'm a KKKK!' replied the juve, becoming progressively angrier.

'Not yet – not till you kill me, you ain't,' goaded Dredd.

This was too much for the juve, who flung himself bodily at Dredd. The lean, sinewy Judge neatly side-stepped the charging teen who stumbled and fell just short of flinging himself off the skedway, five hundred feet up from ground level. Another charge, another side-step and the juve went sprawling again.

'Stand still so I can kill you!' bawled the juve.

'Can't just kill me, boy – gotta do it stupidly,' Dredd reminded the youngster.

'Oh yeah,' mumbled the youth absent-mindedly and plucked a cigar from his pocket, along with a flare. 'This cigar is packed with enough concentrated hi-ex to kill anyone within a hundred metres, Dredd. Get ready to die!' The juve lit the flare, placing the cigar in his mouth.

'Smoking is illegal except in an authorised smoka-torium,' grimaced Dredd and kicked the cigar out of the juve's mouth, along with several of his teeth. Another boot to the solar plexus sent the KKKK prospect stumbling backwards into the roving reporter, gasping for air.

'Excuse me, sir, a moment of your time?' asked Whiti of the winded teen. 'What's your name and what block do you come from?'

'Buh-Billy Boyle and – ah – I come from – huh –

Roger Clinton Block,' panted the juve through a mouthful of blood and enamel chippings.

'This your first murder/suicide attempt?' enquired Whiti, beaming for the camera.

'Yeh-yes.'

'Well, good luck and thanks for being such a great guest on our show!' smarmed Whiti as he hoisted the inept Billy back onto his feet and propelled him towards Judge Dredd.

'Back for more, huh?' questioned Dredd rhetorically as he slammed a fist into Billy's nose, crushing the bones into tiny fragments. 'You punks don't know when to stop, do you?' Billy swayed on the spot and Dredd followed up with an uppercut to the jaw and a knee-thrust squarely into the juve's crotch.

Billy creased over on the ground and rolled around, cursing silently.

'Attempted Judge murder – twenty years,' Dredd passed sentence, accompanying the charges with a solid boot into the body of his opponent.

'Attempted suicide – five years.' One hand was ground into the skedway by a heavy boot.

'Bleeding on a Judge – two months.' Billy was hoisted up off the ground and cuffed cross the face.

'Citizen using a Judges-only skedway – one year.' Two broken ribs.

'Jaywalking – ten months.' Dislocated knee.

'Being stupid in a built-up area – one year.' Broken jaw, and Billy was out cold in a heap by the side of the skedway. 'Total sentence – twenty-eight years. No remission. Case dismissed.' Dredd strode back to his Lawmaster and reopened the storage pod. 'Control, you can send in that catch-wagon now – perp's just about ready for you.'

* * *

Back at Control, the monitor Judge was aghast.

'That was brutal – totally unnecessary!' he stammered.

'No wonder they put you on monitor duty, if you're going to be so soft. Dredd made an example of the perp – you can guarantee KKKK suicide/ murder attempts on Judges drop by at least fifty per cent after that little display. More, once the tri-D stations repeat it on their news bulletins,' answered the supervisor with grim satisfaction.

'Well, looks like it's not over yet, ma'am,' said the monitor Judge, pointing at the screen. 'The tri-D presenter could be next!'

Whiti Vitaliev could barely contain his glee at such a scoop. He only made two mistakes. The first was going to Dredd immediately afterwards for a follow-up interview.

'Judge Dredd – a stunning and some might say shocking display of physical prowess and law-keeping there,' gushed the roving reporter. 'How do you feel?'

Dredd glared at Vitaliev for a moment, then returned to pulling on his gauntlets and strapping his utility belt around his waist.

'Any comment to make about the wave of attacks on the Judges by KKKK wannabees?' probed the journalist hopefully.

Dredd finished checking that his Lawgiver was fully loaded then turned and stared straight into the hovering camera. 'Anybody wants to take on a Judge, they can come and take on me – all-comers welcome! Now get out of my face.' Dredd started to mount his Lawmaster but Vitaliev wouldn't take drokk off for an answer. That was his second mistake.

'What about accusations of police brutality against – ' His question was cut short by a fist in the face and the sound of Dredd's handcuffs clicking into place around the reporter's wrists.

'You were warned. Three months for interfering with a Judge,' growled Dredd.

'Bud I – '

'Six now. Any more for any more?'

Vitaliev turned to his camera for the last time. 'This ib Whiti Bitalieb, signib off.'

During a cadet's training to become a Judge, they had to face many tests and assessments. One of the most dangerous and feared by all cadets was the arduous assessment under action conditions in the Cursed Earth. This was known amongst all cadets as the Hotdog Run. The future of every cadet depended upon how they acquitted themselves during this test.

Cadets had to take the Hotdog Run as part of their twelfth-year assessments. If they failed, they were instantly expelled from the Academy of Law, without right of appeal. Failure can also be fatal – sometimes cadets were failed and required to find their own way back to Mega-City One without aid or accompaniment. Many never finished the treacherous journey back to the city wall. Other cadets were adjudged borderline cases. For these, it was within the authority of the presiding Judge for such cadets to be suspended until such time as their tutors deemed them ready to retake the assessment.

A Hotdog Run was supervised by a senior Street Judge, with another Judge as observer, in case the leader missed a significant error by one of the cadets. Each squad was made up of seven cadets, selected randomly from the year's intake to avoid any bias. Cadets were assessed on both their individual performances and on their ability to function together as a team.

For each Hotdog Run the squad was assigned a task to complete in the Cursed Earth, usually within a forty-eight hour period. These ranged from routine patrols of outlying norm settlements, or hunting fugitives from Mega-City One, through to taking on squads of marauding mutant monsters.

Once the task had been completed, the senior Judge gave his assessment on each candidate's abilities. Frequently some cadets didn't survive long enough to hear the supervising Judge's opinion – the Cursed Earth was a dangerous place, especially for twelfth-year cadets with little or no real combat experience.

Hotdog Run assessments had only recently been resumed, after the harrowing zombie warfare nicknamed Judgement Day. It had all begun while Judge Dredd was leading a Hotdog Run deep into the Cursed Earth to investigate a loss of communication with a mining station. The cadets quickly discovered the reason behind the breakdown – the mining station had been overrun by zombies! Within minutes the squad was surrounded by more than a million zombies, the walking dead raised from their graves by the power of an alien superfiend, Sabbat the Necromagus.

The fighting was desperate and hopeless, but at the moment when all seemed lost, the zombies turned and began marching on Mega-City One, forgetting the handful of survivors. Dredd led the cadets back to the city through an army of the undead, getting nearly everyone back alive.

Even after the zombie war had raged its course, it was not safe to send Hotdog Run squads back out into the radioactive wasteland for months afterwards. The events of Judgement Day exposed a seam of magic and evil in the land best left buried, and hover-wagons patrolling the Cursed Earth had reported many strange sightings.

Now, months later, Hotdog Runs were about to be resumed. And it was Judge Dredd who had been selected to lead out the first patrol of cadets into the radioactive wasteland that lurked outside the battered walls of Mega-City One.

'Judge Dredd! Always a pleasure to see you back here at the Academy!' beamed Judge-tutor Marcus, head of assessments at the Academy of Law.

'Hmph. This lot better be an improvement on Brisco,' grunted the lean, laconic lawkeeper.

Marcus looked down at the ground, embarrassed. Harold Brisco had been hand-picked by Marcus as the Roll of Honour cadet from his intake. Brisco was assigned to Dredd for rookie assessment but proved to be a sleeper, planted in the Academy of Law as part of an elaborate revenge scheme against Dredd and the city. Only a last-ditch appeal to the rookie's years of training by Dredd had prevented Brisco from handing over the fate of the city to the vindictive genius Roland Savage. Afterwards Brisco had disappeared, seemingly gone rogue, with all the training and expertise of a top-rank cadet – and all his weapons. Marcus could sense that Dredd would never let him forget his mistake. The Judge-tutor looked up again, levelling his gaze at Dredd.

'You know as well as I do, Dredd, cadets are chosen randomly for Hotdog Runs. These seven candidates for assessment range from the adequate to the excellent.' Dredd said nothing, and Marcus continued with his briefing.

'Coster, Patrick. A natural leader, probably one of the best cadets in the current intake.' As Marcus spoke, a three-dimensional hologram image of Coster's head appeared from the holovision unit built into his desk. Coster was black, with a scar running the length of his young face down the left side. 'Perhaps too rash, too willing to take risks. Doesn't wait for others to catch up.

'Agnew, Brian.' On the holovid, Coster's image was replaced with a projection of a baby-faced Caucasian youth, with blond, short-cropped hair. 'Young for his intake and physically weaker than the others in this squad. But has shown resilience beyond our expectations.

'Singh, Nita.' Now the face of a young Indian woman appeared. 'Her family emigrated here ten years ago. A late induction to the Academy but one of the best of her year.

'Archer, Julian.' Red-haired and red-faced, a little overweight judging by the jowls forming around the chin. 'In danger of failing, has only just scraped through so far, mostly thanks to his friendship with Singh.

'Jenks, Kate.' Curly brown hair and a freckled face, but no smile seemed possible on these grim female features. 'Headstrong and argumentative – a danger to herself and those around her. Yet one of our most effective cadets. Fearless, to the detriment of those around her.

'Zender, Timothy.' A sensitive, worried face was

the last to appear on the holovid unit, with eyes of deepest blue. 'Transferred across from the Psi Academy recently. Was inducted there with high Psi readings as a five year old, but these seemed to have been dulled rather than enhanced by puberty – unusual in that respect. Again, a borderline case, not up to the rough and tumble of Street Judging, I suspect.'

Marcus looked at Dredd, searching for signs of reaction or opinion in that stony face, but finding none visible. What goes on inside that head, the Judge-tutor found himself wondering. Was Dredd a soulless machine or just as human as the next person, simply better trained at hiding what went on inside him? But the chin remained resolute, the glare hard and unyielding – Marcus would find no answers looking at the face of Judge Dredd. After another moment's consideration, the object of his ponderings spoke.

'They ready?'

'The cadets have been notified. They're waiting in their dormitories for the order to mobilise,' said Marcus. 'Who's your assistant for the run?'

'Chung.'

'A good Judge – I trained her myself,' said Marcus, allowing a little self-satisfaction to creep into his voice.

'We'll see. Mobilise the candidates – I'll meet them in the briefing room in ten.' Dredd stood up and marched from Marcus's office, his stride regular and even, his uniform gleaming in the harsh lighting.

Marcus activated the Academy's communications system and ordered the seven cadets to the briefing room in the basement. 'Good luck,' he offered as his final words to the cadets, switching off the microphone. 'You'll need it,' he muttered to himself darkly.

Nita was polishing the eagle-shaped badge on her uniform for the sixth time in the last hour when the call finally came through. Archer jogged past her bed in the unisex dormitory, puffing slightly.

'Didn't you hear? We've got five minutes to report to the basement briefing room!' he panted.

'Jovus Drokk!' exclaimed Nita. Grabbing her white cadet's helmet, she shoved Archer in front of her and they started running towards the nearest turbo-lift. Two minutes later they walked into the briefing room to find Judge Dredd already standing at the front of the chamber. Next to him were a Tek-Judge, a Judge with some Sino-Cit blood in her, and a three-dimensional projection unit. But the excited cadet only had eyes for Dredd, or Old Stony Face as he was universally known among the cadet ranks. Stories about Dredd, his brutality to cadets under assessment and his exploits were almost mythic in status, but this was the first time she had seen him in the flesh. Somehow, she had expected him to be taller.

Suppressing a grin, she pushed Archer into one of the long, hard benches facing the front of the briefing room and dropped into the space beside him, which proved to be a tight squeeze.

'Archer! Shove over! Boy, you've got to lose some weight, or you'll never graduate,' she whispered out of the corner of her mouth.

'Don't say that, you'll make me hungry again!' moaned the other cadet plaintively.

The three Judges at the front were still talking amongst themselves and Nita took the opportunity to study them more closely. She ignored the Tek-Judge – she was probably only here to explain technical details of their mission. Grud, she hoped they would have something more exciting to do than retrieving a satellite or mapping out some new anomaly from the ground! Cadet Singh wanted action and lots of it. The other two Judges would be the guides to that action.

The Judge of Sino-Cit extraction interested Nita. Relations between the American mega-cities and the Sino-Cits had been strained for years, and the nuking of Sino-City One during Judgement Day had not assisted matters. It had been one of five mega-cities around the world nuked to prevent Sabbat turning them into zombie factories after their primary defences were overrun. The decision to nuke had not been easy, according to lectures Nita had attended at the Academy. It took a council representing nearly all the world's Judges more than a day to agree that the procedure was absolutely necessary. Representatives from Sino-Cit had been conspicuous by their absence from the summit, declining all assistance. The nuking of their main city had not endeared the world council of Judges to the Sino-Cits.

Nita had heard rumours it was Dredd himself who had suggested nuking the five cities, a drastic but necessary move. So what was a Sino-Cit-descended Judge doing in Mega-City One, she wondered. She could only assume that the Judge was, like herself, an immigrant or the offspring of immigrants. Nita's family had come to Mega-City One a decade before from the impoverished Indo City, hoping to give their children a better future. Nita was accepted as a late inductee to the Academy of Law, making her a rarity among her intake of cadets. She had been picked on at first for being strange, foreign, a latecomer to the intake. But she had worked hard, sometimes twice as hard as the others, it had seemed to Nita, to prove herself. Now she was near the top of her intake, she was sure of it. A good result from the Hotdog Run would ensure that placing when their final ranks were assessed.

Next to the Chinese Judge stood Dredd, lean of body and hard of face. After the initial shock of seeing him for the first time, Nita began to appreciate Dredd's obvious physical qualities. Not an ounce of fat hung on his body, just lean muscle, nothing showy or extravagant, simply a body honed to the perfection of fitness for the tasks it faced. And that chin! Tales about Dredd's jaw were the stuff of legend, whispered late at night from cadet to cadet in the dormitories. Firm, unyielding, tougher than the most reinforced leathereen, harder than rockcrete. No wonder he's called Old Stony Face, smiled Nita. She wiped the grin from her face as Dredd turned to call the cadets to order.

'Attention!' he barked and the silence was immediate. 'Tek-Judge Suzanne Mooney will explain our mission. Listen carefully – what you hear could make the difference between life and death.' Dredd nodded to the Tek-Judge, who activated the tri-D projection unit. Light surged up from its mouth and the briefing-room lights dimmed gradually in response. A three-dimensional map showed the Cursed Earth, Mega-City One and a path leading to the centre of the radioactive desert. In the centre was a small, black spot.

'Your mission is to investigate a "black spot" that has appeared in the Cursed Earth. Two Justice

43

Department aircraft have crashed in the area of the black spot, one on a routine surveillance patrol, the second while investigating the loss of the first. Rather than risk any more aircraft, we're sending you in to find the cause of this anomaly.'

'Yeah, why risk valuable aircraft when you can just send us?' quipped Nita to Archer, who could barely contain his giggles. Dredd's head spun round to search out the source of the interruption.

'Who spoke?' he demanded.

Nita sheepishly put up an arm.

'Share your wisdom with us, cadet.'

'I, er, was just wondering why we hadn't used satellites to investigate the black spot,' replied Nita, thinking fast.

'Good question – Mooney?'

'The black spot is at the very centre of the Cursed Earth, an area of intense residual radioactivity,' explained the Tek-Judge. 'Our most sophisticated scanning satellites are unable to give us a clear picture of what's going on down there.'

'That's where we come in,' grunted Dredd. Now the other Judge spoke up.

'Any other information you can give us?' she asked, her voice surprisingly soft for a Street Judge.

'Just that you'll need radiation cloaks for much of the journey and you'll be issued with some extra sensing equipment for your Lawmasters. It should take you two days to reach the edge of the black spot,' concluded Mooney, deactivating the tri-D unit. The room's lighting increased again in response, the cadets blinking to adjust. Dredd surveyed their young faces before speaking.

'This will be the first Hotdog Run for more than a year, so things'll be pretty lawless out there. Be ready. We go through the city gates at dawn, but you'll need to be ready at least two hours earlier. That's all – dismissed!'

The cadets filed out, a long, sleepless night ahead of them before rising early to collect their equipment and prepare for the most important days of their lives.

In the briefing room, Dredd and Chung remained behind to hear more details about the case from Mooney. Once she was sure the cadets were gone, the Tek-Judge recalibrated her tri-D projector. Instead of a simple location guide to the black spot, it now showed the face of a frightened woman, frozen in a single moment.

'Okay, now tell us what you wouldn't tell them,' said Dredd. Both he and Chung moved closer to the projection unit for a better view.

'This is a recording of the final moments of the second flight to crash in the black spot. They managed to beam this transmission out through the radiation haze, how we don't know. This is the pilot, Judge Tina Wilding,' explained Mooney before activating the recording.

'We've been . . . pulled into . . . some kind of . . . vortex – ' shouted Wilding, her voice barely audible for white noise and the sound of her ship tearing itself apart around her. 'Can't pull . . . away . . . cannnnnnnnnnnnnnnn – '

Mooney halted the projection abruptly.

'After that she starts to speak in some kind of gibberish, almost like another language. But it's nothing our analysts can pin-point and it defeated our translator programs too.' The Tek-Judge's face was grim. 'The only words we could discern in the rest of the transmission were "towers", "bones,

bones" and "the windmills". We've got no idea what they mean.'

'Terrif,' commented Dredd dryly. 'Anything else?'

'That's it.' Mooney began packing the tri-D unit away as Dredd and Chung filed from the room. A few moments later another uniformed figure slipped into the room. It stayed in the shadows at one end of the chamber and spoke in quiet, hushed tones.

'So?'

Mooney turned around, quite startled. After a moment she recognised the other person. 'Oh – it's you! Drokk, I wish you wouldn't sneak around like that!'

'We must be covert if we are to succeed. Did they believe you?' enquired the figure.

'Seemed to – no obvious suspicions,' replied the Tek-Judge.

'Good,' cooed the figure. A Lawgiver was drawn, a special silencer clamped around its barrel. 'Goodbye.'

'Hey, what are you – '

Mooney's words and her life were cut short by a bullet as it spat from the gun and thudded into her forehead. The Tek-Judge's brains left a crimson mess on the wall behind her.

'Sorry, no witnesses allowed,' murmured the figure as it slipped away into the shadows.

Nita rose at oh-five-hundred hours the next morning. After hasty ablutions she just had time to wolf down some rations before going to the Armoury for her weapons. Spare rounds of ammunition were slotted into the pouches on the utility belt around her waist, along with stumm gas and frag grenades. A gleaming boot knife slotted into its sheath moulded into the side of her right boot – Nita was left-handed.

Finally, the Lawgiver. A brand new hand-gun was given to her, carefully placed in her palm. Within seconds her palmprint and heat signature were implanted into the weapon's tiny memory chip. Now if anyone else tried to fire her Lawgiver it would explode in their face. The palmprint signature was actually taken while Nita was wearing her kevlar-reinforced gauntlets, something which had always perplexed her during lectures about the weapons of a Judge at the Academy.

'How can the gun read or recognise my palmprint through my gauntlet?' she asked the Judge-armourer dealing with the cadets.

'Simple,' replied the supervisor, opening out the palm of her gauntlet-clad hand to demonstrate. 'This gauze fabric over your palm isn't just there to help you grip things better. It's also designed to easily transmit your heat signature through itself – a bit like electricity through wiring.'

Nita shook her head, still not understanding. It's a good thing I'm not planning to become a Tek-Judge, she told herself ruefully.

Last of all she gathered with the other cadets at the motor pool to be issued with their Lawmaster bikes. During the course of their training to date, they had spent many hours on the seat of a Lawmaster. The ability to handle the complex machinery of the motorcycle was an essential part of becoming a successful Street Judge. Nita had excelled at this part of her training, unlike her friend Julian. Archer had already wrecked two practice Lawmasters in training sessions on the live ammunition courses, where cadets had to dodge explosions, taking evasive action or dying in the attempt.

At the motor pool Archer was having problems again. His Lawmaster's on-board computer was dysfunctional and kept trying to go onto auto without authorisation.

'What'd you do, Archer – sit on the computer screen by mistake?' taunted Cadet Kate Jenks.

'Shut up,' growled Nita, trying to keep the anger from her voice. She had never liked Jenks, who was certainly one of the most fearless among the cadets, but also arrogant and headstrong. Jenks did not suffer fools gladly and she made a point of picking on Archer, or so it seemed to Nita.

'Why should I? It's probably true,' laughed Jenks.

Nita started to dismount from her Lawmaster. Archer tried to put a restraining hand out but she brushed it away. 'It's okay, Nita.'

'No, it isn't!' She strode up to Jenks, who had also dismounted. 'I'm warning you now, Jenks – leave Archer alone or else.'

'Or else what? Little chubby Julian too fat to fight his own battles? What you gonna do about it – punjab!' Jenks was still laughing at her own joke when Nita's fist smashed into her left eye, the first of a dozen blows pummelling her to the ground.

'You stupid, drokkin' bigot, I'm gonna smash that grin right off your – '

'What in Grud's name is going on here?' demanded a booming voice. The cadets fell back into ranks beside their bikes, just Jenks left on the ground, a trickle of blood running from the side of her mouth. Nita stood over her, triumphant for a moment before realising how much trouble she was in.

Judge Emma Chung strode into the motor pool, helmet under one arm and anger all over her face. She came to a halt beside the cowed Jenks, who was picking herself up from the ground. 'Well?'

'It was Singh, ma'am, she started it. She began punching me for no apparent reason. I tried to defend myself but – '

'She's lying!' cried out Nita. 'She started it. She called me a – '

'I heard what she called you. Racism may almost be a thing of the past in Mega-City One, but still the bigots remain,' said Chung sadly, shaking her head. 'I should knock both of your heads together and have you expelled – the pair of you!'

Nita and Jenks stared at the floor intensely, not daring to look up.

'But then we'd lose two potentially excellent Judges for a stupid incident. Singh, consider yourself on your first and last warning – what Jenks did gave you no right to attack her. Hitting another Judge is unforgivable; we should be fighting crime, not each other.'

Jenks allowed herself a quiet smile of triumph but it didn't last long.

'And you can stop smirking Jenks, you're on your last warning too!'

'But she – '

'Don't lie to me again, you'll only make things worse. Now wipe the blood away and get on your bikes, all of you. Judge Dredd'll be here any moment.'

The sun was just rising over the Black Atlantic to the east of Mega-City One as the six cadets and two Judges rode their bikes to the gates in the wall on the other side of the city. The sturdy metal gates had been reinforced following the relentless attacks upon it by the zombie army during Judgement Day. Now massive reinforcing slabs of rockcrete were built into the superstructure of each of the double doors. It took nearly a minute to have the gates opened, even using the massive hydraulic system created for this purpose.

Finally, the gates were open. As dawn's early light touched the West Wall for the first time that day, Judge Dredd led the six-strong squad of cadets out into the Cursed Earth, with Judge Chung bringing up the rear of the column. Behind them the gates moved shut again, with much whining of hydraulic pumps and a final, ominous boom.

In the middle of the column, Nita glanced back at the gates in her wing mirrors. She looked across at Archer, who was glancing nervously around at the wasted landscape. 'Now the fun really begins,' said Nita cheerfully. Archer just gulped.

A crackle and then Judge Chung's voice was in Nita's ears: 'Drop back a metre, Singh. Maintain your formation.'

'Yes, ma'am!' replied the cadet and quickly followed the instructions. She settled in her seat and concentrated on the road – they had a long, hard ride ahead. It would take at least two days to reach the edge of the black spot, riding non-stop. Two days was a long time in the Cursed Earth.

CHAPTER TWO

'It's not right, Mister 'arke, it's just not right.'

'What are you yabbering about now, my semi-simian associate?' inquired an imperious voice.

'Stealing from these old Atomic War graves, I just don't thinks it right,' said the heavy-set individual carrying a selection of digging implements.

'It's not stealing, my fine fellow! Think of it as, er, liberating these valuable relics from their resting places, to make them available again to an eagerly awaiting marketplace,' replied the taller of the two, conspicuously weighed down with nothing more than a battered top hat and a few pretensions of intelligentsia.

'Well, if you says so, Mister 'arke,' grumbled his companion.

'I do, Mister Burr, I most certainly do. Why, it would be a crime to neglect the loot – er, important artefacts – any longer. And with business being a bit slow . . .'

Harke and Burr were antique dealers. Antique and Curious read the legend on their storefront. Harke had always regretted not checking Burr's spelling abilities before he let his partner loose on a spot of signwriting. Based in the Cursed Earth township of Dunedin, the pair frequently roamed the surrounding countryside in search of valuables to sell to gullible customers. Rarely was any of their

51

stock actually worth a fraction of the asking price, but that didn't trouble Harke's conscience, if he actually possessed one. '*Caveat emptor*,' he frequently announced with all due authority whenever Burr questioned the wisdom of their activities. But then, it was always Burr who had to sort out aggrieved customers with a bit of 'the ruff stuff', as he called it.

But now their business had fallen on hard times, with the people of Dunedin wise to their schemes and sidelines in the dodgy and the dubious. Tourists were few and far between and most passing trade in the Cursed Earth was more trouble than it was worth, and frequently fatal for somebody. So now they were reduced to the odd spot of grave-robbing to replenish their worthless stock.

It had taken more than three hours for their horse and cart to reach the military graveyard on the outskirts of Dunedin, thanks to the recalcitrant nature of their mutant nag, Hercules. If the antagonistic animal knew the legends about his namesake's prodigious strength, he certainly didn't attempt to emulate him.

Now the dubious duo were traversing the last few yards on foot through the overgrown perimeters of the cemetery. During the horrors of the civil war, individual funeral ceremonies had been abandoned in favour of mass graves to save time and resources. Each mass grave was marked by a single slab of rockcrete, just three words burnt into the headstone by laserblade: LEST WE FORGET.

'Yes, this'll do nicely,' announced Harke grandly, his breath issuing forth as steam in the night atmosphere. 'Start here, Mister Burr.'

'Couldn't we at least come back in the daytime,

Mister 'arke, when I could sees what I's doing? This place ain't 'alf spooky at night . . .' Burr's eyes darted around nervously beneath the brim of his bowler hat.

'Nonsense, nonsense. Just start digging,' urged Harke, drawing his greatcoat closer around his bony shoulders. 'There's nothing to harm us here – it's as quiet as the – '

'Urrrrrrrrrrrrrrr.'

'Please, Mister Burr! I know the natural social graces don't come easily to you, but try to keep your bodily noises to yourself, if you can,' admonished Harke.

Burr stood frozen, a pickaxe poised comically in mid-swing, motionless in his hands. 'It wasn't me, Mister 'arke.'

'Well it certainly wasn't me, if that's what you're suggesting,' said Harke haughtily, adjusting his precious pair of pince-nez eyeglasses.

'Well, if it wasn't me, and it wasn't you – 'oo was it?' asked Burr fearfully.

'Ahh! It was – err – ' Before Harke had time to formulate an answer, a terrible noise like the sound of human flesh tearing away from the bone rent the air. And with it came a stench of death and decay, pungent and putrid, attacking the nostrils and filling up the senses.

'Urrrrrrrrrrrrrrrrr!'

Suddenly something burst from the ground between their feet, a human hand but reduced to bones, a few ligaments and strips of flesh and skin hanging loosely from it. The hand turned left and right, almost as if it were trying to sniff out its quarry.

'Oh my Grud – ' began Harke.

Then there were dozens of hands punching out of

53

the musky soil, reaching upwards, grasping, searching. And the air was filled with the moans of the dead, summoned to awareness again, brought back for some terrible purpose.

Harke and Burr looked at each other for a moment. Neither were possessed of any Psi abilities they were aware of – Harke doubted his associate was possessed of many mental abilities at all – but at that moment they shared a single, all-encompassing thought.

'RUN!' they screamed at each other and took to their heels, digging implements still falling to the ground as the pair vaulted the cemetery wall and sped towards town, only just stopping to collect Hercules and their cart.

Hundreds of miles to the east, the last rays of sunlight were disappearing over the horizon when Judge Dredd called the squad to a halt for the night. He turned around to face the six cadets, speaking to the one nearest.

'What's your name, Cadet?'

'Coster, sir.'

'Where do you recommend we pitch camp for the night, Coster? How about in that valley we just passed through?'

'Negative, sir. The area had no protective cover – we'd be sitting ducks in event of any attack,' replied Coster. 'I recommend we camp on the top of that rocky bluff. Any attackers would be visible long before they could get to us and it would be an easy position to defend.'

'Good. You're assigned to establish camp and position the bikes.'

'Yes, sir!'

While Coster organised the other cadets into teams of two to take care of the necessary tasks for establishing a secure base for the night, Dredd called Chung aside.

'What do you think of them so far?'

Chung thought carefully before answering, aware that Dredd would be submitting a report on how she had handled herself, just as they both would do for each of the cadets.

'There's some tension between Jenks and Singh which could cause problems later on. Other than that, they seem like a typical cross-section of abilities and flaws. Hard to judge until we get into a combat situation.'

'I agree. Tomorrow we're going into gila-munja territory. That should shake them up a bit.'

'You think they're up to that?' asked Chung, trying to keep the concern out of her voice.

'We're here to test them, not coddle them, Chung!'

'Yes, sir.'

Dredd dismounted from his Lawmaster and strode up the hillside to examine the campsite. Within seconds he was bawling out Agnew and Zender for failing to activate their bike computers' motion-sensors.

'Not everything is visible to the human eye out here, as you'll find out tomorrow. What's the use in having special sensing equipment built into your bikes if you don't use it?' he demanded angrily.

'Yes, sir. Err, no, sir!' stammered the nervous cadets.

Chung just smiled to herself, remembering her own Hotdog Run, five years before. Dredd had been the supervising Judge then too, and she had been terrified of him, cowering every time she felt his steely gaze sweep over her. But somehow, by some miracle she'd survived the ordeal and gone on to graduate in the top ten per cent of her cadet intake. The Judge noticed one of the cadets standing on guard duty, looking nervous and afraid, and started walking towards them.

Nita was not terrified, she was not afraid. She had drilled and trained for moments like this most of her young life. But that didn't stop her jumping when a hand suddenly fell on her shoulder-pad.

'Jovus Drokking – '

'Careful what you say, cadet, your next words could be your last in uniform.'

Nita turned round to find Judge Chung standing behind her, a wry smile playing around her lips. 'Sorry, ma'am, I wasn't expecting anything to approach me from behind.'

'At least you're honest, unlike your friend Jenks.'

'Hah! She's no friend of mine!' exclaimed Nita. She could feel the blood flushing her face with anger again, just at the memory of the other cadet's taunts.

'She really got at you, didn't she?' probed Chung, her eyes searching Nita's face for a response.

'Yes, ma'am, she did. I've gone through a lot to get into the Academy and I've had to work twice as hard as the others to be accepted because I'm an immigrant, an outsider – '

'And you believe you should be treated differently because of that?'

'Not at all! I should be treated exactly the same as everyone else. I just want to finish my training and become a good Judge,' affirmed Nita.

'Well, if it's any consolation, you have my sympathies. I know how you feel, I got much the same treatment when I was a cad. Just don't let them know they're getting to you and they'll soon get bored and give up,' confided Chung. After a moment's silence she added: 'Just because I've told you this, don't expect any special treatment from me either.'

'I wouldn't dream of it,' said Nita. She glanced up the bluff to where Dredd was sitting, writing something by the light of his bike lamps. 'What's he really like – Old Stony Face?'

'Hard, but fair. But mostly hard. Do well on this mission and he'll give you a good report. Mess up and you'll be failed and sent back to the Big Meg on your own without a moment's warning.'

Cadet Archer joined the pair as they hiked back up the hill to the squad's encampment. 'Old Stony Face has put us on half-rations, says we could be out here for several extra days – I'll starve to death before we get back home!'

Chung and Nita burst out laughing at Julian's pained expression. 'Out of all of us, you're carrying the most body fat, you'd last longest without food,' laughed Nita.

Extract from the personal log of Judge Dredd, dated December 7, 2115AD:

'*HOTDOG RUN HAS PROCEEDED ACCORDING TO PLAN SO FAR. HAVE PITCHED CAMP ON DEAD MAN'S BLUFF FOR THE NIGHT. JUDGE CHUNG PROVING TO BE AN ABLE ASSOCIATE IN ASSESSMENT.*

'*CADETS A MIXED GROUP. COSTER IS POSSIBLE LEADERSHIP MATERIAL. AGNEW AND ZENDER WARNED FOR FAILING TO ACTIVATE BIKE SENSORS AT CAMP – A BAD*

SLIP, COULD COST LIVES. SINGH SEEMS NERVOUS BUT ABLE. JENKS AN OBVIOUS TROUBLE-MAKER, WILL NEED TO BE WATCHED CLOSELY. JUST A MATTER OF TIME BEFORE ARCHER FAILS.

'*TOMORROW WILL TAKE CADS INTO GILA-MUNJA TERRITORY. THOSE WHO SURVIVE COULD MAKE GOOD STREET JUDGES.*'

Nita was awake well before dawn, the screaming of dog-vultures as they flapped overhead reminding her of the cries of beggars on the streets of Indo City. She sat bolt upright, as for a moment it seemed she had been transported back to the old country, the place she still thought of at the back of her mind as home. But then the smell hit her, the stench of sulphur and rotting flesh and death, like the embrace of a corpse. She was not five any more, she was not living in Indo City. She was seventeen years old, her name was Nita Singh and she was a Cadet Judge on a Hotdog Run in the Cursed Earth.

'What a way to wake up!' she muttered and nudged awake the slumbering Archer, still dead to the world and dreaming of a large breakfast, she had no doubt.

Nita stood up and looked down from the bluff at their surroundings. The final few klicks had been completed in near-darkness the night before and only now did she get a chance to take in their surroundings. The previous day they had covered more than seven hundred klicks but the terrain had been hard to remember, a mixture of desert, rocks and mountains soon blending into one long sandy-brown blur.

Now they had obviously crossed over into one of the zones of heavy radiation. Instead of blue, the sky was purple directly above her, blending downwards to the horizon through shades of pink to finish a blood red, as if the earth itself was raw and wounded. The ground was parched and yellow, like old paper, with just the occasional green of a mutated cactus breaking the monotony. No trees, no bushes, no shrubs, virtually no sign of life.

'Grud, what a horrible place,' Nita commented, pulling her radiation cloak closer around her shoulders. Her tutors at the Academy had been right – out here it was coldest just before the dawn – weird!

Moments later she spotted a moving dot appear on the horizon. Soon it was joined by another, then another, then more, all travelling in single file, the line growing ever longer, snaking towards them from the west.

'Judge Dredd – something's coming from the – ' began Nita but her words were cut off by a gruff voice at her shoulder.

'I see 'em.' Dredd stood beside her, staring out at the caravan slowly approaching them. After a few moments he turned and bellowed an order at the slumbering cadets: 'Get up – now!'

The sun was just clearing the horizon as Dredd issued a steady stream of orders to the bleary-eyed squad. Chung stood behind him, alert and ready for action.

'We've got a convoy coming out of the west. Coster – what should we do?' Dredd demanded.

'Determine whether they're hostile, sir!'

'And how do you suggest we do that?'

'Observe first to assess their intentions, then send a small team to approach the convoy. Sir!' barked back Coster.

'Jenks, I want you and Archer to maintain surveillance. Coster, you and Zender will join me when we approach the convoy. The rest of you, prepare to move out before oh-seven-hundred hours,' commanded Dredd.

'Yes, sir!' The cadets quickly set to their tasks, but before moving away Dredd approached Singh and said just three words.

'Well spotted, cadet.'

'Comes on, 'ercules, just a bit farther!' implored Burr.

'Can't you make this nag go any faster, Mister Burr?' inquired Harke irritably.

'I'm sorry, Mister 'arke, but 'ercules 'ere ain't designed for speed. 'E's a beast of burden, not a thoroughbred racing stallion,' explained Burr.

'Just like his master,' muttered Harke under his breath. Their primitive horse-drawn cart rattled along slowly, to the annoyance of the other vehicles behind them in the convoy fleeing Dunedin.

The dubious duo's tale of zombies rising from the grave had been ignored by all and sundry when the two rogues returned to Dunedin in great haste the night before. For a start, no one really believed a word spoken by Harke, and Burr was considered a relatively harmless simpleton who had fallen into bad company. But neither were considered men of their words or great intellects. So stories of zombies and the dead rising from their graves were roundly dismissed – the township had been through all of that during Judgement Day last year, so surely there were very few dead left in their graves to be raised anyway?

But when the zombies started knocking on front doors the next morning, asking after 'the child',

Harke and Burr's unlikely anecdote suddenly gained a very large degree of credence – it's hard to argue with the evidence of your own eyes, especially when it's coming in through your windows.

The exodus had begun before dawn, as hundreds of frightened families fled the norm township, seeking refuge from the undead hordes roaming their streets. The people of Dunedin were hardly a mobile lot, most having lived in the same homes all their lives, so fleeing town had proved problematic, requiring all manner of strange jalopies and cart-horses to be brought forth from retirement or just plain neglect.

Now the majority of the town were fleeing in any direction possible. Harke and Burr had actually been the first to leave, but the unwilling nature of their nag had slowed them down so much that the rest of the population had already overtaken them or turned off for a better route out of Dunedin.

'My good Grud, I've just had a brainstorm!' cried Harke aloud. Beside him, Burr began to feel distinctly nervous – Harke's last three brainstorms had led to the pair being chased by killer mummies, attacked by gigantic mutant vampire hamsters and last night's escapade in the local war cemetery. Brainstorms like that, Burr had decided, he could do without.

'We'll go back!' announced Harke triumphantly. 'What a fool, why didn't I think of this before? We'll go back!'

'Back where?' asked Burr dubiously, not really wanting to know the answer, but knowing how much Harke hated it when rhetorical statements were left hanging around like Burr's old socks ('They leave an

61

unsightly and frequently odorous mess, my dear fellow!')

'Back to Dunedin, of course! Why, the entire town will be deserted – think of the valuables left behind in the mad rush to flee a few roaming corpses. Wealth beyond the dreams of avarice!' Harke's eyes were starting to glaze over.

Burr had seen that look before and it only meant one thing – trouble. 'Look, Mister 'arke, I don't know nuthin' 'bout any dreams of yours. All I wants is a quiet life and enuff creds to keep a roof over me 'ead and the occasional pint of synthi-ale in me 'and.'

'But, my dear fellow, you just don't understand. All the creds you'll ever need wait for us back in Dunedin!'

'I'm sorry, Mister 'arke, but we ain't going back and that's me final word on the matter!' Burr folded his arms, resolute – for once he would not be swayed by his associate's gentle voice of persuasion.

Fortunately, there was outside intervention before Harke could begin bending his partner's will to his own way. A roar of mighty motorcycle engines, and the antique dealers found themselves surrounded by Judges.

'Crivens!' gasped Burr.

After observing the convoy for more than ten minutes, Dredd led Coster and Zender down onto the plain where their Lawmasters quickly covered the distance to the ragtag caravan of makeshift vehicles and carts. The trio were quickly directed to the last vehicle in the convoy for an explanation for the exodus.

'Zombies! The hundead, walking and everythink!' explained Burr, his arms waving animatedly.

Coster had been carefully monitoring the duo's response to questioning on his handheld lie-detector, nicknamed the 'Birdie'. He nodded to Dredd, indicating the pair were probably telling the truth.

The senior Judge examined the terrified twosome for a full minute, his eyes sweeping back and forth between them. Finally he spoke. 'All right, go about your business.'

'Yes, sir. Thank you, your honour,' repeated Harke over and over, oozing obsequiousness from every pore. Burr flicked the reins in his hands and the not-so-mighty Hercules stumbled on, following the rest of the caravan, which was disappearing away over the horizon.

Once the convoy had disappeared completely from view, Dredd and the cadets returned to the rest of the squad and reported what they had learnt.

'Could it be some after-effect of Judgement Day, sir? Perhaps Sabbat returning to haunt us again?' ventured Agnew, his eyes full of fear. During the final hours of the terrible war with the zombies, even cadets from the Academy were drafted into the front lines during the last assault from the undead hordes. Agnew had watched several of his comrades die that day, the first time he had truly seen death in all its horror. He didn't want to relive that experience again in his lifetime.

'Possible, but unlikely,' replied Chung. 'I accompanied an international team of Judges to Sabbat's final resting place outside Hondo City. Any sign of activity from Sabbat and the whole world would know about it in moments.'

'Something else then, which we don't have the resources or manpower to properly investigate. Archer – recommendations?' demanded Dredd.

'Um, we should record the site of the, er, um, phenomenon and send a message pod back to Mega-City One. Err, sir,' stammered the chubby cadet nervously.

'Good – see to it. But be quick, we move out in five minutes. Everybody else, check your weaponry. We're heading into gila-munja territory next.'

Gila-munja – a name to strike fear into the hearts of Cursed Earth travellers and inhabitants everywhere. No one truly knows where they came from, perhaps the mutated results of fallout from the Atomic Wars, perhaps the result of some twisted experimentation. No matter, because all you need to know is this: they're deadly!

The gila-munja are a tribe of mutant assassins, based in several regions of the Cursed Earth. They possess a special kind of chameleon skin which enables them to blend perfectly with any surrounding. It gives them first-rate camouflage and makes them virtually impossible for the untrained eye to spot – you and me, in other words!

You won't see the drokkers coming, but if they get you, at least they'll kill you fast. At the end of each arm they have massive crescent-shaped claws with razor-sharp teeth built into the edges, excellent for cutting or tearing at the bodies of their victims, capable of penetrating solid rockcrete. These guys are nasty!

Worst of all, the venom they exude kills instantly, with no known anti-venom in existence. One scratch and you'll be dead within five seconds. Basically, if

you meet the gila-munja, you're as good as dead.
Everybody got that?

*(Extract from 'Hitchhiking across the Cursed
Earth on less than Five Creds a Day', by Cecil B.
de Cleene, published 2114AD by Dead Juve's
Press)*

'Well? What do the signs and spore tell you,
deputy?'

'They came this way, all right, yes sirree.' Crouching on the ground, a battered, dusty figure examined
faint marks and scratches in the soil. He picked up a
shred of flaky, reptilian skin, rolling it between his
three lumpy digits, feeling the texture. Next he held
it up to the two nostrils set into his face, sniffing long
and hard, his bulbous eyes examining every detail.
After a moment's contemplation, he spoke again.
'Definitely the shedding from a gila-munja. I'd say
this skin's been off the beast three, maybe four days.
It's crusty, but still kinda soft inside.'

The hunchbacked mutant stood up again, his spare
hand still clutching the reins of his mutie mule.
'They're headed home, back to their lair – 'bout
thirty miles from here.'

A few paces away stood a coal-black steed, its
blood-red eyes testament to Cursed Earth lineage.
Any animal that lived in this radioactive wasteland
had long since adapted to the inhospitable conditions, the fall-out, the fierce dust-storms and the
many vicious predators. This steed was rippling with
muscles and menace. In another time, another place
it would have made someone a fortune. Now it was
simply transportation for one of the angriest souls in
all the Cursed Earth.

Atop the black horse sat a grim-faced man, lean

and sinewy of body, with a face to chill the marrow. Beneath black, bushy eyebrows gleamed two hard, flinty eyes. A hawk-like nose and grim slit of a mouth completed the features, the jutting jawline bristling with five o'clock shadow, even though the sun had only just risen.

His long grey hair was pulled back from the face severely, and his garb was just as brutal. Brick-red jeans over unembroidered cowboy boots with harsh, two-inch spurs attached; a long brown riding coat, its tails flapping slightly in the early morning breeze, pulled over a black shirt with a clean white dog-collar pulled taut around the neck. Two ammunition belts were slung round the thin waist, a gun-filled holster hanging at each side. Finally, a wide-brimmed circular hat was pulled low over those grim, piercing eyes. The upright figure shifted in the saddle before speaking in a voice full of menace and hellfire.

'We ride on. The Lord's work is not yet over.' He turned his horse towards the direction their quarry had been heading. As he did, a beam of sunlight caught a glint of metal on his chest, pinned over his left breast. Two words were visible, burned into the badge: OUTLANDS MARSHAL.

'Yes, sir, Preacher Cain!' responded his deputy, quickly getting into the saddle of his humble mount. 'That's definitely the way they went, all right, or my name ain't Resurrection Joe!'

The pair rode off into the distance.

The tiny metal shape, barely bigger than a fist, flew low, hard and fast like a bullet from a gun. But unlike any bullet, its minute forward-sensing equipment detected any obstacles ahead and the missile swerved or flew upwards to avoid them, dropping back close to the ground again when it sensed the path was safe.

A tiny nuclear cell propelled the missile forwards, ventings along its side helping it ride the hot air slowly rising from the radioactive wasteland as the orange sun overhead heated the poisoned soil. Still the missile flew on, ignoring long-abandoned conurbations and small settlements, homing instead on the strong signal transmitted from the highest point in Mega-City One, the recently reconstructed Mega-City Museum.

As the missile flew unerringly towards its target, it triggered an electronic sensing post a hundred klicks from the city boundary, the West Wall. In the monitoring defence centre, this activated an alarm on one of the screens. A Judge quickly picked up a headset and sat at the terminal, activating a three-dimensional projection unit set into the equipment.

'Show me,' he murmured into the voice-response mike. Light was flung up from the unit and a tiny speck could be seen, glowing brighter within the lightstream.

'Magnify.' The object grew brighter and larger, growing until it filled the lightstream. 'Stop.' A pause. 'What is it?'

From the ear-piece a mechanical voice issued: 'Justice Department message pod, fired from a Lawmaster bike on patrol in the Cursed Earth, homing on the Department's signal beacon atop the Mega-City Museum. Estimated time of arrival, two minutes and thirty-eight – '

'Intercept with a jamming signal and have the pod home in on the following location,' interrupted the monitoring Judge, dictating a series of co-ordinates.

* * *

Minutes later the monitoring Judge was presenting the unopened pod to his superior.

'You haven't opened this?' demanded the seated Judge, his uniform gleaming darkly like the skin of a black snake. A skull motif was incorporated into the elbow- and shoulder-pads.

'No, sir. I followed your orders explicitly.'

Despite this assurance, the senior Judge still checked the seals were intact before breaking them open. 'All right, return to your post. Keep me informed of any comings or goings from the Cursed Earth.'

'Yes, sir, of course, sir!' The monitoring Judge snapped to attention, saluted and, turning on his heels, marched from the chamber. After he had departed, the remaining Judge pulled the message chip from the pod and slotted it into his desktop reader. A holographic image of Archer appeared, reporting the information about the zombie attack. The Judge watched the message twice more, then activated his vid-phone, ensuring the scrambler was functioning first.

'Dredd's sent in a message pod, with information about a zombie attack on a small norm settlement, but nothing else so far.'

On screen a face could barely be made out, shrouded in shadows and static – scramblers played havoc with communications on vid-phones, a price paid for secrecy. 'Anything else, any sign he's suspicious?' asked the person at the other end of the call.

'Nothing.'

'Erase the message, destroy the pod. Keep up the good work and you'll be rewarded when the time comes – out!' The call cut off abruptly.

In the chamber, the seated Judge leaned forward and touched a control on the message reader. Within moments the now-blank disc was ejected. The Judge crushed the silicon wafer between his fingers, then wiped the powdered residue from his fingers. No trace of the message remained.

'Archer, what can you tell us about that conurbation?'

The squad of cadets and Judges was stopped on a hillside, above an abandoned city, most of its buildings just bombed-out husks, hot winds off the surrounding desert whistling through its wizened structures, creating strange moans and clangs, the sounds of decay and forgotten urban follies long left dead.

'Er, this is, um, the remains of the city of Beakersville, population before the war more than eighty thousand, population today estimated to be, um . . .' The nervous cadet stammered and stalled for time as his Lawmaster's on-board computer struggled to recall the data from its memory banks. The local levels of radioactivity were adversely affecting its function. '. . . Er, about zero. Sir.'

'We can see that, Archer, for ourselves. What else?' asked Dredd tersely.

'Last aerial survey undertaken more than a year ago, before Judgement Day, sir,' replied Archer with a little more assurance, as his bike screen cleared. 'At that time, the area was believed to be, er . . .' His voice trembled a little at the last words as he spoke them: 'Heavily infested with gila-munja.'

Dredd turned to another of his charges. 'Jenks – tactics?'

'Frontal attack, go in all guns blazing. Flush 'em out into the open, they'll be easier to pick off,' replied the cadet confidently.

'Your tactics stink, Jenks! We'd be the ones being picked off! Zender – what do you say?'

'Spray the immediate area with heat-seekers to take out the front guard. That'll bring them out into the open,' ventured Zender carefully, waiting for Dredd to tear a strip off him too.

'Good thinking, Zender. Anything else?'

'Yes, my bike sensors show the area is low in radiation, due to the sheltering nature of its location in this depression. Recommend we remove our radiation cloaks to help free our movements when we go in, in case of any hand-to-hand,' added Zender, growing in confidence.

'You don't fight hand-to-hand with gila-munja, boy, they don't give you a chance! But losing the cloaks will aid mobility – everyone comply,' ordered Dredd, slipping his own from his shoulders and stowing it in the storage pods built in the rear of his Lawmaster. Once the squad was ready, he barked a final order.

'Coster, up front with me. Chung, you take the point with Archer. Set your Lawgivers to heat-seeker. Let's ride!'

A Judge's standard-issue weapon is a deadly, multi-faceted hand-gun, known as the Lawgiver. It can only be operated by its Judge owner and will self-destruct if unauthorised use is attempted. The Lawgiver has manual and automatic focus and targeting, with an in-built voice-responsive unit capable of controlling its operation, including such functions as choice of cartridge.

The weapon's maximum range is about three miles, but accuracy is naturally poor at this distance. It has six settings:

- Heat-seeker, a general purpose shell, propelled by the unstable element Argon 886. The heat-seeker hunts out its target by having a sensor range of up to twelve inches from it trajectory, seeking out objects of a set temperature, generally the body heat of a human;
- Ricochet, a rubber-tipped missile, able to 'bounce' off non-organic surfaces more than a thousand times in laboratory testing;
- Incendiary, packed with a napalm-derived agent which explodes into a fireball upon impact;
- Armour-piercing, specially coated with miniscule amounts of depleted uranium, able to punch through most armours, penetrates up to six inches through reinforced rockcrete;
- Grenade, an explosive round rarely used, soon to be replaced with the new 'melter' rounds;
- High Explosive, or 'hi-ex', considered far more powerful and accurate than the older grenade cartridge.

(Extract from 'Weapons and their Applications in Lawkeeping' (revised edition), by Judge-Armourer Jackson, due to be published January, 2116 AD)

The outpost sentinels had spotted the squad approaching long before it had even reached the outskirts of Beakersville. Runners were sent back to the lair, deep within the ruins.

Beakersville had long since been picked clean, now just a carcass of twisted metal and rockcrete, so raiding parties had to be sent out, further and further from the lair. Soon it would be time to move on, find a new lair. The last raiding party had been a disaster, barely bringing back enough meat to last its members the return journey. Added to this, the pack had encountered and enraged a new foe, armed with twin pistols and riding a jet-black steed. Mutiny was brewing among the ranks when the word came back from the sentinels: Judges approaching!

The leader shifted on his throne of human skulls, still sharpening the teeth of his giant claws on the skeleton of some long-dead unfortunate. Good! These fools on their metal chariots would be easy fodder for his people, providing good cheer and good feeding for several days. That would silence his rivals for the leadership.

He stood up. Let the Judges come, he announced in a series of gutteral growlings. Tonight we shall feast on human flesh again. And I will tear open the skull of their leader and suck out his brains myself! To war!

The gila-munja arose and filtered out to the edges of Beakersville, near-invisible wraiths awaiting the chance of battle, of conquest, of slaughter.

CHAPTER THREE

'THE CADETS FOUGHT WELL AGAINST WHAT PROVED TO BE AN OVERWHELMING NUMBER OF GILA-MUNJA. SPECIAL COMMENDATIONS GO TO THE TWO CADETS WHO DID NOT SURVIVE THE BATTLE. THE INTERVENTION OF THE STRANGER WAS A TURNING POINT . . .'

(EXTRACT FROM THE PERSONAL LOG OF JUDGE DREDD, DATED DECEMBER 8, 2115 AD)

'Fire heat-seekers – now!'

The squad began firing their Lawgivers at the bombed-out buildings below, shooting round after round of heat-seekers into the rubble, varying their aim to get a wide spread of bullets across the approach to the deserted city. Within seconds, dark green blood-stains began to appear on the walls and rockcrete strewn around, the bodies of gila-munja becoming apparent as they died and lost control over their chameleon abilities.

'Rapid fire – fire at will!' Dredd commanded and the hail of gunfire continued, a torrent of death falling onto the area below them. After a full three minutes of firing, reloading and firing again, Dredd called the carnage to a halt. 'Reload,' ordered the grim-faced Judge as he surveyed the scene before them.

Dozens, nearly a hundred corpses could be seen, and the vicious green staining leading away from the edge of the town into its centre testified to many more wounded having retreated. Chung moved her bike to beside Dredd and spoke to him in hushed tones.

'Grud, there's nearly a hundred down there – how many do you think are in the main lair?' she asked.

'Five times that number, maybe more,' estimated Dredd. 'They'll be regrouping – we should go in now, while they're still disorganised.' He glanced round at the cadets, then gave the order to move in. The squad rode down the side of the bluff and into the remains of Beakersville, maintaining a standard two-by-two formation. Dredd stayed at the front with Coster, behind them came Agnew and Zender. Nita and Archer rode as the next pair, with Chung and Jenks bringing up the rear.

They all rode in silence, looking around at the carnage of corpses as they passed the front line of dead gila-munja. Then they had passed the first crumbling buildings, and the dry orange dirt of the Cursed Earth disappeared behind them. The squad rode quietly towards the centre of Beakersville for nearly ten minutes – then the blackness came from the sky.

'The Death Belt is a vast belt of flying garbage that hovers over areas of the Cursed Earth. After the Atomic Wars, terrible winds attacked the surviving settlements, almost as if nature were fighting back against the humans that were hurting it with their conflict. Houses, cars, rocks and debris were hurled high into the air and fragments stayed there, forever suspended by the hot air-currents rising up from the parched wasteland below.

Worst of all, radiation-mutated vermin were swept

up into the sky too and some learnt to live in the Death Belt, jumping from rock to rock, feeding off the garbage. The rats learnt to glide on the air-currents and when the winds would sweep down to scour the earth, the rats would come down too, searching for prey. Because of their terrible mutated fangs and deadly poisonous bite, the vermin were soon given a new name – the Devil's Lapdogs.'

(Extract from 'Flora and Fauna of the Cursed Earth', by Prof. S. J. Millipitt, 2111 AD)

'D'you think we shot all of them, Nita?' Cadet Archer was glancing nervously from one side of the road to the other, searching for any sign of the gila-munja.

'Hardly likely, Julian,' replied his friend, also scanning their barren surroundings. 'We picked off quite a few, but I'd guess that was just the outpost guards – the real thing is yet to come!'

'Oh boy,' mumbled Archer and tried to remember the last full meal he'd had. 'D'you think we'll stop to eat soon?'

Behind them, Chung could hear their conversation and nearly laughed out loud. Instead she contacted the pair on her helmet radio. 'Archer, if we stopped now, we'd be the ones getting eaten, not the other way around!'

'Oh boy.'

Nita felt the hairs on the back of her neck stand up, a disquieting sensation. Glancing around at their surroundings, she couldn't help noticing how hard it was becoming to see more than thirty feet from the main road. She radioed ahead to Dredd. 'Sir, is it my imagination, or is it getting darker all of a sudden?'

Dredd turned in the seat of his Lawmaster and looked at the sky around them. Directly behind them, a huge black cloud had appeared in the last few minutes. Dredd looked closer and realised that the cloud was moving – no, not moving – pulsating. The cloud was no cloud, it was alive!

'Jovus Drokk – the Death Belt! Everybody take cover!' he bellowed into his helmet radio and swerved his bike off the road violently. As it screeched to a halt behind a crumbling wall, the Judge threw himself to the ground behind it, Lawgiver already drawn and ready to fire. The rest of the squad followed his lead, finding cover behind walls, the sides of buildings, anything.

For a full minute the cloud hovered overhead and almost seemed ready to move on. Then suddenly it plunged downwards towards them and the air was alive with rocks and teeth and pain as the Death Belt slashed at the landscape, its deadly predators leaping off to attack anything that moved.

'Nobody move and they won't attack you,' muttered Dredd over his helmet radio to the others.

On the other side of the road, Nita and Archer were behind a low wall, using their bikes as a shield. The air-currents swirled and then moved around behind them. In moments they were surrounded by a moving, pulsating carpet of vermin.

'I can't take this . . .' whispered Archer out the side of his mouth.

'Hold on!' urged Nita, but the rats had heard their whispers and the flow slowed and stopped. The pair were surrounded, with no way of escaping. Nita looked to her Lawmaster – if only she could activate its siren, maybe that would draw the vermin away from the others.

A single rat jumped up, onto the seat, almost as if it sensed her thoughts. Nita thought for a moment it was actually two rats, then the full horror hit her – it was one rat, but with two heads! Her stomach heaved and she almost vomited, but managed to contain the stream of bile. The double-headed monster stared at her and the cadet almost felt as if it was trying to hypnotise her, as if she were some tiny creature about to be devoured.

Around them, the rest of the vermin seemed to be closing in, just waiting for the signal from their leader, the king rat. It could only be moments before the pair of them were torn apart by thousands of pairs of tiny, vicious incisors. Nita suppressed a shudder of disgust and whispered to Archer, who was frozen with terror.

'Julian, can you hear me?'

A whimper, a slight nod of the head.

'When I say now, vault over this wall and run like drokk, all right? You got that?'

Just a nod.

Nita kept her eyes locked on the twin-headed monster, but let her hand slip down to the stock of her Lawgiver, protruding from its boot holster. The closest rat tried to take a nip out of her, nearly scaring the cadet to death, but only got a mouthful of gauntlet. Thank Grud for kevlar, thought Nita as she gripped the handle of her weapon.

The king rat sensed her movement and its back haunches flexed and rippled. It's getting ready to jump, Nita realised.

'Now!' she screamed and everything seemed to happen at once, almost in slow motion. As she screamed, a wailing sound filled the air. The rat king jumped, lips pulled back from both mouths, exposing black, razor-sharp teeth and fetid green saliva, launching itself at her face. Beside Nita, Archer – in probably the most athletic moment of his life, Nita joked afterwards – virtually somersaulted backwards over the wall behind them.

While all this happened, Nita ripped the Lawgiver free of her boot holster, bringing it up into the air. At the same time her free hand involuntarily flung out in front of her, grabbing the rat just before it could sink its teeth into the flesh of her face.

The rat squealed in rage and thrashed its heads around, biting great chunks out of the gauntlet encasing her hand. Nita, ignoring everything else, held the barrel of the Lawgiver up to the rat's heads with her free hand.

'You want to eat something?' she sneered. 'Eat this!' The first bullet blew both the rat's heads off but Nita threw the convulsing, hairy, bloated body to the ground and kept firing at it, round after round thudding into the body, until just a red smear was left. Then she sank back against the wall, slumped to the ground and threw up violently.

As the rats surrounded them, Judge Chung found herself and Jenks trapped in the corner of a building, with just her Lawmaster for cover. Then she remembered a lecture Dredd had once given at the Academy during her time as a cadet, more than ten years before. He had just returned from the great trek across the Cursed Earth to deliver a viral antidote to Mega-City Two, on the opposite coast of the land that had once been the United States of America.

Judge-tutors at the Academy thought it would be valuable for the cadets to hear about Dredd's experiences. In particular Chung remembered having nightmares for days afterwards because of Dredd's account of having to fight hordes of mutant rats in a town called Deliverance – the Devil's Lapdogs, that was the name he had given them. Then she remembered how the monsters had been defeated.

Emma Chung turned to whisper to Jenks beside her. 'Whatever I do, don't move,' she hissed.

'You can count on it!'

Chung gave herself a moment to clear her thoughts, concentrating only on the task ahead. She closed her eyes, reinforcing the same image over and over again in her head. Finally, she was ready. She flung herself onto her Lawmaster, and its engines roared into life. She let the revs build up for a moment, then released the brake and screamed away across the carpet of vermin, her back wheel spinning as it tried to get a grip on the moving, pulsating surface below it. The bike shot onto clear road and Chung activated the siren, pumping up the volume to maximum, until its screeching wail could be heard for miles.

'Don't leave me, you bitch!' screamed Jenks.

(On the other side of the road Nita screamed 'Now!')

At the sound of the siren all the rats turned, the high-pitched noise an irresistible lure. As one, they raced off, following the siren. Jenks found herself alone, her chest heaving for breath. She sank to the ground, her face white, her legs shaking.

Chung looked back to see the black swarm following her. The hunch had been right and hopefully all the rats were following her and leaving the others behind, safe. Now Chung just had to save herself!

'Only one thing for it,' she told herself and surveyed the path ahead. Just in front it widened out on one side, an area clear of rubble. 'Bike to auto!' she commanded, the on-board computer taking control of all functions. It would keep the Lawmaster upright and moving at this speed, avoiding oncoming objects where possible for hundreds, even thousands of miles until commanded to stop or prevented from continuing.

Chung pulled herself up by the handlebars, hoisting her legs and feet up onto the seat. Then, just as the bike reached the clear area, she flung herself off, curling into a ball and rolling ten, twenty, thirty metres before finally stopping. The wailing Lawmaster continued its journey and the Devil's Lapdogs bolted after it, ignoring their former quarry.

Emma Chung picked herself up and brushed the worst of the dirt and dust off her uniform. Dredd was a stickler for a clean uniform and correct appearance; she'd read his comportment volumes often enough to know that! The Judge pulled her Lawgiver from its boot holster and started the long walk back to where the rest of the squad were.

Dredd had watched Chung ride out on her Lawmaster, sirens wailing, drawing the rats away from the other squad members. 'Good thinking,' he muttered. Within minutes he had reformed the squad. Fortunately there had been no casualties.

'What about Judge Chung?' asked Nita.

'As I recall, she does a good speed roll,' replied Dredd. 'Now, we have too – '

It was at this moment that the gila-munja attacked.

* * * *

80

The pair had been riding for more than three hours since their last stop, but the leader never slackened his pace, never deviated from the path. Behind him, his deputy looked down at the ground occasionally, just to make sure they were on the right track, but the blood-stains and scraps of clothing told their own story. After a while, Resurrection Joe had stopped looking.

'Reckon the reverend can smell those sinners ahead,' he told himself. The bulbous-eyed mutant looked ahead at his commander and remembered their first meeting, nearly eight months before.

Joe had been run out of a town called Intolerance, aptly named, he discovered, when a posse tried to string him up from the nearest tree. Fortunately the locals weren't too good at tying knots. The reverend had wandered along a few hours later and shot the rope from around his neck. Once he told the preacher his story – Joe had been a bit perplexed by his saviour's identity but actions always spoke louder'n words – the reverend decided to go and teach the inhabitants of Intolerance a few lessons about brotherly love. Joe decided to tag along.

Within five minutes of arriving in town the locals were preparing for a double-lynching, with Joe's neck back in the noose, this time accompanied by his 'mutie-lover friend'. Sixty seconds later the posse was dead by the hand and hand-guns of the reverend – divine retribution he'd called it, when Joe asked for an explanation.

Well, all this had kinda appealed to Joe and when the reverend introduced himself as Preacher Cain, a man with a mission to clean up the Cursed Earth, Joe had been proud to become his deputy. They had some real adventures since then, that was for sure, but even today Joe wasn't sure who the preacher really was. Why, he spoke a mean Bible verse but he also had the best shootin' eye Joe'd ever seen and Joe'd been a member of the Texas City Buffalo Soldier mutie irregulars a few years back. Hell, those boys had nothin' on the reverend!

Joe knew his boss wore the badge of a Texas City Outlands Marshal, but then again, he also wore a priest's collar, so it was kinda hard to know which one to believe. Despite all that, Joe knew he could trust the reverend with his life. Together, well, they made a pretty formidable team – the preacher with his shootin' from the hip and preachin' from the lip and Joe, the best scout, tracker and gila-munja hunter in the whole, dang territories.

It was gila-munja they were tracking now, a whole pack of them that'd attacked a churchload of believers several days before. Joe and the preacher had stumbled across the massacre while searching for a place to rest up. But once they uncovered the atrocity, the reverend had seemed to lose all his weariness, Joe remembered. Instead Preacher Cain was transformed, like a man born again.

The trail was more than a day old when they picked it up but the pair had tracked the gila-munja through the badlands to their lair. Now the marshal and his deputy stood atop the bluff that a few hours before had hosted Dredd and his charges.

'Seems someone's done our work for us,' remarked Joe, looking down at the dozens of gila-munja corpses.

'Not all our work – listen,' grimaced Cain, smoke rising, woody and pungent, from the stub of cheroot protruding from his gritted teeth.

Joe cocked his head to one side and could just hear, faintly, the sounds of screaming and gunfire.

'Let's ride!' shouted Cain and jagged his finely honed spurs into the flanks of his black steed. With a cry they jumped over the bluff and charged straight down the hillside, the tails of Cain's long coat flailing behind. Joe gee-upped his mule and trotted after the reverend. It always seemed his place to follow behind, but then the reverend was better at the fightin' and shootin', so it made sense for him to go first. Leastways that was how Joe figured it.

'This is the promised land, the new Eden – it's time to cleanse away the serpents!' bellowed Cain quixotically.

'Here we go again,' muttered Joe to himself less enthusiastically, trailing along in Preacher Cain's trail of red dust.

A scream, and Nita turned to see Zender's face, agonised with pain, furious with rage and shock. Looking down, she could see a crescent-shaped claw, hot red blood glistening on its razor-toothed edge, jagging through Zender's chest. Behind him, the simmering shape of a gila-munja, lips peeled back from its jaws to reveal green-stained fangs, almost like a smile.

Nita spun round on the spot and for a moment thought her eyes were playing tricks on her. Their surroundings seemed to shimmer and blur. Then she realised the terrible truth – she was not looking at their true surroundings, she was seeing the chameleon skin of hundreds of gila-munja, creating the illusion of what lay beyond them.

'We're trapped – surrounded!' the cadet cried out before she could stop herself. From beside her,

Zender's body was dragged away by the gila-munja that had killed him, towards the rest of the pack. The sensation of slavering, primeval hunger was almost overpowering. Already the creature who had murdered Zender was tearing the uniform away from the dead cadet's body, the better to pick the flesh from his bones while it was still warm and succulent.

'Leave him alone,' barked Dredd, aiming his Lawgiver at that part of the pack. 'Incendiary!' He fired three rounds, each exploding into a fireball as it hit a target. For a moment the gila-munja held back, shocked by the ferocity of the Judge's weapon. Dredd took that moment to shout a few desperate orders to his charges.

'Call your bikes – we'll need the extra ammunition. Fall back into a circle – standard defensive formation. And watch each other's backs. If you want to live, help each other!'

Suddenly he was gone, running straight at the gila-munja pack where the density was lightest. 'Rapid fire!' he commanded the Lawgiver which began to mow down row after row of the mutated monsters in front of him. Burying his boot knife in the chest of another, he burst through the surrounding circle, gila-munja pouring after him. 'Bike to me!' Dredd shouted into his helmet mike.

In the centre of the swarm the five surviving cadets had pulled themselves into a circle, back to back, Lawgivers in their hands, ready to fire. Nita glanced around at the others.

To her left Archer was clutching his weapon with both hands, its barrel visibly shaking. 'What are they waiting for?' he whispered. Around them the circle of gila-munja stood, moving slowly with low gutteral growls and flashing claws, but not attacking yet.

On Nita's right Jenks kept shifting her weight from foot to foot, sweat pouring down her face. 'I don't know, but I don't want to stay here to die finding out with you guys!'

'You move an inch and I'll kill you myself!' hissed Coster viciously. 'You heard what Dredd said – we stay here and that's an order!'

On the other side of Jenks from Nita, Agnew's manner belied his baby-faced visage. 'Lock and load, people. Looks like they're getting ready to make their move.'

Nita pulled her attention to their foes and knew Agnew was right. With a rustling, hissing noise, the carnivorous creatures were slowly closing in around them, the pincers of their claws clacking together ominously. Nita pulled a spare ammunition clip from her belt and jammed it between her teeth, ready for rapid reloading.

'Get ready – pick a clear target before you fire – ' murmured Coster.

'Who died and made you leader?' spat Jenks.

'You if you don't shut up Jenks!' yelled back Coster, the scar on his face a livid red, flushed with anger. 'Get ready – FIRE!'

The five juves fired volley after volley of shots into the pack, emptying their clips of bullets and rapidly reloading as quickly as they could. Dozens, perhaps a hundred monsters fell before this hail of fire but still the gila-munja surged forwards. The creatures moved as one entity, unafraid to sacrifice themslves to advance the common cause of slaughter and destruction.

'Go for you grenades!' bellowed Coster above the

fury of the firefight. Flicking open the pouches of his belt, he plucked half a dozen thumb-sized frag grenades out and lobbed them behind the front line of attackers. Within seconds the other were following suit.

The first grenade landed beside the pack leader, who stood at the back of his swarming legions. He just had time to fling himself aside when it exploded, taking off one of his massively muscled arms and a chunk of his torso. Green, viscous blood began pumping out onto the rubble of Beakersville. The pack leader staggered away, back to the lair.

Explosion after explosion tore through the ranks of the gila-munja, killing nearly half the attackers. But still the cadets were hugely outnumbered and the pack was closing in, now just a few feet away from reaching them, clambering over the corpses of their own fallen to reach the quintet.

'Where the hell's Dredd?' yelled Nita.

'He's abandoned us! Left us for dead, the drokker!' cried out Jenks.

'He'll be back,' testified Coster, resolute and firm.

'No he won't, he's left us for dead. I'm not dying here with you fools!' screamed Jenks. Breaking ranks from the others, she ran at the line where Dredd had broken through, mowing down gila-munja in her path by setting her Lawgiver to rapid fire. For a moment the monsters fell back and a path opened up. Jenks burst through it to the beyond.

'Jenks – NO!' screamed Coster furiously.

'I'm going after her!' shouted Agnew and before anyone could stop him, the youngest of the cadets threw himself after the deserter.

Nita turned her head just in time to see the path through the monsters close in around Agnew.

Moments later there was a terrible cry, then nothing but a low rumbling noise like the sound of thunder but deeper, almost as if it were coming from the very earth. Then it was joined by a high-pitched wailing, so intense and finely tuned, it was almost beyond the hearing of the teenagers.

All around them the gila-munja paused for a moment, seeming to stumble in their approach, as if unsure or disorientated.

'What is it?' asked Nita.

'Who knows – just keep firing!' replied Archer, his voice filled with a rare resolve. The three of them fell into a new, triangular formation, shielding each other with their backs. Clip after clip, round after round they fired into the gila-munja, the ground turned to mud with the blood of their opponents. Still the wailing grew louder and more piercing. The monsters did not retreat, did not attack, they just milled around as if unsure of their actions or location.

A metal click and Nita reached for another clip from her belt – there were none. 'I'm out!' she shouted. Moments later Archer and Coster were also left without ammunition.

'All I've got left is one frag grenade,' said Coster grimly. He glanced around at the other two. 'Did you see what they did to Agnew?'

Nita and Archer just nodded. They knew what was coming next. Coster swallowed hard before continuing.

'They're gonna attack again any minute. I say when they come, let's take some of those drokkers out with us! You guys in?'

Nita and Archer exchanged glances, then each

nodded their agreement. The three cadets put their hands on the release trigger of the frag grenade.

Nita turned to look at the gila-munja, who seemed to be regrouping, preparing to attack again.

'Here they come –'

Chung had been walking for more than ten minutes when she stumbled across the gila-munja as they prepared their massive attack on Dredd and the cadets.

'Sweet Jovus, there must be more than five hundred of them!' she gasped under her breath. Without her Lawmaster, she had no way of warning the squad without being killed herself. The best way of helping them was a covert attack on the attackers when the ambush came.

Judge Chung didn't have long to wait. By the time she'd moved to a better vantage point atop the remains of a building, the battle had just begun. When Dredd made his bid to break through the lines, Chung poured three clips into the gila-munja hordes directly ahead of him, clearing the path for his break out. Chung didn't realise her own actions had not gone unnoticed.

Within moments she was under attack herself from half a dozen creatures, only escaping with a desperate leap from the semi-destroyed building, twenty feet to the ground below, leaving a frag grenade behind to finish off her attackers.

Hitting the ground, rolling, jumping up and running, Chung saw Jenks burst through the lines and run away from the fight, tears streaming down the cadet's face as she flung her helmet away. Behind her, the terrible death-screams of Agnew rent the air.

'The little bitch is deserting!' spat Chung angrily and ran after Jenks, determined to bring her back to fight alongside the others, and to die with them if necessary.

Dredd burst through the gila-munja hordes, which seemed to fall away before him. 'Bike to me!' he shouted into his helmet mike.

Nearby his Lawmaster's engines burst into life, roaring with power. The on-board computer quickly tracked his location by homing in on the tracking device built into his helmet. Within moments of Dredd barking his order, the Lawmaster was racing towards him.

Seconds later Dredd threw himslf into the seat and rode hell for leather back to the battle. Reaching the perimeter of the clearing where the fighting was taking place, he yelled a new order to his machine: 'Bike cannon – rapid fire!'

The twin barrels mounted either side of the Lawmaster's front tyre began spitting death at the gila-munja hordes in front of it. The monsters turned and half a dozen charged at Dredd head-on.

At that moment a stray frag grenade soared overhead, to drop directly into Dredd's path.

'Drokk – grenade!' Dredd tried to brake and turn away but the bike slid out from under him, crushing most of the creatures flinging themselves at him. The Judge hit the ground rolling, keeping his body turning over and over to minimise injury. Finally he stopped, thumping heavily into a rock-solid object.

Groggily Dredd turned over to see a gila-munja towering over him, its fang-filled face almost drawn in a smile, great globs of saliva hanging from its jaws. The monster raised a claw, about to attack with a single, fatal thrust down towards the chest. Then the frag grenade exploded, ripping its head off.

The massive body toppled over on top of the Judge, crushing the wind from his body, smashing Dredd's helmet-clad face against the rocky ground. Then there was just blackness.

Nita looked grimly around as the gila-munja closed in for a final attack, the last surge.

'Here they come – ' she said, and the three cadets tensed for a moment, about to release the trigger mechanism on the frag grenade.

Then there was the report of a weapon, firing over and over again, and the rumbling in the ground grew ever louder. The gila-munja checked for a moment. Then he arrived.

Jenks ran and ran and ran, she didn't know where to or why, she just kept running, trying to get away from those monsters. Behind her she could swear she could hear the feet of at least a dozen gila-munja following her. She dared not look back, lest they overwhelm her. Still she ran on but the footfalls behind her grew heavier and closer all the time. Then she felt a claw rake at her back and legs and she was falling, stumbling, sprawling, a monster tearing at her. Jenks flailed, desperately doing anything she could to stay alive –

'Be still, drokk you!' yelled Chung, slapping the hysterical cadet across the face several times. 'It's me, Judge Chung!'

Jenks lay quite still for a moment, then burst into tears, great heaving sobs wracking her chest and throat.

'Why did you run? Why did you desert the others?' demanded Chung angrily.

'I – I – ' sobbed Jenks.

'Tell me, damn you!'

'I – I – ' cried Jenks, but now terror filled her face and a quivering hand pointed past Chung, behind her. The Judge turned and began to stand, taking in the horror around them.

'Grud on a greenie!' whispered Emma Chung. She had fought the zombie millions during Judgement Day and survived the horrors of the Dark Judges' reign over Mega-City One during Necropolis, but she had never seen anything like this before.

They were in a charnel-house. Around them were the bodies of at least a thousand victims of the gila-munja. Some were mere skeletons, the bones picked clean, some of them broken open for the marrow to be sucked from inside. Other corpses were still partially intact, just sections torn away, some of the flesh hanging from the putrefying bodies as maggots crawled cross the surface of old wounds and cuts. Still others hung nearly intact, suspended from the ceiling in the way that game had been hung by human hunters centuries before. The corpses were a mixture of human and mutant, but they all had one thing in common: fear. Those whose faces were still visible were stricken with a terrible visage of agony and pain and fear.

Chung retched twice before she was even aware of it. After a few moments to recover, she turned back to the petrified Jenks, who seemed rooted to the spot.

'You've led us into their lair! Sweet Jovus . . .' Chung realised Jenks was simply frozen with terror. She slapped the cadet across the face – once, twice, three times and more. Finally, Jenks blinked and looked at the ground.

'I'm sorry, I'm so sorry – ' she stammered.

'Save it for Dredd, make your apologies to him. We've got to get out of here now!' Chung hauled the cadet to her feet and they turned to leave. But a shadow was blocking the entrance way.

It was the gila-munja pack leader.

'Get thee behind me, spawn of Satan!'

Nita had never seen a live horse before, only diagrams in tedious history lectures about DNA-cloning and regeneration techniques and how these had been used to reintroduce many species to parts of the planet at the end of the twenty-first century. The horse had been the largest animal to be success-fully reintroduced – anything bigger had proved problematic. Nita had never realised horses could grow to be so big!

The jet-black steed appeared from nowhere, leap-ing over the advancing gila-munja with a mighty bound. It stopped almost immediately, reined in by its rider, and it was only then that Nita realised this massive animal had someone riding it. Seated on the horse was a whipcord-thin figure, armed with two ridiculously large-barrelled pistols which he began firing indiscriminately into the attacking creatures. At the same time he seemed to be shouting, as if quoting from something or someone – Nita didn't recognise the words.

'Vengeance is mine, saith the Lord!' Each shot took out at least three gila-munja and the pistols seemed to hold more than thirty rounds each – an advantage of the massive calibre, Nita surmised later.

'Blessed are the peacemakers, for they shall be called the sons of God!' Another group of monsters was mowed down by this dynamic figure, blasting away with a fervour and accuracy to match any Street Judge.

'Ask and ye shall receive!' Within a few minutes, the gila-munja ranks had been cut by more than half; just a few dozen left. Nita realised she was still holding the frag grenade. Releasing the trigger mechanism, she launched it into the rabble of ravenous creatures, who were starting to beat a hasty retreat away from this new entry to the battle, a foe the gila-munja had recently grown to hate.

Now the horse and its rider were chasing the monsters! Nita could barely believe her eyes. Then, before she could call out a warning, three gila-munja appeared from the rubble, their chameleon skin hiding their attack until the last possible moment. The trio flung themselves at the horse and its rider, sending them tumbling to the ground. One of the gila-munja stood over the fallen man, ready to slay this demon that plagued them.

'No!' cried out a croaky voice from the other side of the clearing. Nita turned to see a tiny hunchbacked figure atop some mutant creature, twirling a strange device above his head. Some sort of brown leathereen, it had a hoop at its end which he swung in a great circle in the air, creating a high-pitched wailing.

The trio of cadets turned back to see the gila-munja confused again, the sound seemingly throwing the monsters off-balance for a moment. Then three shots rang out, clear and sharp like a bell ringing.

The three gila-munja standing over their tormentor looked surprised, small holes appearing in their foreheads. Then they tumbled to the ground, rolling over to reveal the back halves of their glistening, scaled heads plastered over the rocks and rubble behind them. A putrid smell of death and sweat and fear hung in the air, along with the strangely mouth-watering scent of slowly roasting gila-munja flesh, as the victims of incendiary bullets slowly burnt away.

From the shadows Judge Dredd emerged, his uniform torn in several places, one kneepad torn away, cuts and scratches visible across his face. In his hand was a still-smoking Lawgiver.

'So what happened to Chung and Jenks?'

'We're dead. We're dead. We're dead. We're dead –'

'Shut the drokk up!' hissed Judge Chung at the cadet as they stood facing the gila-munja pack leader. 'If we don't panic, we can get out of this death-house alive!'

'Some chance!' exclaimed Jenks sarcastically.

'If you'd bothered to look, you'd see he's wounded, missing an arm. I reckon that makes us about even,' grimaced Chung, looking around for possible weapons. She'd lost her Lawgiver and belt when attacked by the gila-munja earlier; Jenks had abandoned her own while fleeing the firefight. Stupid girl: looks like we'll have to do this the hard way, thought Emma.

'So – you kill here often?' she said to the angry, bleeding pack leader, getting just a grunt for her troubles. 'Not much of a conversationalist, are we?' Behind her back, the Judge gestured for Jenks to circle around to the opposite side that she was approaching their foe from.

The pack leader noticed the target splitting apart,

94

his viciously scarred head swivelling from side to side slowly to take in their movements.

'Not big on peripheral vision, huh?' continued Chung gamely. 'We'll have to see what we can do about that.' She looked to Jenks, who had now circled around to the wounded side of the pack leader.

'Are we ready?' asked Chung politely. 'Now!'

The pair flung themselves at the monster, desperately trying to grab hold of its remaining arm while avoiding the venom-laden teeth of its claw. The monster fought for all it was worth, but the wound had cost it a lot of blood and sapped its strength. Finally, with a last effort, Chung grabbed the claw and turned it back on its owner, plunging the razor-sharp teeth into the gila-munja's neck. The claw flexed involuntarily, slashing again and again at the nerves and veins. In moments, the monster was dead.

Chung and Jenks collapsed back onto the ground, panting with exhaustion. Finally, the Judge turned to the cadet.

'Thanks. But I'm going to recommend Judge Dredd fail you. Because if he doesn't, I will!'

CHAPTER FOUR

'So what's your story?'

It was more than an hour since the firefight with the gila-munja, and the cadets had spent the intervening period counting corpses and checking all the gila-munja were dead. The task had been arduous and delicate – even in death, the claws of a gila-munja held enough venom to kill a human outright.

During that time Chung and Jenks had reappeared, the Judge leading the cadet in front of her. Nita tried to catch Jenks' attention but the disgraced juve kept her eyes downcast, avoiding them all. Nita noticed Chung take Dredd to one side for a few moments – to report the cadet's desertion, she wondered – but Dredd's face remained as grim and resolute as ever, blank of emotion or reaction.

Nita, Archer and Coster had been aided in the body count by the strange mutant who had brought up the rear when the gunfighter in religious garb had burst upon the scene, guns ablaze. Nita was startled to discover the mutant was a friendly, personable little man.

'Joe's the name, Resurrection Joe. Don't mind me, I'm just a humble deputy for the reverend there,' said the hunchbacked fellow.

'You saved our skins, that's for sure!' said Archer excitedly, the adrenalin of combat still flooding through him like liquid fire. 'Where'd you come from?'

Joe explained how they'd been tracking the gila-munja for days. While he spoke, Nita noticed Coster kept away from the little man, almost as if he was contagious. She approached the cadet quietly.

'What's wrong with you? He hasn't got the plague, you know, and they did save our lives,' she whispered.

'He's a mutant, can't you see?' replied Coster.

'So what? He's a mutant, you're black, I'm brown, so what? Maybe we should judge a person by their actions, not by their colour or genetic structure!' said Nita, starting to feel the old anger welling up inside her.

'But the Law states – '

'Drokk the Law! This isn't about textbooks, this is about survival and finding allies where you can! And if you can't see that, you don't deserve to be a Judge!' Nita stormed off to help Joe and Archer finish the body-count on the other side of the clearing.

Nearby, Dredd and Chung were talking with the mysterious stranger, who was tending to his mutant steed.

'So what's your story?' repeated Dredd. After a long silence, the tall figure let go of his horse's front left hoof and stood upright, turning to glare at his interrogators.

'Name's Preacher Cain,' he growled, all flinty eyes and jutting jawline.

'Anyone can wear a dog-collar. What's your authority?' snarled Dredd, his lip curling.

Cain just pulled back his long, battered riding coat to reveal a metal star pinned to his left breast.

97

Emblazoned into the metal were the words: OUT-LANDS MARSHAL. 'That enough authority for you?'

'You're a way out of the territories. This ain't your jurisdiction, Cain.'

'Hot pursuit, we been hunting these servants of Satan for nearly a week, up from below the border. Reckon that makes it my jurisdiction,' replied the preacher gruffly.

'Yeah?'

'Yeah!'

'Yeah?' In the background, Judge Chung rolled her eyes and suppressed a smile. Any minute now they'll start arguing about who's got the biggest gun, she thought.

'Yeah!' continued Cain. By now the two hard men had squared up to each other and were standing just inches apart, their chins almost touching each other. 'Anyways, from what I saw, you boys wouldn't have survived without our help!'

'Is that so?' demanded Dredd.

'Yeah!'

'Yeah?'

Chung couldn't take any more of this rampant machismo and strolled off to supervise the cadets. 'Men!' she muttered to herself darkly as Dredd and Cain set to jabbing each other in the chest.

Soon afterwards the pair emerged into the clearing, looking a little scuffed and dusty. The scowls across their faces persuaded Chung, Joe and the cadets to refrain from asking any questions.

'Time to leave, deputy. Our work here is done, but the Lord's crusade must continue!' announced Cain. Joe snapped to attention and quickly mounted his patient mule. Moments later, Cain too was ready to ride, but there was just time for some parting unpleasantries.

'Keep to your own territories next time!' advised Dredd, a thunderous aspect on his face.

'And you!' Cain jabbed his spurs viciously into his steed and galloped away. Resurrection Joe just had time for a quick wave and smile to Nita and Archer before following his master out of sight.

Dredd looked down at the white helmets of Agnew and Zender, which had been found after the battle. The white casings were cracked open and spattered with blood and other tissue. 'Coster! Singh!'

The pair snapped to attention. 'Yes sir!'

'Start digging two graves. You are authorised to use the bike lasers to break open the ground if necessary.'

'But sir, the – ' began Coster.

'Just do it!' snapped Dredd. 'We bury our dead, we don't leave them to the dog-vultures as carrion!'

'Yes sir!'

It took more than an hour to hollow out two shallow graves. The work was hot, dirty and exhausting, but Nita counted herself lucky. Archer and Jenks had been assigned to gather together the remains of the fallen cadets for burial.

Finally, Zender and Agnew were laid to rest in the centre of the clearing where they had fallen in battle. Cairns were built over each grave from the rubble of the destroyed and battered buildings around them. Chung drove a metal stake into the ground at the head of each grave and the cadets' white helmets were placed atop the stakes as markers. Then Dredd and Chung pulled out their Lawgivers and fired the final salute over the resting places.

Standing to one side, the four cadets dealt with their emotions as well as they could. Coster remained unmoved, at least outwardly, while Jenks still kept her eyes cast down, knowing she was the reason Agnew had died. Nita could hear her friend Archer sniffing beside her, trying to hold back tears. But she let the tears flow freely down her face. Nita had been taught it was right to mourn by her family, and she wasn't going to stop now, even for the almighty Justice Department.

The burial over, Dredd called the cadets to attention to make a rare and brusque speech.

'Cadets, most of you handled yourselves well in battle. The numbers of gila-munja were almost overwhelming yet the conflict was won, despite outside interference. The loss of Zender and Agnew was – unfortunate. However, the actions of one amongst you was unforgivable. Cadet Jenks – step forward!'

Nita watched her fellow cadet move out of line, Jenks' gauntlet-clad hands visibly shaking.

'I – I'm sorry, sir, I panicked and ran – '

'You deserted your fellow cadets. You ran from the enemy, and in doing so led another cadet to his death. You've been a trouble-maker since the start of this Hotdog Run – don't think I don't know about that little incident between you and Singh. I know everything, Jenks. Everything!' By now Dredd was thrusting his face so close to the cowering cadet that his helmet was banging against hers.

'I – I'm sorry, I – I – ' stammered Jenks.

'Kate Jenks, I hereby fail you on this Cursed Earth assessment,' announced Dredd formally, making sure the other cadets could hear every word.

'You will return to Mega-City One, alone, and report your failure to the Academy of Law, from where you will be expelled forthwith. Do you understand this instruction?'

'I – I – ' Jenks was crying openly by now, tears streaming down her face.

'DO YOU UNDERSTAND?' demanded Dredd.

'Yes, sir.' Jenks managed to pull herself together, wiping the tears from her face. Snapping to attention, she pulled on her helmet, strode to her Lawmaster and rode away, heading back to Mega-City One.

Nita watched Jenks drive away towards an uncertain future. The journey back to Mega-City One was difficult enough as part of a squad like theirs, on your own it was ten times as deadly. If Jenks survived the trip, she faced expulsion from the Academy, possible brain-surgery to remove elements of her Judge training and aggression, to help her fit back into the community as a normal citizen. Even then, she would be an outcast for the rest of her life, unable to apply for any kind of employment. Failure was something no cadet liked to contemplate but which each one feared. 'Death before failure' was often the motto of cadets in the Academy of Law and they meant every word of it. The harsh sound of Dredd's voice brought Nita snapping back to reality.

'Cadets! Check your bikes, reload your ammunition and prepare to move out – we ride in five minutes.'

'Yes, sir!' replied Nita, Archer and Coster in unison, setting about the task. There were only three cadets now, but the mission would continue until it was completed, as per Justice Department regulations. According to cadet rumours, the most cadets Dredd had ever passed in a single Hotdog Run assessment was two and that was considered exceptional. Chances were, at least one of the three left was going to fail.

Dredd turned to Chung. 'You can take Zender's Lawmaster until we get back to Mega-City One. Suggest we reload from the ammunition and stores inside Agnew's bike, share them amongst the rest, then destroy the bike.'

Chung nodded. When she had speed-rolled off her bike, she had set its auto-destruct to destroy the attack from the Devil's Lapdogs. Now she would have to ride one of the dead cadets' bikes. However, the other bike could not be left intact in the Cursed Earth, in case it should fall into the wrong hands: standard Justice Department procedure required the machine be destroyed if at all possible. 'I'll set the auto-destruct,' she told Dredd.

Within minutes, the squad – now reduced to five members – was riding out of Beakersville. Behind them the auto-destruct exploded Agnew's bike, sending a mushrooming fireball high into the air. Nita watched the black clouds hanging in the sky behind them, dark against the orange skyline of radioactive haze, until a voice spoke in her ear, through the helmet radio.

'Don't look back, Singh. We have to go forward,' said Judge Emma Chung.

'Yes, ma'am.'

Kate Jenks was stunned and surprised when she heard the explosion far behind her. Braking and turning to the left, she looked back to see the fireball rise above the rubble that had once been Beakersville.

'Of course. Destroying one of the bikes – probably Agnew's,' she told herself, trying to push the sounds of his dying screams out of her mind, but knowing they would haunt her for the rest of her life. Unfortunately, that would not be for very long.

When the tall one on the black beast appeared, the gila-munja were terrified. Days before, this foe with hands that spat death had killed many of their number. They had stumbled back to their northern lair, beaten and hungry, with little to show for their raiding party but scars and fallen warriors. There was murmurings of a revolt against the pack leader and the dark one was first choice to replace the leader.

The dark one was named for his scaly hide, which was unusually dusky in its natural, non-chameleonic state. He was young and strong, full of the arrogance of youth, never beaten in battle, sure of his own invincibility. He had long coveted all that the pack leader possessed but none could challenge the leader, except by combat to the death. The dark one bided his time, built up his own following and waited for his chance.

When the tall one appeared, atop his steed of night and dealing death by the dozen, the dark one made his bid. The pack leader was wounded and had fled the field of war. Now the dark one claimed the pack as his own and called them away, leaving those still loyal to the pack leader to die at the hands of the tall one.

Several hours later, nearly a hundred gila-munja were following the dark one eastwards to another part of the Cursed Earth, looking for a new lair. Already the dark one was being proclaimed pack leader of the new tribe. Now, he just needed an act, a sign to cement his authority.

Suddenly a booming, bellowing call of metal and fire came from the west, from behind them. The pack turned as one to see the fire leap skywards. Only the dark one noticed the lone rider in the canyon below them, who had also stopped to look back at the fireball. The skin around the new pack leader's mouth stretched sideways and a long, saliva-coated length of tensile flesh slipped out, running itself lovingly around the edges of the mouth. A trickle of saliva hung, then dropped slowly to the ground.

Kate Jenks turned back to the path ahead and gunned the accelerator of her Lawmaster. For the last few minutes she was sure she could hear something, like the sound of flesh slapping against flesh, but she couldn't be sure. The high canyon walls round her acted as an echo-chamber, turning the tiniest noise into a resounding one.

'Time to go back and face the music – no future out here,' she told herself grimly and the wheels began turning. Suddenly the walls around her seemed to shimmer and shift, but this was no heat-haze rising from the radioactive desert floor.

Directly in front of her she could make out a shape, its hue a shade darker than the rest. It seemed to rustle and sway from side to side, almost like a slow dance, almost hypnotic . . .

Jenks shook herself out of the reverie and took in her situation. She was surrounded by gila-munja, alone in the middle of the Cursed Earth, rejected and reviled by her fellow Judges, with nothing to go back to but a miserable existence as the lowest of the low, a reject, dishonourably discharged from the Academy of Law.

'You know, guys,' announced Jenks, almost good-humouredly, 'I'd never even contemplated failure before today.' Around her the shimmering shapes began to close in for the kill. 'But then, I'd never contemplated suicide either.' Jenks' hand initiated the auto-destruct countdown. Ten, nine, eight . . .

'Makes you think, doesn't it?'

Five, four, three . . .

'See you in hell, drokkers!'

One, zero.

'Coster, how far to the edge of the black spot?' questioned Dredd, checking the cadet's reply against the indications of his own Lawmaster's in-built sensors.

'Estimate less than two hours, sir. However, the area of navigational disturbance seems to be expanding outwards sir, making exact distances hard to calculate.'

'Hmm,' murmured Dredd. The squad had paused after riding for more than five hours non-stop. By now the worst heat of the day had passed, with just an hour of twilight left to light their way. 'Any townships or settlements ahead?'

Coster switched his bike monitor to the topography memory banks. 'One township, sir, called Lazarus. Mixture of muties and norms, population of less than five hundred. About seventy minutes from our present location.'

Dredd turned to the other cadets. 'Archer – tactics?'

'Suggest we continue but find a camp-site just short of Lazarus for the night,' replied the slightly chubby cadet in even, measured tones.

'Why?' quizzed the senior Judge.

'Reaching Lazarus would leave us riding in darkness – dangerous in this terrain, against unknown enemies. Also, it's better if we stay outside settlements at night, easier to defend ourselves. And strangers arriving this late in the day, even Judges, aren't likely to be welcome.'

'Good. Singh – any other reasons?' asked Dredd.

'The black spot could be caused by someone or generated from something within the settlement. Better to arrive first thing, fresh and able to find out what we want, with the element of surprise on our side,' answered Nita, thinking quickly. She hadn't been ready for the question because she had been watching her friend Archer. The Hotdog Run seemed to have been the making of him, he was now far more self-assured and confident. Nita had had her doubts that he would survive the trip into this forbidding territory, let alone prosper in it, but he had proved her wrong.

Dredd considered for a moment before announcing his decision. 'We ride for another forty minutes then find the best camp-site we can for the night. Move out!'

The two bikers had never seen anything like it in all their days. The pair had left Mega-City One nearly a year before, in search of freedom, the chance to live a little, to see what was left of America.

Of course the Judges had tried to stop them, told them all sorts of horror stories about muties and acid rain, rad-storms and dinosaurs, bandits and monsters, two thousand klicks of coast-to-coast hell, the Judges had called it. But to this pair, that didn't sound like hell. That sounded like a party!

So the two bikers had zoomed out of the gates in the West Wall to one of the greatest adventures of their lives. Just like the Judges said, there were dinosaurs (recreated from the DNA inside the blood cells of fossils, then cloned up to full size and kept in huge natural reserves), mutants and even two crazed mechanoids out to destroy the world. But the pair had survived the encounter and gone on to several other, even more exciting escapades since.

But what they were now looking at, this beat everything they had seen and experienced since leaving Mega-City One all those months ago.

One of the pair, all flaming orange hair and unbridled body odours, turned to his companion. 'Hey, Ryder, man, like, what is it?'

By comparison, his partner was decidedly more low-key, a mane of long black hair swept back from the face, eyes protected by expansive, pitch-black sunglasses. 'I don't know, Sleeze, but one thing's for sure . . .' He lowered his shades to get a closer look, horror filling his features. 'It ain't cool. Let's get the drokk outta here!'

'You said it, man!' Twin bursts of acceleration, a squeal of tyres and the pair were burning rubber, heading as fast as they possibly could in the opposite direction.

Behind them, the darkness edged outwards, in an ever-expanding circle of black.

In Mega-City One, the furtive monitoring Judge was maintaining his covert surveillance over the city's sensor systems. Besides the West Wall sensors, he was also operating intercept programmes on all radio communications from and to the Cursed Earth, as well as satellite monitoring systems. But the monitoring Judge had one advantage over his counterparts in the main Control despatch and monitoring centre – an extra satellite in space, placed there three years before in geostationary orbit in the skies west of Mega-City One. It was the sensors on that satellite he was monitoring when his superior appeared behind him.

'Anything?' asked the senior Judge, startling the Judge sat at the secret monitors.

'What the – ? Oh, it's you, sir! Sorry, you startled me, nearly jumped out of my – '

'Yes, yes. Now tell me – do you have anything more to report on Dredd's team?'

'Well, they've gone out of range of all the standard Mega-City One sensor systems. I'm only able to track them now on our own satellite,' explained the monitor.

'Where are they?'

'Here, I'll show you.' The monitor activated a holo-projector, which threw up a three-dimensional graphic of the Cursed Earth. In the centre of the image, a small black circle glowed with an evil intensity. Around it a series of small white dots hung in the air. Just to the west of a dot quite near the edge of the black circle was a flashing point of light.

'The black circle is the navigational black spot, where the two h-wagons went down, sir. These white dots are settlements. According to what our satellite is picking up, the black spot is growing, expanding outwards. Quite slowly, but it's already absorbed two such settlements – '

'Yes, yes, what about Dredd's squad?' pressed the senior Judge.

'They're this flashing point here, sir, just coming within range of the black spot.'

The senior Judge leaned closer to the holo-projector to get a better grasp of the positions involved. Suddenly the light beams from the projector shut out and smoke began to pour from the unit. Quickly the monitoring Judge powered down the unit, dousing the fires with his reinforced gauntlets.

'Sorry, sir, that's the third projector I've lost today looking at that area. The black spot seems to send out pulses of some kind of energy, which short out any sensing equipment,' explained the monitor. 'We won't be able to use the satellite again for another six hours, and by then the squad will have entered the black spot.' The monitor was apologetic but his superior seemed unperturbed.

'That's all right, I know everything that I need for now,' said the senior Judge, turning to walk from the secret room. At the door he paused when asked a question.

'Will you need me for anything else, sir?'

The senior Judge pulled his Lawgiver from within his tunic and pointed it at the monitoring Judge. 'No, I don't think so.' He fired once, then again, both shots tearing through the junior Judge's brain. 'Thank you for your assistance.' Adjusting the setting on his weapon to incendiary, he fired three times at the equipment in the tiny room only leaving when the chamber was well ablaze, all evidence of its contents destroyed.

The approaching column appeared to be just a single vehicle for a long time, as Dredd, Chung and the three cadets saw it on the horizon. It was only when they pulled away to one side that the length of the column became apparent from the line of convoy members stretching off into the distance, a massive dust cloud billowing up behind it.

'Interesting,' commented Dredd. 'Archer – what do you make of it?'

'A large convoy, sir. Judging by its haste, they're fleeing something. Or someone. Possibly refugees from some disaster.'

'Possibly,' agreed Dredd, but his voice suggested other reasons could be involved.

It was just after dawn and the squad had just begun the last leg of their journey to the settlement of Lazarus, after camping the night on a nearby hillside. Now their path was blocked by this massive caravan of vehicles, seemingly fleeing whatever lay behind them.

At the front of the column were two bedraggled figures on motorcycles, racing towards the five-strong squad. As they drew near, Dredd signalled for the bikers to stop.

'Hey, man, have you seen what's back there? We ain't stopping for nothing or nobody – '

Dredd's Lawgiver was now aimed at the speaking biker's head, unwavering, resolute, determined.

'Though of course we've got time to speak to these like, nice friendly Judges – right, Ryder?' The orange-haired hippy turned to his companion for support.

'It's cool, Sleeze,' was the minimal reply.

'So, okay man, you got our attention. Like, what d'you wanna know?'

By now the rest of the column had caught up to

them. Dredd motioned for the two bikers to pull to the side and waved the rest of the convoy through.

'Hey, how come they get to, like, keep going man?' protested Sleeze noisily. Dredd pointed his Lawgiver at the two bikers again. 'Oh yeah, I remember now,' said Sleeze sheepishly.

'Where have you come from?' demanded Dredd.

'The west, man, figure it out!'

'Spare me the lip, boy!'

'Uh, yeah, man, be cool. We've come from Lazarus, okay, man?'

'Who are these people? Where are they going?' Now Chung got involved in the questioning, lest Dredd's brusqueness and the bikers' disregard for authority kept them here all day.

'These people? Man, they ARE Lazarus – almost the entire population, y'know? That's right, isn't it, Ryder?' Sleeze turned to his partner for confirmation. Ryder nodded his agreement.

'As for where they're going, man, I'd say just about anywhere away from, like, that thing back there! Now can we, like, go, man?' Sleeze was starting to get edgy and impatient, fidgeting in his seat.

Dredd turned to Archer and Coster, both of whom had been monitoring Sleeze's responses on their Birdie lie detectors. They both nodded, testifying to the truth of the biker's words. The senior Judge turned back to the strange pair. By now, most of the convoy had passed by behind them and was starting to disappear over the horizon, heading eastwards in a hurry.

'What thing? What's happened at Lazarus?' demanded Dredd, determined to find out the true nature of the problem the squad were facing.

111

'Hell, man, what hasn't happened? The dead gettin' outta their graves, animals, folks disappearing, corpses turning up out of nowhere. And then, like, that black stuff on the ground – it ain't natural, man, it just ain't natural!' Next to Sleeze, Ryder was nodding his head in agreement. 'Now, if you wanna know any more,' concluded Sleeze, revving the accelerator on his bike, 'I suggest you go see for yourself, man!'

With that the pair accelerated away.

'Should we pursue them?' asked Coster, ready to make chase. Behind him the last of the convoy went past. Already the pair of bikers had caught up, and were nearly half-way along the caravan of fleeing vehicles.

'No, we'll get no more from those two,' grimaced Dredd. Around them the dust from the convoy's passing began to settle to earth again, specks of orange falling onto their radiation cloaks, like tiny snowflakes. 'Time to find out what's really going on with this black spot – move out!'

'He's coming, the deadman, the dreadman, I see him!'

Blind Mary had no eyes, but she could see the future. She was also one of Soon's favourites. Deep within her mind, he spoke to her.

'A Judge? A Mega-City One Judge?'

'Yes! He is steeped in blood. The souls of billions have fallen before him yet he believes in one thing – the Law. He is dangerous!'

'Good. I shall enjoy punishing him and all his kind for what they did to me.' The voice paused, evil pleasure replaced with curiosity. 'Is he alone?'

'No. Four travel with him. Three are but children,

the other is also a Judge, but not so dangerous as he.'

'Hmm, playthings at best, but the Judges might have their own uses. How long before they reach us?'

'Less than a day, perhaps only hours. They are cautious.'

'Then we must bring them to us. Do they know about the child?'

'No, nothing.'

'What? Look again!' demanded Soon.

'Nothing, my lord, I tell you, nothing!' replied Mary, her voice quaking with fear. It was best not to anger the lord, his furies were legendary among the children of Soon.

'Sssh, Mary, sssh. Be calm! I won't hurt you, I want to reward you,' cooed Soon in her mind. 'You have served me well, come to me now and receive your reward.'

'Thank you, my lord,' said Mary and moved forward, guided by Soon's voice in her head. In moments she stood before him, just inches away from him, from his terrifying, disgusting naked form.

'Touch me, Mary.'

The blind woman slipped forward a hand, stroking over Soon's chest and arms, downwards and then upwards, touching his neck, his chin, his face. Where his mouth should have been was just skin, stretched taut. Mary tried to control her feelings, a mixture of revulsion and passion and fear.

'You know I have no mouth, Mary.'

'Yes, my lord.'

'Yet I have always longed to be kissed. Kiss me Mary, where my mouth should be. Kiss me now,' breathed Soon in her mind, silkily persuasive.

113

'I – I – '

'Kiss me, Mary!'

'Yes, m-my lord.' Trembling, half terrified, Mary leaned forward and pressed her lips against the skin between Soon's chin and twisted nose. Beneath the skin, she could feel his jaws working, his fused, deformed teeth gnashing in pain and frustration. It was horrible, like kissing some smooth, vibrating canvas. Mary tried to pull away but now Soon's clump-like hands were sliding up her body, pushing away the robe from her shoulders, roaming over the curves of her figure.

For a moment she began to succumb to pleasure but then the hands became more insistent, grabbing, pawing, clawing at her, invading, brutal. The more she tried to fight them, the worse it became, the tighter the grip on her naked body, the more vicious the movements. In moments the hands on her seemed to alter, changing, mutating into sharpened talons, growing ever more razor-like.

Now the talons were tearing at her skin, slashing at her like knives. Mary cried out, again and again but to no avail. No one was coming to save her, no one dared oppose the lord, no one ever would again.

She was losing blood at an incredible rate but Soon kept her conscious by shouting into her mind, screaming at her psyche like the cry of a thousand screaming banshees.

'Now do you know what pain feels like, bitch? Do you! This is pain!'

Finally, just as Mary felt blackness creeping over her for the last time, Soon's voice came back to her one more time.

'I've no more use for you, Mary, so I'm going to feast on your mind instead. Time to die!' Maniacal laughter was the last sound her mind heard as Soon plunged his talons through the spaces where her eyes should have been, deep into her brain, waves of psychic energy pouring back through the claws to his own mind.

Their two bodies were locked together for a moment, like two lovers at the ultimate ecstasy. Then Soon stepped away, letting the bloody, hollow husk that had been Blind Mary fall to the glasseen floor like an empty bone bag. With relish he smeared his bloodied talons over his face and chest, slicing little tears into his own skin.

'I do so love a good appetiser, before the main course arrives,' he announced telepathically.

Outside the blackness surged forward.

'There's something strange here, sir,' said Nita into her helmet radio. She had checked the readings again and again but could find no fault in her Lawmaster's on-board sensors. Perhaps checking with the others would resolve the anomaly.

'What is it, Singh?' replied Dredd.

'Well, according to my sensors, we are now entering an area with absolutely no radioactivity. None at all, not even the standard background trace found in the most unspoiled areas of the world, sir.'

'Interesting. Everybody check their sensors,' ordered Dredd, running a systems check himself. Within moments his bike sensors confirmed what Nita and the others were saying – the area they had just entered bore no traces of radiation whatsoever. Dredd called a halt to their progress for a moment.

'Singh, you discovered this – any explanations?'

'Well, Beakersville exhibited minimal radiation, probably because of its geographical position. But this area is very close to the navigational black spot we're investigating. And that is at the centre of the Cursed Earth, ground zero for one of the biggest explosions of the Atomic Wars. By rights, the radiation in this area should be phenomenal . . .' speculated Nita.

'Yes, but do you have any explanations?' asked Dredd again.

'Not really, sir, no,' replied Nita humbly.

'Anybody do any better?'

A pause, and then Chung spoke up. 'Obviously, there must be some connection to the navigational black spot. We must be nearly on top of it by now, Lazarus is just a couple of klicks away. I suggest we keep going forward – it could be that the black spot knocks out radiation just as effectively as it knocked out the systems on the Justice Department's two aircraft.'

'Feasible,' nodded Dredd. 'We proceed.' The squad continued onwards, not noticing the broken-down farmhouse hidden away to one side by some bizarre rock formations.

'Have they gone?'

The old mutant woman at the window nodded, then closed the wooden shutters and turned away. 'We should have stopped them, or at least warned them,' she said wearily. 'We could soon need their help ourselves.'

Beside her another mutant eldster was fingering the harsh fabric of her cloak. 'No! You know the prophecy as well as I do – "One shall come, unknowing, unseeing, and that one will be the guardian". Those poor people out there, they're just fodder – the guardian will come later, mark my words!'

116

Now a third old woman chipped into the argument. 'Well, all I can say is, they should hurry. At this rate, the blackness will get to us before your great guardian does. I tell you, we should have fled Lazarus with the others!'

After that the argument turned to bickering, until a light, almost lilting voice hushed the others to silence. 'The guardian is coming. We must wait here, or be lost.'

The three old women nodded, knowing the voice always spoke the truth. It had always been that way, and always would be so.

'Grud on a greenie!' exclaimed Nita before she could stop herself. The squad had soon found the settlement of Lazarus and was riding through when they saw him, appearing as if from nowhere directly in their path.

The man was bleeding from his side, his hands and feet. Blood poured from his eyes, which he clutched at with bewildered hands. 'My eyes! My eyes! They took my eyes!'

The squad braked and swerved as one to avoid the stricken figure as it staggered around in circles in the centre of the road. Drawing his Lawgiver, Dredd cautiously approached the forlorn figure, wary for any deception.

'Who are you?' the Judge asked, stopping beyond arm's reach.

'My eyes, my eyes,' the man kept sobbing. Dredd circled the loner before signalling the others over to give assistance. Nita brought the medical supplies in her storage pods with her. Among her specialist studies at the Academy had been three months spent working with the Med-Judges.

Once the bleeding was staunched and dressings applied, Dredd returned to his original question. 'Who are you?'

'My name is N-Novar,' stammered the wounded man. His simple clothes were in tatters, stained with blood, excrement and the desert dust. 'I was taken captive, pulled into the asylum. They were doing te-terrible things there. Don't make me go back! You can't!' He started screaming.

'Don't worry, we won't,' assured Chung, looking to Dredd. The senior Judge was rubbing his chin between thumb and forefinger thoughtfully.

'The asylum, hmm,' mused Dredd, but didn't offer any explanation of his line of thought. Instead he returned to questioning Novar. 'Where is this asylum? Is it in the black place?'

'Over there, to the west,' said Novar weakly. 'You have to enter the black zone to get to it. Please, don't make me go back . . .'

'Tell me about the black zone!' demanded Dredd urgently.

Nita looked up and shook her head. 'He's passed out, lack of blood. Without emergency surgery he'll die soon.'

'Unless we find out more about this asylum, a lot more people could be in danger of dying!' barked back Dredd brusquely. But even the stone-faced Judge accepted that the unconscious Novar could answer no more questions for the moment. He walked back to his Lawmaster, followed by Judge Chung.

'He mentioned an asylum and you reacted. Why?' she asked Dredd.

'A vague recollection, nothing more. The Justice Department used to run an asylum out here in the

Cursed Earth. I remember once having an insane perp sent there when the psycho-cubes were full. But that was back in the 80's, nearly thirty years ago. The entire place was closed down after some incident in '95. I'd forgotten all about it, can't even recall the location,' muttered Dredd darkly. 'It was called . . . Erebus!'

The Judge strode back to Novar and tried to prod him awake. 'The name Erebus mean anything to you, boy?' But whatever secrets Novar held stayed locked inside his unconscious mind. 'Could've done with a Psi on this trip,' commented Dredd. He mused for a full minute before announcing his decision. 'We go on, into this black zone. All these things happening in one area, it can't be coincidence.' Dredd turned to mount his Lawmaster.

'What about Novar?' asked Nita.

'We leave him behind, he's no use to us now,' said Dredd blankly.

'But he'll die! I'll stay behind and look after him,' offered Nita.

'You'll come with the rest of us,' growled Dredd. 'You said he was going to die anyway. No point in wasting any more medical supplies on him. Everybody – mount up!'

Nita thought about protesting further but the dark look on Dredd's face dissuaded her. And Dredd's logic, however harsh, was correct. Better to find the cause of suffering like this and stop it at the source; attack the cause, rather than treat the symptoms. That had been one of her first lessons while working with the Med-Judges, and it applied just as well here.

In less than a minute all five squad members were on their bikes and ready to ride. 'Draw your Lawgivers,' ordered Dredd. 'We don't know exactly what we're up against but we need to be ready for anything. Move out!'

The Hotdog Run rode away down the road, around a corner and into the black zone. From that moment they were as good as dead.

When they were gone, Novar heard a familiar voice in his head. 'Arise, Novar, your illnesses are healed!'

Novar opened his newly restored eyes and sat upright. He pulled the bloody bandages from his body and looked down to find all trace of his wounds gone, the skin unbroken, unblemished by scar or injury. 'Have they come to you, my lord?' Novar asked the air.

The reply echoed through his mind. 'Oh yes! I shall have fun with my newest arrivals, oh yes! You've done well, Novar. Return to Erebus,' said Soon telepathically.

'Thank you, my lord,' murmured Novar and stood up, brushing the dust from his clothes and body, before setting off along the road, following the path recently taken by Judge Dredd, Chung and the three cadets.

In the centre of the black zone, Soon laughed inside his mind. He loved to have a new plaything, and five at once! What a day this was going to be.

Part Two: Two days ago

CHAPTER ONE

The sensors built into the West Wall picked up the approaching object first, when it was still two miles away. The automatic systems primed the missile defence systems and locked onto the target while alerting the sentry Judges on duty of the incoming object.

Judges Blundell and Fynes sat atop the massive gun emplacement, staring out into the radioactive haze beyond the wall. Both had seen duty on the wall during Judgement Day, when Judge Dredd had ordered it set ablaze to keep the zombie hordes out of Mega-City One. The fighting had been brutal, hand-to-hand combat with the undead, and both men counted themselves fortunate to have survived. By comparison, returning to sentry duty now the wall had been reconstructed seemed uneventful, even dull at times. But they didn't complain or seek a transfer – the pair felt they deserved some quieter duties for a while. The horrors of the zombie war still haunted many Judges. . .

When the alert came Blundell was first to react, pulling his high-powered binoculars up to his eyes, scanning the horizon for approaching vehicles. Fynes busied himself checking the post's weaponry was armed and ready, poised to take manual control should the automatic missile defence systems proved ineffective.

'Bike coming in,' announced Blundell, still watching the object's progress towards them. It was now less than a mile away, just at the edge of his range of vision, even with the ocular enhancements.

'Lawmaster?'

'Wait . . . yes. But there doesn't seem to be a rider . . .'

'It's coming in on auto? Could be booby-trapped.' Fynes pulled his long-gun up to his shoulder, sighting on the incoming bike. With this weapon he could shoot a tiny radbug at a klick, being a long-gun specialist. Fynes had a right to be cautious: just three weeks earlier a vehicle had approached the city walls, laden with hi-ex, another attempt by muties to decoy the guards while an assault was launched elsewhere on the wall.

'Hold your fire,' advised his partner. 'I was wrong – there is a passenger, looks like a Judge. But they aren't riding the bike, they're lashed to it!' Blundell pulled the binoculars away from his face. 'Alert the gates and get a med-team down there, now!'

'All right, someone wanna tell us what happened?'

Chief Judge McGruder was furious. It had taken nearly an hour for the news of the bike's arrival to be transmitted through the chain of command to her, despite express orders that all news of arrivals from the Cursed Earth should go to her first, no matter how trivial.

Judge Dredd's Hotdog Run had been sent out on a routine mission two weeks before, a trip expected to take four days, five at the maximum. Since then there had been no sign of them, no message pods, nothing. It was totally out of character for Dredd to ignore standard procedure, therefore something must have gone wrong – badly wrong.

Normally, the disappearance of a Hotdog Run squad would not concern the chief Judge, but Dredd was no ordinary Judge and right now McGruder needed all the senior Judges she could get.

She had first been Chief Judge more than a decade ago, after heading the highly secretive Special Judicial Squad, the SJS – the Judges who judged the Judges themselves. Her term had been highly successful but she had resigned after an error of judgement cost many lives, mostly those of good Judges. A woman of honour, McGruder had chosen to take the Long Walk into the Cursed Earth, one of the few options open to a Judge when they resigned. The Long Walk was meant to be a journey of no return, a former Judge dispensing justice to the wild, untamed radioactive wasteland until they died – but McGruder came back.

Several years after she had resigned, Dredd had become disillusioned with the justice system and also took the Long Walk into the Cursed Earth. There he learnt that his arch-enemy Judge Death and the Dark Judges had taken control of Mega-City One in Dredd's absence, turning it into a necropolis. Dredd decided to return to the Big Meg and try to save the city once more.

Along the way he met McGruder in the desert. Long years in the Cursed Earth had mutated her body and fried parts of her brain. Stubble grew from her chin and she sometimes gave hints of displaying a split personality, always talking in the royal 'we'. Despite this, the pair had teamed up and gone back

123

to Mega-City One. Their arrival was the turning point in the conflict and the Dark Judges were eventually routed.

The conflict over, McGruder had reassumed the role of Chief Judge, her replacement having been personally murdered by Judge Death. At the time, the city needed leadership, someone to pull it around. But more and more, Chief Judge McGruder became an isolated figure, at one point disbanding the Council of Five, her immediate advisers. The Council had met irregularly since then, such as during the multiple crises of the mayoral election day, but the Chief Judge seemed to regard her role as that of a dictator, not an individual elected from the membership of the Council of Five. Strictly speaking, she was not legally Chief Judge but no one had officially challenged her authority – not yet, anyway.

McGruder had come to depend on a small team of senior Judges for advice, particularly Hershey, whom some believed she was grooming as her successor, and Joe Dredd. But even Dredd had been in conflict with her recently, particularly over the controversial Project Mechanismo, a plan to introduce robo-judges to help a depleted human contingent of Judges enforce the Law.

Now Dredd was missing, taking away one of McGruder's most powerful allies in the Justice Department. While Dredd remained loyal to McGruder, the Street Judges would continue to support her, and they made up the bulk of all Judges. But the Chief Judge had been hearing whispers of a conspiracy against her, a few mutinous elements trying to stir up feelings against her leadership. Now with Dredd gone, that mutiny could only blossom.

'Well? Haven't lost the power of speech, have you?' demanded McGruder, her hard, flinty eyes boring into the face of her adjunct, Gault.

'A – er – communications breakdown, Chief Judge,' he stammered, avoiding her gaze.

'Yeah? Well, if it happens again, we'll break you down to rookie again, patrolling the Slab! You got that, Gault?' she warned.

'Yes, ma'am! This way, ma'am!' replied the adjunct, leading her into the central med-bays. Ahead of them a team of robo-docs and Med-Judges were clustered around an isolation tank. They stepped aside to allow the Chief Judge a closer view of the contents.

'She's in here, ma'am,' announced Gault unnecessarily and got a withering glare for his trouble. A nod of dismissal sent him scurrying away. Meanwhile, McGruder began to circle the tank, striding slowly to view it from all angles.

Inside floated the naked body of a woman, held in suspension by heavy, viscous fluids of green and yellow. Lighting from the bottom of the tank illuminated the body, an oxygen mask clamped over the nose and mouth supplied air, and other piping trailed away to one side.

The body was a mess, torn and charred. Much of the left arm was missing, seemingly sliced off, just a flap of skin hanging away from the stump. One leg was badly ruptured, muscle, tendons and bone exposed. Terrible burns ran the length of the body and parts of the hair and scalp had been torn away. The remaining hand was broken, fingers ripped backwards, fingernails missing, one stabbed into the palm of the hand.

The face was worst of all, almost a parody of a

human visage. The left ear was missing, the right eye had been plucked out and a long flap of skin from around the mouth was gone too, exposing the teeth and jaw and gums inside the mouth. Across the woman's chest a word had been clawed, slashed into the skin and soft flesh: FODDER.

'Sweet Jovus,' murmured the Chief Judge, taking in the horrific damage. Finally, she turned to the deputy head of the Med Division, Judge Julia Tierney, one eyebrow raised questioningly.

'Her name is Judge Emma Chung. Graduated in the Academy class of '10, in the top ten per cent of her intake. Been on the streets nearly five years, records show her to have been an outstanding Judge – ' said Tierney tonelessly.

'Have been?'

'She's dead, or as good as. What you see in that tank is the result of more than an hour of exacting microsurgery. She arrived at the gates in a bodybag made from scraps of her own uniform, lashed to a Lawmaster running on auto. She was in worse shape than her uniform. It's a miracle we've managed to put the pieces together again. How she survived the trip across the Cursed Earth. . .'

'Can she talk?'

'Talk? Chief Judge, this woman can't even breath without assistance from life-support systems. We read no brain activity, no motor functions, nothing. That tank is the only thing keeping her alive!' exclaimed the Med-Judge.

McGruder was unfazed. 'What about a Psi-scan?'

'Already tried, nothing,' replied Tierney dismissively.

'Can you revive her?'

'Yes, but she'd have seconds of life, a minute at most – '

'Do it.'

'But that would kill her, that's murder!' Tierney's face was flushed with anger, horrified at what McGruder was demanding.

'You said she's dead already, what can it matter? Do it, and that's an order, Tierney,' said the Chief Judge, her voice hard and steely.

'But what can you hope to gain? I've already told you she's brain-dead and – '

McGruder grabbed the Med-Judge by the throat and lifted her bodily off the ground, spitting words into her face.

'Chung's already dead but we've still got six cadets and the best damned Judge in the city out there. Now we want to know what's happened to them and she's the only one who can tell us. Either you revive her or else we'll have your badge for breakfast and find somebody else who will do as they're told. Understand?'

'I – I – '

'Do you understand?' demanded McGruder, not shouting, just a voice full of menace and eyes to chill the soul.

'Y-Yes, Chief Judge,' stammered Tierney.

'Good,' smiled McGruder, lowering the Med-Judge back to the floor again. 'Let us know when she's ready to talk and have a Psi Judge standing by. A good one!' With that the Chief Judge strode from the room with a face like thunder.

Unnoticed by the others, one of the Med-Judges slipped away to report the incident to his colleagues.

* * *

Three hours later, Chung was finally ready for her revival. A special chamber had been set up for the event, rigged with monitoring equipment manned by teks and Psi Judges. Every aspect of Chung's behaviour, her responses to questions, her breathing, even her heartbeat would be checked to see if she was able to communicate to them.

Beside all this were the many support systems keeping her alive, Tierney and the other Med-Judges assigned to Chung's care, plus an elite group of senior Judges – Shenker, head of Psi Division; Sagassi, from the SJS; Collins, from the teks; and Chief Judge McGruder. Last to arrive was Judge Barbara Hershey, Council of Five member and rising star within the Justice Department. She was frequently considered third in the unofficial command structure of Mega-City One, after McGruder and Dredd. In fact, during the zombie warfare of Judgement Day, she had been left in charge while Dredd and the Chief Judge had gone to an international Judges' conference in Hondo City to plan a global strategy against the threat. Among Hershey's duties were overseeing the running of the Academy, so the loss of the Hotdog Run squad was important to her, especially the first run out of the city since Judgement Day. Once Hershey had arrived, McGruder gave the nod for Tierney to begin the revival.

For long minutes nothing happened as Tierney and her team poured some of the most dangerous, proactive drugs and chemicals in their pharmacopoeial armoury into Chung. Finally, there was a flutter on the monitors as heart and brainwave activity increased. The signals increased and stabilised, moving close to normal levels. Tierney pulled the breathing mask away from Chung's face.

'You've got a minute, probably less,' the Med-Judge warned McGruder. The Chief Judge stepped up to the raised bed on which Chung lay and whispered into her ear.

'Chung? Chung – this is Chief Judge McGruder, can you hear us?'

Nothing, no response came.

'Chung? Chung – can you hear us? Respond in any way you can, woman!'

Still no reply.

'Chung? Chung – '

'It's hopeless, I told you it was – ' said Tierney, moving to intercede. McGruder shoved her away, back from the bed.

'We keep trying! We've got to know what happened to that Hotdog Run!' insisted the older woman.

'Please, Chief Judge, I must ask you to – '

'Wait.'

The voice was Hershey's. While everyone else had been watching the conflict between the Chief Judge and Tierney, Hershey had kept looking at Chung, hoping against hope for a sign of life. Now Hershey was pointing at Chung's hand, which had moved fractionally in the last few moments.

'It's nothing, the muscles reacting to the drugs,' said Tierney dismissively, but the Chief Judge ignored her, returning to Chung's side.

'Chung, can you hear us?'

The mouth moved, just fractionally, but a hoarse sound emerged. 'Yes.'

'What happened to you?'

For long, agonising moments there was nothing, then remarkably, Chung's face began to shake and a single tear rolled out the side of her left eye. Sobbing noises welled up from her throat – she was crying!

'Chung, what happened to you?' pleaded McGruder.

The dying Judge shook her head from side to side, as if denying something, but the tears kept flowing.

'Please, tell us!'

Judge Chung sobbed, bitter tears running down her face. 'He killed them, all of them, one by one. It was terrible, horrible what he did to them, to – to me,' she cried, shaking her head more violently now.

'Who killed them?' McGruder demanded.

'Dredd,' replied Chung, her voice just a whisper now, her face contorted, almost as if it was twisting itself into a different shape.

'She's in terrible pain, I must stop this now!' Tierney stepped forward but now it was Hershey who prevented her from intervening, a heavy, gauntlet-clad hand clamping down on the Med-Judge's shoulder.

McGruder was crouching by Chung now, one hand shaking the mutilated body, demanding more, a different answer, anything but this.

Chung turned her face towards McGruder's so close they were almost touching, and stared at the Chief Judge with her remaining eye. 'I'm sorry,' she whispered, and then her head drooped to the side for the last time.

'Get her back!' demanded McGruder.

'I can't – she's dead,' said Tierney simply. The other Med-Judges nodded their heads, concurring. But McGruder wouldn't give up, motioning for a Psi Judge to come forward and do a post-mortem Psi probe. After a few moments, the Judge stepped away from the body, shaking his head.

'Sorry, just a few images – the sound of screams, a jumble of corpses on a floor, blood, and one word, one name: Dredd. After that, just mental static. . .'

'No, we can't accept that. Dredd kill six cadets and torture Chung? Impossible!' spat the Chief Judge.

'But that would seem to be the truth of the matter,' chipped in Judge Sagassi of the SJS, speaking for the first time since entering the chamber. 'And if it's true, then it's our duty to hunt him down – and see that Justice is done.' Sagassi was stern-faced but a smile played around his eyes. A vocal opponent of McGruder's, he seemed determined to force the issue.

McGruder fumed for a minute before reaching a decision. 'We don't have all the facts available to us to choose a course of action yet. Gather all information available about this incident – we call a Council of Five meeting for twelve hundred hours, two hours from now. Don't be late!' With that she strode from the room, smacking one gauntlet-clad fist into another as she left.

'Basically, what little we've discovered in the past two hours corroborates what Chung said – '

'Or doesn't contradict it,' interrupted Hershey, to the ire of Sagassi, who had been addressing the council meeting. 'We still have no proof, except the words of a dying woman, drugged to the eyeballs.'

'Eyeball, Judge Hershey. Dredd had obviously ripped the other one from her face. Perhaps it offended him,' speculated the SJS Judge, enjoying his biblical paraphrasing.

'Wild speculation, Chief Judge,' countered Hershey.

McGruder held up a hand, silencing the two bickering councillors. The Chief Judge sighed wearily before speaking.

'Tell us the facts of the case – Sagassi, you go first please.' The ambitious SJS representative stood up and began pacing slowly around the circular meeting room, one hand stroking his ginger moustache as he spoke.

'The Hotdog Run squad left Mega-City One two weeks ago on a routine mission that should have taken four days to complete, five at the outside. Since then there has been no sign, nor words, no message pods, nothing – until the arrival of the unfortunate Judge Emma Chung this morning.' Sagassi paused, turning to look at Hershey as he delivered his next statement. 'She testified that Judge Dredd butchered the cadets and brutally attacked her. Since Chung was in no state to do anything, Dredd obviously bundled her up and sent her back to Mega-City One on her bike as some kind of grisly talisman. We can only speculate that he has been driven insane by radiation sickness and some incident happened to trigger this frenzied killing spree.

'The question now is what to do about it. I took the liberty of ordering satellite surveillance of the route the Hotdog Run was supposed to take, and also sent out a Gunbird to investigate, with orders to carry out a low-level ground search. The results of these searches should be available within the next few minutes.' Now Sagassi stopped pacing, having completed a full circle of the table, and stood behind his high-backed chair.

'Chief Judge, you must authorise a full investigation of what happened to the Hotdog Run. I will personally lead the hunt for Dredd. When we find him, we will bring him back to face justice. We must do so now!' he thundered, pounding his fist on the council table for emphasis.

'And if he protests his innocence, or resists arrest?' asked McGruder, already knowing the answer.

'Resistance can only be taken as an admission of guilt, so he would be killed, like any other fugitive murderer. That's the Law,' concluded Sagassi with an oily smile, slipping back into his seat.

'Hmph,' grunted McGruder. 'Hershey?'

The thirty-year-old Judge got to her feet, pushing her chair away from the table. If Sagassi was going to turn this into an inquisition, it was time to state a few facts, she thought. Hershey brushed a few strands of her chin-length black hair from her face and began.

'The facts restated by Judge Sagassi – such as they are – are not disputed, but their interpretation must be. He also omits several important details which I have discovered through my own investigations.' Hershey pushed back her seat and began to slowly walk around the chamber, travelling in the opposite rotation to that followed by Sagassi.

'For example, he says the squad left the city on a routine mission two weeks ago. True enough, but he does not report that the squad's mission was changed, completely altered just an hour before they were briefed. There seems to be no official record of why the mission was changed, or upon whose authority. In fact, the Tek-Judge who briefed them has disappeared without a trace. I'm having Control check the records of his movements but Tek Division have no knowledge of her whereabouts. Do they, Judge Collins?'

The head of the Tek Division shifted uncomfortably in his chair. 'Er, yes, that's right. The last notation we have is that she was summoned at short notice to give the briefing to the Hotdog Run squad. After that, she just seems to have, well, vanished. That's confirmed by Control.'

'Curious,' commented McGruder. 'Continue, Hershey.'

'Thank you. According to Control's logs for the West Wall, the Hotdog Run's mission was to investigate a new lair of gila-munja which had sprung up near the remains of Milwaukee, an unusually northern location for a breed that prefers the badlands around Texas City,' said Hershey.

'That's right!' interrupted Sagassi.

'Wrong!' spat back Hershey vehemently. 'The squad was sent deep into the Cursed Earth to investigate a navigational black spot that has appeared in the centre of the wasteland, nearly a thousand klicks away!'

Sagassi was laughing now. 'Ridiculous! On what evidence do you base these so-called "facts"?'

Hershey pulled a slim volume from a pocket in her tunic and flung it onto the table, sliding it across to Sagassi's seat. 'On the evidence in that book – Dredd's personal log of the journey!' Sagassi rifled through the pages while she kept talking and walking around the table. 'He meticulously noted the true nature of their mission and records the route they followed. Among the events recorded are the deaths of two of the cadets in a firefight with gila-munja, the failing of a third and meetings with refugees from a spreading blackness, emanating from the centre of the Cursed Earth.'

'This proves nothing!' replied Sagassi. 'Anybody could have written these words.'

'It's been confirmed as Dredd's handwriting by Tek Division calligraphy analysis programs,' chipped in Collins, happy to report something positive.

'It still proves nothing – the words of a mass murderer count for nothing,' insisted Sagassi.

'Perhaps, but we don't know that Dredd is a murderer yet,' maintained Hershey. 'Among the other data in that journal, Dredd reports sending a message pod back to Mega-City One. I've checked with the sentry Judges on duty when that pod would have arrived and they confirm seeing such a message pod cross from the Cursed Earth into Mega-City One, yet it never reached the collection point. It must have been intercepted by something – or some-one.' She stared directly at Sagassi now, almost accusing him with her piercing blue-grey eyes.

'If you're accusing me of – ' he fumed.

'I accuse no one,' smiled Hershey. 'Not until all the facts are available, that is.' Before the conflict could grow into a full-blooded shouting match, the vid-phone in front of Collins' chair began to buzz insistently.

'Excuse me,' mumbled the Tek-Judge, activating the unit. 'Yes, what is it?'

'Control here. We have the results of the scans,' replied a monitor Judge from its small display.

'Put 'em on the big screen,' interjected McGruder, waving a hand at a massive tri-D viewer set into the far wall of the meeting room. Collins nodded and switched the communication across. The face of the monitor Judge appeared on the floor-to-ceiling viewer, bulging out through the wonders of tri-D to give the impression of three dimensions.

'We scanned the area requested by Judge Sagassi and indeed recorded a massive build-up of gila-munja, judging by the body units showing up on the infra-red readings. But there was no sign of typical Lawmaster fuel emmissions, not even the traces which can usually be picked up more than two weeks afterwards,' stated the monitor emotionlessly.

'Hmmm,' pondered the Chief Judge, casting a dismissive eye at the head of SJS, who was looking a little less confident than before. Back on screen, the monitor was continuing.

'We also scanned the route suggested by Judge Hershey and trace readings seem to confirm a group of Lawmasters travelled in the direction she indicated. From what we can determine, this group on Lawmasters encountered a large pack of gila-munja – the area is so awash with blood, it could be picked up by the sensors on our satellites!'

'Ridiculous!' scoffed Sagassi.

'No, it's quite possible with the advances we've made,' enthused Collins, but a glare from Sagassi shut him up.

'We paid particular attention to the area at the centre of the Cursed Earth but our sensors were unable to probe within a thirty-klick radius of the area. It seems the high concentration of radiation is burning out all sensors on the satellite,' continued the monitor.

'Why haven't we picked this up before?' asked McGruder.

'Because it wasn't happening before,' replied the monitor. 'This is a new phenomenon, and one with no available explanation, ma'am.'

'Thank you,' grunted the Chief Judge ungraciously and motioned for Collins to cut the transmission. She turned to the rest of the Council. 'Well, that would seem to bear out the contents of the journal, at least in part. Do you have anything more on this black spot, Hershey?'

'Not yet. An initial records check showed no sign of two aircraft having crashed in the area, as Dredd and his team were told, but we're searching further.'

'I think I can help Judge Hershey there,' volunteered Sagassi. 'I seem to recall some report crossing my desk about the loss of a minor surveillance h-wagon going down in the Cursed Earth recently. I believe the SJS sent out another aircraft to investigate but I, er, heard no more about it. . .'

'Surveillance flight? You mean spying?' Hershey delighted in making Sagassi squirm, he did it so well.

'We must protect ourselves from outside intervention, and the SJS sometimes works at the forefront of this area, as you well know,' replied the red-faced Judge.

Hershey turned to her superior. 'Chief Judge, there is obviously much more to this case than meets the eye. I suggest we launch a much fuller investigation, to find out what is going on within the ranks of the SJS. For more than a year now, since the Tooth incident, they have been storming around like – '

'Chief Judge, I must object to this slanderous – ' stormed Sagassi, now red-faced and shaking with rage.

'Shut it, both of you!' bellowed McGruder, silencing the pair in an instant. 'We're not here to discuss your squabbles, we're here to find out what's really happened to Dredd and those cadets, and decide

137

what to do next!' Silence for a moment, then the Chief Judge continued, thoughtfully stroking the slight stubble about her chin. 'Collins, any word from the Gunbird conducting the low-level search yet?'

'Just coming through now, Chief Judge,' replied Collins, his eyes fixed on the monitor in front of him. 'I'll put it on screen.'

The council turned back to the wall monitor, to see a flash of static, then a wildly vibrating image, the face of the Gunbird's pilot. Blood was pouring from his nose and ears, and smoke had blackened his face. His eyes held only desperate determination.

'Gunbird six to Control, do you copy?' demanded the pilot, half-pleading, half-sobbing. 'Do you copy?'

'There's something jamming our reply to them. Control are trying to break through it now,' explained Collins in a whisper to the rest of the council.

'The rest of the crew – are – d-dead. We were hit by some force, I can't explain what. It was almost as if a hand was reaching up to grab us from the sky,' continued the pilot. 'It – this force – crippled our engines, blew out the weapons systems, shredded the back half of the Gunbird. I don't know how long I can keep her up – '

Behind the pilot, the councillors could see fire raging inside the cockpit, about to engulf the pilot. 'Eject, man, eject!' pleaded Hershey but the pilot stayed in his seat.

'We saw – horrors – a place like some living hell – and the windmills – may Grud forgive me,' mumbled the pilot, losing consciousness. Moments later, the transmission cut abruptly.

The councillors sat in silence, some staring at the static-filled screen, others looking down at the table in front of them. After what seemed like hours but was only moments, Collins spoke.

'Control says the Gunbird has crashed fifty klicks outside the West Wall. No survivors.'

'Terrif,' said McGruder dryly. 'Well, we can't find out what's going on from satellites or by using our airfleet. That leaves one option – a hand-picked team to investigate on the ground, following in the footsteps of Dredd and the Hotdog Run. They can find out what's happened to the squad and investigate this black spot at the same time – it's obvious the two matters are closely interwoven. Any suggestions who should go?' The Chief Judge looked around the table, staring into the eyes of the other councillors. 'Shenker, you haven't spoken yet, you start.'

The head of Psi Division sat forward in his chair, elbows on the table, fingers of each hand steepling together, light gleaming from his bald pate. 'Obviously, the best choice is one Judge from each of our major divisions, to give the best cross-section of abilities and expertise.'

McGruder nodded. 'Who from the Psis?'

Shenker pondered before speaking, the trait of a true Psi, never willing to easily commit or jump to a conclusion. 'Unfortunately, Anderson is still on the assignment in space, so she is out of the question.' In fact, Anderson had quit the Justice Department a few months before, but this was not common knowledge, even among the Council of Five. Shenker and McGruder had a private agreement not to discuss the matter openly, in case Cassandra Anderson – one of the city's top Psi talents – changed her mind.

Until something happened to indicate a change one way or the other, Anderson remained 'on assignment' in space. After more consideration, Shenker spoke again. 'I suggest Psi-Judge Karyn. She's worked with Dredd twice before, on the Raptaur case, and against Roland Savage a few months ago. She knows some of his methods and has shown special resilience under stressful situations.'

'Good,' agreed McGruder. 'Hershey? From the Street Judges, any suggestions?'

'Judge Lynn Miller. Acquitted herself well as acting sector chief when the Nelson Rockefeller orbital suburb crashed to earth. Tough, resourceful, never gives up.'

'Agreed. Collins, one of your teks?'

'Claire Tupolua, a bit of a loner, but one of the best.'

'Good. Now how do we get them close to this black spot? It's obvious Gunbirds or Lawmasters aren't up to the job.'

'May I suggest the new, redesigned Killdozer, the Mark III? We've just updated and enhanced the weapons systems and manoeuvrability. It's probably the best little mover on sixteen wheels around, perfect for Cursed Earth terrain,' urged Collins, warming to his topic. 'Comes equipped with a dozen war-droids, six all-terrain Quasar bikes and enough firepower to level a small mountain. Accelerates from –'

'All right, all right, we get the idea!' protested McGruder, a hand held up to stop the flow of technical data. 'Anyone else got any suggestions?'

'I have,' said Hershey. 'The team'll need a stringer, an all-rounder to fill the gaps. May I suggest Judge Kevin Brighton? He's fresh out of the Acad-

140

emy but a good prospect, and he knows several of the missing cadets personally. He's likely to bring a few fresh ideas to the squad.'

'That's settled then,' concluded the Chief Judge. 'Collins here can assign his best driver to the kill-dozer, and the team will leave tomorrow at dawn. Now, unless there's – '

'Anything else? Yes, there certainly is!' interjected Sagassi angrily. 'I suggest – no, demand! – I demand an SJS Judge be included in the team for this mission. As yet we've had nothing to disprove what Judge Chung told us, yet you all seem to have decided Dredd's innocent! As far as I'm concerned this is a murder investigation and Judge Dredd is the prime suspect!' Sagassi sat back in his seat, arms folded, ready for war.

'Quite frankly, Chief Judge, you can't – ' began Hershey but McGruder cut her off quickly.

'I am forced to agree with Judge Sagassi. If he would like to suggest a candidate for the task, we will happily include them in the squad,' she said calmly. Hershey was nearly apoplectic, but Sagassi merely smiled.

'Judge Emil Nyder, I think.'

'That's settled then. Six judges including the driver, to find out what's happened to Dredd and the six cadets. Dismissed,' announced McGruder and strode from the meeting room, Hershey in hot pursuit. The younger woman caught up with her superior as they entered McGruder's office.

'Why in the name of Grud did you agree to having an SJS Judge included?' demanded Hershey.

'Because Sagassi was right, that's why,' replied the Chief Judge, dropping into the chair behind her

141

desk, her shoulders slumping forward. Weary fingers rubbed at her eyes. 'Grud, I'm tired.'

'Chief Judge, at least let me accompany the mission. I don't trust Sagassi as far as I could spit him, and his henchman Nyder is even worse!'

'No, you're staying right here, Hershey. With Joe gone, maybe even dead, I need all the friends I can get right now. Besides, I've got another job for you.'

CHAPTER TWO

And then he was running, helter-skelter, legs pumping like pistons, his chest gasping for breath, a taste like blood in his mouth, yet dry and arid like a desert baked red. And no matter how hard he ran, the hunter was always faster, closing in on him with every step he took.

Bullets and grenades began to explode in the air around him, forcing the runner to redouble his efforts, but like some nightmare, the ground seemed to swallow up his energy, sapping it straight from his legs, until he seemed to be running on the spot. Behind him the terrible rasping breath of his chaser wheezed ever louder behind him, until he could feel it upon his neck. But still he did not dare look around, afraid of what manner of monster could be chasing him. . .

Then he was sprawling, sure a brutal shove in the small of the back had undone him. Limbs sprawled outwards, face thudded into blood-soaked soil, the smell hot, musky, all too human. Sweat soaked his body, urine trickled down his legs, curling and cling-ing. A boot thudded into his side, kicking his torso over and the sun blazed down into his eyes, dazzling, blinding.

And a figure bent over, leering over him, blocking out the blazing sunshine, replacing it once again with that vicious visage, all teeth and leering grin, a dribble of fetid slime hanging from the stubble-encased chin, evil eyes hidden behind a flashing visor. The figure leaned forward, closer still, until its face was just inches from him, almost touching, like a lover seeking a kiss, but this kiss was deadly, he knew that, had always known it. Now it was truer than ever.

The leering, jackal-faced pursuer pulled a weapon from its side, a hand-gun of some sort, and thrust it upwards against the underside of his jaw.

'Time to die, creep!' grinned the figure, pulling back the trigger on its weapon.

The hunted, the victim turned his head slightly and caught sight of a thin slice of metal welded to his killer's chest. A single word was emblazoned upon it: DREDD. The victim screwed up his eyes desperately as his murderer repeated the final message, pulling back the trigger, the bullet rushing forward in the chamber, just a moment away from tearing into his jawline, ripping through the mouth and upwards, exploding inside the brain.

'Time to die, creep!'

Jonah sat bolt upright, his chest heaving, his body and the simple fabrics encasing it soaked in sweat. A nightmare! It had just been a nightmare!

But not just any nightmare, he remembered almost instantly. The same terrible, tortuous ramshackle assemblage of horrors and hatred that had haunted so many past evenings. Every night he lay down, praying never to see that fearsome face again, and every night it returned, as constant as the orange dust on the floor, blown in from outside the spartan lean-to shack.

Jonah swung his lean, muscular legs round onto the floor and groaned, clutching a hand to his heavily bandaged head. The pain still nagged and stabbed at him, blurring his vision a little and throwing him off-balance. Still, his wounds were slowly healing, the old woman who was treating him said so, and Jonah had no reason to doubt her. She seemed wise and knowing in such matters, and had shown him only kindness, like the other poor souls trying to eke out a living on this small stretch of land.

Jonah sat for a moment on the edge of the hard bench, only a thin blanket stretched over its length for comfort. He wished he could remember more of how he'd come to this place – years? Days ago? With no memory of the time before being here, it could be either. All he could remember was the nightmare, over and over again, echoing that same word, etched across the demon's chest: DREDD.

What did it mean? Why was he, a simple farm-hand, tormented by these horrific images of some brutal killer? Jonah shrugged to himself and stood up, pulling on the simple garb of his role in life – sturdy dungarees, a well-worn blue shirt and a pair of heavy brown boots that had seen better days. Jonah did not look forward to the rainy season, when the water would flood upwards through the holes in the soles of his boots. Until then, they would suffice.

Outside, the dark blue shadows of the night was slowly being replaced by the first rays of sunlight, burning through the orange clouds on the horizon from the east. Dawn was coming and it was time he was about his chores. Since coming to the farm, Jonah had settled easily into a self-imposed regime of hard work and a minimum of rest. He enjoyed working the land, which seemed unusually fertile and almost lush compared to the barren soils that surrounded it.

Only once had he left the farm, to visit the nearby settlement to pick up some supplies. In reality, it had been an excuse – he had really gone there in the hope that something, anything, would trigger a memory, help explain the mysteries of his past. But the people had all been hostile, unwelcoming to strangers. So he had come back to the farm and resigned himself to his fate. It was not an unhappy life, and if the pain became too much for him, there was always the soothing presence of the little girl.

She had cared for him, along with the eldest of the womenfolk, visiting him daily, helping to change his dressings. When she was around, Jonah always felt better, as if a weight had been lifted from his shoulders. And the child seemed to speak with a wisdom beyond its years, with eyes to soothe away any pain.

Yes, this was a good life, Jonah decided, clouded only by those nightmares. Soon he would be fully healed and fit to move on. But – if the folk of the farm would have him – he hoped to stay, give them back something for his kindness. A gentle smile played around his lips as he stepped out of the shack and surveyed the surrounding fields. It was the least he could do.

The farm was small, but bountiful in its yield. Jonah's shack leaned against the main building, an eight-roomed structure, none of the chambers much bigger than his own small lodging. The walls were a mixture of packed dirt, chunks of rockcrete and metal from a previous building on the site, a few wooden-shuttered windows dotting the walls. Around the building stood a sturdy corral of metal poles and rockcrete slabs, encircling the main building and a few sheds used for storing equipment. Beyond the corral, a handful of fields, a rare spring bubbling out of a rock formation in one of them. A single dirt-track led out past another rock formation, this one quite bizarrely shaped, the track soon joining the main route into the nearby settlement.

All the water they needed came from the spring, and the carefully cultivated fields provided enough food for the small community living on the farm to get by. In that, Jonah knew they were unusual – outside the farm's boundaries was a barren, sterile desert, not fit for man nor beast. While he worked to repair some of the fence poles in the corral, Jonah considered the members of the community.

They were a curious group. The three old women, all mutants, kept their cloaks and their secrets drawn closely around them; the little girl and her soothing smile; and the others, a handful of mutant men who rarely spoke but still worked hard beside Jonah in the fields. The men appeared almost frightened of the old women, yet Jonah cold see nothing about the trio to strike fear. Still, to each their own, that was his motto.

It took him nearly two hours to repair the corral fence and by then his head and back were throbbing with a dull, aching pain. The sun was up and already his body was soaked with sweat from labouring beneath its harsh rays. Finally the metal clanging sounded, the signal for the men to stop work and break their overnight fast. Jonah and his fellow workers trudged into the main building, after washing briskly from a barrel of murky water.

Once inside, they sat at a communal bench in the largest chamber at the centre of the building, where bowls of fruit and vegetables awaited them, with pitchers of water to quench the heartiest thirst. But before they could begin, the old women led them in reciting a daily refrain.

'All praise the land, that provides for our needs. All praise the earth, for giving up its water. All praise the sun, for ripening our crops. All praise the one, for giving us hope.'

That last sentence Jonah could not understand but none of the other men would explain it to him, and he decided against asking the old women about it. Jonah had tried asking the little girl, but she had just smiled.

'Everyone needs hope, Jonah, you know that!' she had told him, and ran off to play.

As he left the main building that day, he was aware of the three old women following his movements with their beady eyes. But they said nothing, so he had just gone back to his duties. Maybe he did understand why the other men feared them, after all.

'This is the guardian, this frail man who is chased by shadows in his sleep? He barely remembers his own name!' the tallest of the old women scoffed, watching as Jonah left after the meal. She turned to her sisters, her dark eyes blazing with vehemence. 'Surely we cannot trust our fate to such as he!'

'I concur,' nodded the third woman, her face deeply lined, weather-beaten like the surrounding countryside. 'He is unworthy of the task. He may even be a spy, sent to find out more about – '

'Hush! We dare not speak the name, not with the emissaries of evil walking the earth in search of. . .' The second woman trailed off, her short, squat

148

frame a comic counterpoint to the upright, spindly figures of her companions. 'If this is the guardian, then guardian he is, no matter how we may doubt him. It is spoken.'

'I know it is spoken, you silly old – ' raged the tall one, but she was cut short by a gentle voice in their minds, words of wisdom quieting their debate.

'Jonah is the guardian, there is more to him than meets the eye. When the time comes, he will be the difference between hope and despair, life and death,' said the voice, sure, confident, rich and warm.

'But – ' the first woman began to protest.

'It is spoken, you know it must be true.'

'It is spoken,' agreed the old woman, trying to put her doubts aside.

'It is spoken,' echoed the other two.

'And so it shall be,' replied the voice.

As Jonah rose that morning, nearly a thousand klicks to the east the killdozer snarled and burst forth from the great gates in the West Wall of Mega-City One. On board were six Judges, each with their own reasons for being on board. Ahead of them lay some of the deadliest terrain known to man, and several unpleasant surprises.

Sitting up front in the cockpit were the driver/navigator, Judge Bill Raimes, and the leader for the mission, Judge Lynn Miller. She was an unusual choice for such a role, just two years out of the Academy, but Miller had already proven herself to be an exceptional judge.

After graduating in the top ten of her intake, Miller had volunteered for posting to the Nelson Rockefeller Orbital Suburb. It was said at the Academy that six months on Nelson Rockefeller was worth five years on the streets of the Big Meg, so the ambitious young Judge had become the first person in history to volunteer for such a posting. Others had thought her mad, and indeed the six months had been the most dangerous Miller had ever known. But she had come out of it with three citations for bravery and a reputation of going for guts or glory, and usually grabbing the glory.

Her greatest test had come when the orbiting slum satellite, normally in geostationary orbit above Mega-City One, had been sabotaged and fell to earth amidst on-board block wars, rioting and the slaughter of most of her colleagues. The satellite had crashed into several citi-blocks at the east edge of the city, smashed through a section of the sea wall, flooding several sectors with the vile polluted inpourings of the Black Atlantic, and finally splashed down in the oxygen-starved ocean.

Miller was among a handful of survivors and had lost both legs and one eye in the mayhem of screaming metal colliding with solid rockcrete. But she had lived, and new limbs – cloned from her own DNA blood samples – had been delicately grafted in place of the lost ones. Her remaining human eye had been plucked out by the Med-Judges and both eyeballs replaced with considerably superior bionic implants, giving her 20/20 night vision and a vastly improved long-distance and peripheral sight.

That had all been four long months ago. Since then she had been in physical rehab, regaining the use of her new limbs. It had been long, hard and tedious but she had mastered them now – in fact just days before she had posted her best-ever rating in the 'Shooting Match' live simulation assessment, just a fraction out from a perfect one. Only one significant physical change since the satellite fell to earth remained unchanged – the length of her hair.

Miller knew a Judge was not meant to be vain or self-aggrandising, but she had always been particularly fond of her silky-soft strawberry-blonde hair. When she had awoken in the wards at Med Division, she was shocked to discover her beloved locks were gone, burnt off in the impact and subsequent explosions aboard the Nelson Rockefeller. What was worse, when it grew back, her hair was now pure white, shockingly so, as if she had been given the fright of her life. Not too far wrong, smiled Miller ruefully, as she looked out the cockpit at the terrain ahead.

The ground was dusty and baked dry, massive cracks fracturing its surface, a few hardy weeds the only sign of plant life. The chemical warfare that had followed the Atomic War had made certain little or no life would ever flourish in vast regions of this radioactive wasteland. The windswept desert advanced far towards the horizon, where distant pyramids could be seen, the tips of the Appalachian Mountains, a treacherous and forbidding piece of countryside.

'Well, how does she handle?' Miller asked the driver.

'Like a dream,' smiled Raimes, a thin-faced black Judge with intense, thoughtful eyes. 'I did a lot of the test driving for the Mark III when it was being developed last year. They've made a few improvements even I didn't spot!'

'Such as?' enquired Lynn, happy to indulge him. If Raimes appreciated his task, she would get the best work out of him, plus she was genuinely interested. Miller had once considered joining the Tek-Judges, but her ambitious nature had got the better of her.

'For a start, the weapons targeting systems are the equal of anything on the West Wall, and the long-range sensors have uplinks to all the major satellite surveillance systems. Using them, we could spot a radfly coming at a hundred klicks!' enthused Raimes.

'Good. I've got a hunch we'll need all the help we can get on this mission,' noted Miller. The crew had all been fully briefed by Judge Hershey the night before, under the watchful eye of SJS Judge Sagassi. It wasn't overtly stated but Miller could read between the lines: there was a lot riding on this mission.

'We've got two hours before you need to make a decision, but what route do you want to take round the mountains?' asked Raimes. 'I can start plotting in the course now.'

'I've already analysed the route taken by Dredd and the Hotdog Run,' answered Miller, pulling the battered personal log from a pouch on her belt. 'They took the traditional northern bypass, then headed south until rejoining the main western route. However, the log notes nothing of interest during that part of the run. So I propose we go straight over the top. What do you think?'

Raimes smiled broadly. 'I like it! Give me a chance to see what this baby can really do.'

'And it'll save us nearly three hours on our journey time. Since every second could be vital. . .'

'You're the boss,' agreed the driver and he started punching course projections into the navi-comp.

* * *

'How long have you been a Judge, Tupolua?'

'Nearly fourteen years. Why do you ask, Brighton?'

'Me? I've been a Judge just four months. All I've done since they told me I was coming on this mission is wonder why I was selected,' replied the young lawkeeper. He and Tek-Judge Claire Tupolua were in the rear section of the killdozer, checking the systems and making sure the war-droids were all fully operational and ready for immediate action.

The older Judge considered for a moment, resting a weary arm on the bulkhead above her face. 'Probably that's the reason – your age. Remember we're hunting for a Hotdog Run squad, full of seventeen-year-old cadets. Cadets can act strangely, almost bizarrely under pressure, do things a normal Judge would never think of. But you, you've barely ceased being a cadet yourself! Out of all of us, I imagine you'd make the best guess at what those cadets might have done.'

'Yeah! Yeah, I suppose you're right!' smiled Brighton cheerfully. It had been preying on his mind over the past day since receiving the assignment, but the senior Tek-Judge's assessment of the situation fitted the facts. The excited young Judge decided to share something with her. 'I know one of the missing cadets. . .'

Tupolua had gone back to her work, tightening the fittings on one of the storage bulkheads, but she kept listening to her young assistant. 'Which one?'

'Singh, Nita Singh. She is – was – a real prospect, coming top of her intake, real honour-roll material. She was only a few months younger than me,' muttered Brighton quietly, withdrawing into himself.

'Hey! We don't know she's dead yet. We don't know any of them are dead for sure – 'cept Chung, of course,' said Tupolua firmly. Fourteen years as a Judge meant you saw a lot of death, lost a lot of fellow Judges – you didn't have time to get sentimental.

But word about Chung's terrible injuries and the allegations that Dredd was responsible had blazed through the Justice Department like wildfire. Brighton had only met Dredd once, but once had been enough – the fearsome Judge certainly deserved his nickname, Old Stony Face.

'D'you think Dredd killed the cadets like everyone says, Tupolua?' asked the young Judge.

'No, I don't. I've worked with Dredd and he ain't a murderer. Sure, he's killed, but only in the line of duty. Judge Dredd ain't a murderer, and don't you ever forget that!' Tupolua waved a heavy torque-wrench at Brighton for emphasis. The junior law-keeper just nodded.

In the tiny sleeper quarters inside the killdozer, Psi Judge Karyn was not enjoying herself.

Life on the vehicle was divided into strict rotations, each of eight hours duration. For one rotation, one pair would sit up front in the cockpit, one Judge driving, the other acting as look-out and helping to navigate. Raimes, Tupolua and Nyder were all qualified to pilot the killdozer. The next rotation, that pair would shift to maintenance and prep work, making sure the vehicle continued smoothly on its journey and that all systems, including the twelve war-droids, were ready for deployment at a moment's notice. The final rotation would see this

154

pair shift to the sleeping quarters for rest and refreshment.

The rotation system was designed to give each Judge a total of eight hours of rest and relaxation per day, as well as prevent boredom. Unfortunately for Karyn, she had been paired with the exceedingly unlikeable Judge Emil Nyder of the SJS. Staying on good terms with someone while sandwiched together in a space only large enough to store a Lawmaster was bad enough, but sharing that area with an individual as obnoxious and repulsive as Nyder was pure purgatory, Karyn had decided.

Not only was Nyder boorish, dull and unpleasant, he had all the wit of an enraged horde of gila-munja but none of the charm, the Psi Judge believed. Worst of all, he snored. Times like this I wish I was better at mind control than being a precog, Karyn thought. I could will him to shut up, for a start!

She brushed a few errant strands of her curly, flame-red hair away from her face and tried to concentrate beyond the groaning, snorting noise thundering from the squeaky bunk directly above her. She too had heard the allegations that Dredd had gone rogue, slaughtering a squad of cadets and sending Chung back to the city as a bag of body parts lashed to a Lawmaster.

Karyn had trouble believing a word of it but she had been brought in by Hershey for a post-mortem scan of Chung, secretly, once the body had been released for its judicial funeral and disposal at Resyk. By the time the Psi Judge had been given access, the body had been dead more than three hours, making the scan haphazard at best.

It had taken time, long minutes, but Karyn finally gained access to the remnants of Chung's mind, only to find it a burnt-out shell, just a few latent images remaining. These proved little one way or the other, simply adding to her unease about the whole case: the sound of the cadets screaming, Dredd firing his Lawgiver over and over and over. . . Karyn had reported her findings to Hershey but could make little sense of them.

'I'm glad Shenker suggested you for the mission,' Hershey had told her privately. The two female Judges had worked together previously, deciphering the final words of Psi Judge Jong, which had given vital clues to stopping a major threat to Mega-City One some months earlier. 'You've worked with Dredd, you know him. Now Sagassi wants to turn this into a witch-hunt, and I'm sure his crony Nyder will do everything possible to turn the evidence against Dredd. I'm counting on you to find out the truth – no matter what it may be.'

Karyn had just nodded, for the first time becoming aware of the political powerbroking at work within the upper echelons of the Justice Department.

'You're a precog, aren't you?' Hershey had asked. 'Sensed anything about the future of this investigation?'

Karyn paused before answering – most precognitive visions came as jumbled puzzles, like a handful of scrambled jigsaw parts, never giving her the whole picture at once, just fragments. Explaining the nature of such visions to non-Psis always proved problematic.

'I sense a power struggle, a battle between good and evil,' she ventured at last.

'Here in the city?'

'No, on a much wider scale. Yes, almost a war, a crusade, I suppose you could call it. . .'

156

'Who will win?'

Karyn shook her head. 'The outcome is unclear, but much blood will flow before this is ended.'

'Terrif,' murmured Hershey.

Now, nearly twelve hours later, Karyn pondered her own words. She hadn't told Hershey everything, hadn't mentioned the nightmare of the twisted-face monster, his one eye beaming across the Cursed Earth like the searchlights atop the West Wall, searching, always searching – but for what?

Karyn closed her eyes and slipped into a trance, somehow managing to blot out the buzzsaw snoring from Nyder in the bunk above. Over and over in her mind she repeated a single word: 'Soon, soon, soon. . .'

Deep in the heart of Erebus, Soon was floating.

Levitation was one of the newest talents he had acquired, absorbing the latent Psi talents of the lesser inmates of the asylum. One by one the unfortunates were brought before him. Transfixed by his stare, some whimpered, some babbled madly, a few grovelled or prayed before him. But all suffered the same terrible fate.

Soon's hands would embrace them, then inflict and invade them, turning into blades, to syringes, to thrashing needles, imparting exquisite pain as they drained the victim of blood, of soul, of psyche, of their life essence. Then the hollow husks of what had once been human would clatter to the translucent glasseen, just the scent of urine and rotting meat hanging in the air to mark the passing of another life.

Soon fed the blood directly into his own veins and arteries until he was almost bloated with it. But the destructive elements within his genetic structure helped absorb this new life, to soothe away the pain of his own DNA rewriting itself over and over again.

The soul Soon had little use for, collecting them as a small boy collects moths and butterflies. The twisted genius liked to imagine them pinned to a wall somewhere inside his mind, wings fluttering, long shafts of steel plunged through their tiny human limbs and torsos, mouths forever screaming in torment.

The psyches, ah, now these he did enjoy. Feeding on a mind was like eating a different meal every day of your life. No boredom, no chance to develop a favourite taste, just constant variety of memories, of experiences, of talents and abilities. Of course, every psyche had its recurrent themes – hope, love, belief, despair, longing – but what Soon really wanted was knowledge and powers, those special talents each person holds deep within themselves, often unknowingly. Soon absorbed the psyche and unlocked those talents, known or latent, taking for his own. For stealing the talents of others, that was his special ability. Soon was a psychic thief, and he stole people's lives away. But not before causing them unbelievable pain at the same time, of course! What would be the fun in it otherwise, he frequently asked himself.

Soon's latest victim had been a mutant of little intelligence who had stumbled into the black zone around Erebus. It had possessed little to interest him except for one, undiscovered talent – the ability to levitate. An animal too stupid to realise its own potential, Soon snorted to himself. But I realise it, and now that potential is mine!

So he floated around the cathedral-like chapel of

horrors he had created in the centre of Erebus' main tower, at the base of this skyscraping citadel of terror. The walls were a mixture of glasseen – stained red with the blood from his early victims, before he learned how to absorb that by-product of his remorseless slaughter – and a cladding of calcium. On closer inspection, the calcium had a grislier origin – it was human bones, laced together with scraps of dried skin and human hair.

As Soon floated, his eye swept over the lattice of skeletal remains, each bone the remnant of another victim. He could remember them all, could savour their life essences still. But his favourites, oh, they had places of honour. Bony, twisted arms upraised beatifically, Soon descended to the ground, alighting on a raised dais at the centre of his private cathedral of death.

Atop the dais stood an altar. Like the walls around it, the altar was formed from human bones. But these were special, because the owners of these remains were still alive. Three faces looked out from the top of the altar, lips drawn back in permanent screams of soundless agony. By all rights, the trio should be dead, their bodies discorporated but their minds kept alive in eternal torment.

Soon's favourite element was the golden trimmings, a finely threaded metallic sheen added to the corners and some of the centre-pieces. It was amazing how far the metal contained in the chains and badges of three cadet Judges would go when reduced to a molecule-width of thickness.

The monstrous master of Erebus looked down at his victims, entombed alive forever. 'Would you like to scream today, my pretties?' he enquired of them telepathically, then – for just a moment – gave them back their power of speech.

Rookie Judges Coster, Archer and Singh screamed.

Karyn was adrift now, deep inside her own psyche, her naked Psi form floating through memories, hopes and dreams. Bolts of blue lightning flashed across the terrain of dusky mind-clouds, her subconscious at work while her body rested. Down, down deeper Karyn let herself fall, searching out that special place where she could see fragments, shards of the future, both possible and permanent.

And still the word echoed round her mind: Soon. Falling further, she had a face to go with the name; a horrible, twisted face, worthy of its twisted owner. The head loomed large above, thrice the size of her Psi form, its single eye closed for the moment, unaware. Karyn examined the face, the whole head, letting herself circle it slowly to take in every feature.

For a start, the whole head was utterly hairless. Not so much bald as purged of hair. No eyebrows, no eyelashes, no facial hair, nothing. The pate was smooth, gleaming, the ears slightly elongated, hugging the sides of the head. The face – that was the horrible aspect.

Just looking at the left side as Karyn saw it, the face was almost normal. An eye, a nose, a prominent cheekbone, a little scar tissue but nothing unusual. But from there the face fell away to the right, almost as if it had been stricken by a frighteningly powerful stroke that had crippled the muscles, pulling them downwards in a palsy. But it was not just muscular deformation; the whole bone structure fell away. No left nostril, just a flap of skin almost melted into the side of the nose; no eye, just a hollow, staring socket; no cheekbone, just slumping skin and hanging flesh. Most bizarre of all, the face had no mouth. A perfectly normal chin, but no mouth, simply skin stretched taut across bone.

Karyn felt horrified and pitiful and sickened, but she choked back her feelings and telepathically spoke to the face, a single word.

'Soon!'

In the bone cathedral, the twisted genius looked around, startled. Who had spoken? Then he realised the voice was inside his mind. How dare someone invade his mind! He must find this upstart, this challenger, and destroy them!

The single eye opened and blazed malevolently at Karyn's Psi form. 'Who dares!' bellowed Soon telepathically.

'What have you done to the children, the cadets?' asked Karyn, trying to get the measure of this monster. Clearly this brooding presence which had been infecting her mind must have a strong connection to the case, or to her own personal future.

'They are my playthings, puppets for my amusement. Would you like to see them?'

'Yes,' ventured Karyn, being careful to mask as much of her own thoughts and feelings as possible. The less time she spent in the presence of this creep the better, she was rapidly concluding.

'Then you shall have your wish,' replied Soon, his eye flicking to the left. Moments later, the screaming visages of the unfortunate trio appeared, soundless, agonised.

'Let them go!' cried out the horrified Psi Judge.

'Oh no, they're mine now. And so are you!' said Soon. A massive, palsied claw of a hand appeared from the ether of the mind to clutch at Karyn's Psi form.

'Got to get out of here! If I die in my Psi form, I'll die in real life as well,' realised Karyn and flung her Psi-self upwards, swimming for consciousness, desperately trying to evade the blindly groping clutches of Soon's grasp. With a final surge, Karyn saw the pure white light of the surface approaching – then she was bursting free –

'Huh! Uh-huh!' she gasped, sitting bolt-upright in the bunk, her body in turmoil. 'Oh Grud, I'm gonna be sick – ' muttered the Psi Judge and bent over, her body retching up bile, convulsing violently.

In the bone cathedral, Soon's brow furrowed angrily. The Psi Judge shouldn't have escaped him. He had been sloppy, lazy after feeding on all this easy meat.

'So the Judges are coming for me, coming to take back their little whelps,' he mused, looking down at the human altar. 'Good! More playthings, more lambs to my slaughterhouse. But these will be better prepared than the others, thanks to that Psi-bitch. Time to find some new recruits for my little army. Novar!'

Instantly, Soon's servant appeared, held in the air before Soon by his master's forceful will. 'Yes, my Lord?'

'The pathetic leavings of this institution are not enough for my appetite. There are Judges coming, we need to prepare them a welcome. Go forth, and bring me back an army. Novar.'

'Yes, my Lord. It shall be done,' intoned Novar,

bowing his head before the floating figure of his master.

'Go!'

Outside, the black zone pulsed outwards again, inching forward, absorbing, putrefying, destroying all in its path. The darkness continued to grow.

Millar had come back from the cockpit to see what all the fuss was about. 'All right, so who can't hold their food?'

The mess had already been cleaned up but the scents of bile and stomach acids still hung in the air, heavy, fetid and unpleasant. A pale-faced Karyn held up a guilty hand, the other clutched to her stomach.

'I've seen the cadets – at least, I've seen three of them,' she announced.

'What! Where?' spluttered Nyder, who had been awoken by Karyn's vomiting fit.

'I was attempting a Psi probe, to see if I could find out any more about the immediate future probabilities,' explained the young Psi Judge. 'Instead I encountered a creep who calls himself Soon. He seems to be holding the cadets prisoner, in some kind of mental and physical stasis. Doesn't seem like the nicest of guys.'

Miller remembered the personal log she had left in the cockpit of the killdozer. 'Which cadets did you see?'

'Judging by the descriptions we were given, Singh, Coster and Archer. They seemed to be in terrible pain.'

'Well, that seems to bear out the account that we have in Dredd's personal log of the Hotdog Run. He wrote that Zender and Agnew were killed during an attack on the squad by gila-munja, while Jenks was failed and sent back to Mega-City One. That leaves Dredd, Chung and the three cadets you mentioned – and we all know what happened to Chung. . .' said Miller.

'This proves nothing!' replied Nyder dismissively. 'How do we know this Soon isn't just a front for Dredd, or that he's even involved? And everyone knows the ramblings of precogs can be interpreted a dozen different ways!'

'Why you stupid, boorish – ' began Karyn, struggling to her feet unsteadily. Miller interceded, keeping the pair apart.

'Alright, you two, break it up. Fighting amongst ourselves will get us nowhere!' The pair grudgingly returned to their places, while Miller thought out loud. 'Dredd's double-zero rated for Psi abilities, so I doubt Soon is a Psi-front for him. As for interpretation of what Karyn experienced, only time will tell who is right.' The team leader looked to the young woman. 'Karyn, did you get any idea or impression where this Soon or the cadets might be?'

The Psi Judge pondered for a moment. 'Not really, but we seem to be heading in the right direction. As we keep moving forward, the latent Psi readings from up ahead are getting stronger. It's almost like I can feel Soon ahead of us, searching, waiting for something – or someone.'

'Us?'

'Could be, but I get the feeling there's something else involved. As if there's the shadow of another presence, but hidden, certainly hidden from Soon. . .'

'Hmm,' muttered Miller. 'Well, we keep going.

164

Karyn, why don't you swap rotations with me and go up with Raimes in the cockpit? I'll stay here with Nyder.'

'Gladly,' replied Karyn, and moved to the front of the killdozer. Nyder watched her go with a sour eye, only to find himself facing the wrath of Judge Lynn Miller.

'As for you, Nyder, I don't trust you – not one little bit. We've got to work as a team on this mission, because if we don't stand united, we'll all die divided. There's no room for your usual SJS bully-boy tactics. You got that, mister?'

'Yes, ma'am!'

'Good! Now go back to sleep – you're on cockpit duties in an hour, so get some rest while you still can.'

Two hundred klicks south of the centre of the black zone, Preacher Cain and his deputy were perplexed.

'I wish I could explain this, reverend, but I can't. I ain't never seen nothin' like it before,' explained the little hunchback scout, crouching by some tracks on the dusty ground.

'Try,' drawled the Texas City outlands marshal.

'Okay. First of all, we got yer standard claw-marks here – that's yer basic gila-munja. But right next to 'em, we got some sort of mutie footprints. And there's something else in here, mixed in, almost like human footprints – dozens of 'em.'

'You ain't making much sense, deputy.'

'I'm sorry 'bout that. These human footprints – well, they ain't proper human, not like normals anyways. The feets making the prints, some are fully formed. Others, they just got some flesh, some bone. Others are like a walking skeleton. To tells you the truth, I don't know what to make of it,' fretted the little mutant, clutching his favourite coonskin cap nervously between his hands. As the best dang tracker, scout and gila-munja hunter in the territories, as he often liked to remind himself, it didn't look good if he was stumped by a set of tracks.

Reverend Cain looked at the ground around them. It wasn't just a trio of tracks, the entire gully they had paused in was trampled with dozens, even hundreds of tracks like those described by his deputy.

Joe hated it when the reverend went silent like this. It usually meant violence was going to follow. Joe had never been on the receiving end of Cain's violence, but he'd been witness to it and the results weren't pretty. Effective, sure enough, but not pretty. The deputy coughed to get his superior's attention.

'Whoever they was, there's at least three, four hundred of them, travelling together and heading due north in a hurry. We going after them?' he asked, hoping against hope the answer would be no for once.

Cain thought long and hard before answering.

'Not yet. First, I want to know more about this heathen enemy before we confront it. Mount up, deputy – we're goin' south!'

'Thank Grud fer that,' whispered Resurrection Joe under his breath and quickly got atop his mutant mule.

It was midday when the stranger appeared at the edge of the farm. Jonah was working to clear away all of the wind-blown debris that had fallen into the rocks around the spring, where it bubbled up from inside the Cursed Earth, purified by the thousands of feet of rock and pebbles beneath the surface. The little girl was watching him work, playing with some of the smaller rocks and giggling to herself. Then she stopped, turned and began to cry out: 'Bad man! Bad man!'

Jonah looked down to see her pointing at a lone figure, standing by the gates at the edge of the farm. He was dressed in black, no trace of the usual orange rad-dust about him, a broad-brimmed hat shielding the stranger's eyes from the harsh noon sun, and casting a dark shadow over his face.

'Bad man! Bad man!' the infant kept crying. Jonah quickly climbed down and pushed her scurrying towards the main building in the compound.

'You go inside, tell the old women. Don't come out again until I say so,' hissed Jonah urgently after her. Then, casually picking up an old pitchfork and passing it back and forth from one hand to the other, he strolled out to the far gate to meet this stranger who had caused the little girl such alarm.

'Yes?'

'My name is Novar. I am a traveller, weary from my travails. May I come in and rest for a short while?' said the stranger, his eyes looking over Jonah's shoulder, taking in the details of the farm's layout.

'For a weary traveller, you seem little fatigued,' replied Jonah. 'Why do you not have rad-dust on your boots? Where is your carriage, or your bags? No one walks without carrying water in these parts, especially not at noon.'

'I lost them,' muttered Novar darkly. 'That is why I need your assistance, and that of the old women inside.'

'Strange how a traveller should know so much about who lives on this farm,' questioned Jonah. He raised the prongs of the pitchfork, holding them in front of his face, pointed directly at the stranger. 'Perhaps you are not a traveller at all?'

'What are you implying?'

'Perhaps it's time you went on your way, stranger – before I'm forced to assist you away,' warned Jonah.

'You'll rue this day,' growled Novar, pausing for one last look over the property. 'I'll return.'

'I'll be ready – punk!' replied Jonah, holding his pitchfork steadfastly in front of him. The pair stared at each other for a few moments more, then Novar turned and strode away into the distance. Curiously, he seemed to disappear from view before the dust clouds could possibly have hidden him.

Jonah watched the stranger disappear, then shook his head. Weird! It was as if he had been speaking with a different voice, one full of resolve and menace. He turned and started walking back to the compound, still puzzled by this visitation. With most of the neighbouring farms now standing empty, perhaps it was best if a guard was posted to watch out for the stranger's return, or other outsiders. It would take a worker away from the fields, so he would have to talk to the old women about it. This morning, the day and the whole world had seemed full of promise and joy. Now, Jonah was not so sure.

'I said he was the guardian, didn't I? He turned the stranger away, didn't he?'

Inside the main building, the old women had observed the confrontation after being alerted by the little girl. Now they returned to their seats, contem-

168

plating what to do next. The tallest still favoured flight.

'The black zone grows ever closer. Soon it will engulf this farm. We must flee before it reaches us!'

'The darkness will surround this farm, but it will never engulf it. While the guardian lives, so shall we,' replied the voice, gentle, soothing.

'Yes, but – '

'There are no alternatives. Others are coming, some to join us, many more against us. The storm clouds are gathering – beyond that, there is only uncertainty.'

'Then surely we should leave now, before this storm of evil breaks over us?' insisted the eldest of the three women, holding a much calloused hand up to support her wrinkled face.

'We live, we die – beyond that, there is only hope,' said the third women, rotund of face and body.

'So shall it always be,' echoed the voice.

It was Nyder who saw the cruciforms first, first one distant on the horizon, then another, then dozens, as the miles disappeared beneath the tracks of the killdozer.

'Miller, you better get up here. There's something you should see,' he called into the vehicle's intercom system. The team leader had left the cockpit a few minutes before to see how Tupolua and Brighton were getting on, now she was being brought back to scan the horizon.

'Sweet Jovus,' she whispered after looking out of the front window at the formation ahead of the killdozer. 'Any signs of life?'

Nyder checked the scanners. 'Nope. Aside from us, there's not a living creature within ten klicks.'

'Take us in close.'

The killdozer drove up to the first of the cruciforms and paused. After donning radiation cloaks, Nyder, Miller and Karyn went outside to examine the grisly creation.

Before them stood more than a hundred crucified corpses, in various stages of decomposition. Some were barely recognisable as human remains, just a few bones, some scraps of clothing and putrefied flesh. Others were only days old, quite dead but not yet picked clean by the dog-vultures and other carrion eaters of the Cursed Earth. On the head of each corpse was a sign, scrawled by some illiterate hand: TAWKIN BAK read one, TOO SMARTE FER O' GOD stated another.

'What the drokk are they?' questioned Nyder.

'Good question – Karyn, you got any answers?' replied Miller, turning the enquiry over to the Psi Judge. Karyn had already removed her helmet, freeing her mass of red ringlets and allowing her to concentrate fully on Psi probing the most recent of the corpses.

'Victims – criminals – something about Dredd. . .' murmured the Psi Judge hesitantly, then shook her head. 'Sorry, that's all I can glean. They've been dead too long.'

'Dredd again! More proof against him!' exclaimed Nyder triumphantly, a broad smile across his ugly face.

'This proves nothing,' retorted Miller. 'And we know from his personal log and the satellite tracings that the Hotdog Run didn't come within fifty klicks of this area!' She was about to continue when she spotted something in the distance. 'What does that sign say?'

'What sign?' asked Karyn and Nyder, almost in unison, glancing around them.

'That one,' pointed Miller towards the foot of the nearby mountains, nearly a mile away. '"THIZ WAYE FER JUZTIZZ!" Back to the killdozer, we'll go a bit closer.'

As they walked back to the mobile mini-fortress, Karyn couldn't resist asking how the team leader had seen the sign from such a distance.

'Bionic eyes may not be pretty, but they have their advantages,' Miller explained.

Once they were driven closer to the sign, a smaller message at the foot of the board was also visible: BY ORDER S of D. 'Curiouser and curiouser,' commented Miller. 'Take us into the mountains, Nyder. Let's see who the S of D really are. Raimes, can you hear me?'

'Copy you,' came the reply through the killdozer intercom system, Raimes' voice as cheerful as ever.

'Better prepare three of the war-droids for use. We could be seeing some action sooner than we expected.'

'That's a roj.'

The killdozer surged forward, hitting the first upslope of the Appalachian Mountains.

'This is where the fun begins,' announced Miller rhetorically.

CHAPTER THREE

Judge Hershey stood back, steadied herself, then punched the citizen full in the face, knocking several of his teeth down his throat. The unfortunate figure, lashed to an interrogation chair, coughed up a mixture of phlegm and blood, along with some chips from his remaining teeth. His face was swollen and already heavily bruised, several of his fingers had been bent back and one eye was completely swollen shut.

'All right, let's try again shall we?' asked Hershey cheerfully. 'Who is plotting against Chief Judge McGruder?'

'I – I don't know all the details, I was just a middleman,' spluttered the prisoner.

'You know, for a Wally Squad Judge who spends all their time working deep undercover, you're a very bad liar,' noted Hershey and cuffed him brutally across the face again. 'Let's try another question then, shall we? Who ordered you to assassinate the Chief Judge?'

'I don't know – her name – I – I was just told a code – word, to sanction the kill, and the name of the victim.'

'Someone whose face you can't see mutters a code word and you take that as an order to kill the Chief Judge? Forgive me if I express my disbelief,' raged Hershey, about to strike the prisoner again. But a

172

gauntlet-clad hand emerged from the darkness behind her to stay the blow.

'Enough, Hershey,' said a quiet voice. Chief Judge McGruder stepped into the light from the darkness at the edge of the interrogation cube, deep inside the Halls of Justice. 'Longman, that's your name, isn't it?'

'Y-Yes, Chief Judge,' mumbled the undercover Judge, blood still dripping from the cuts inflicted on his lips by his own broken teeth.

'Is there anything else you'd like to tell us, Longman?' said the Chief Judge delicately, so quietly the prisoner had to strain to hear her words in his ear above the sound of his own rasping breathing. 'Before we have you shot for high treason, that is. Hmmm?'

'I was just following orders,' sobbed Longman. 'Just following orders.'

'History has proved that to be very little of a defence, boy,' said McGruder wryly. She turned to Hershey. 'Looks like we'll have to kill him. Give us his Lawgiver, Judge Hershey, and then release his left hand from the restraints.' A pause while this was done. 'Now place the Lawgiver in that hand and point it towards his head. That's right, nice and close to the temple – we don't want any ricochets hurting anybody else when he blows his own head off, do we? No, we didn't think so.' Another pause as Hershey knitted her fingers around those of Longman's left hand, forcing them around his grasp as it clutched the trigger. 'Now, if you'll be so kind as to blow his head off please.'

'Yes, Chief Judge,' replied Hershey, starting to tighten the grip of her hand around Longman's fingers, forcing them down on the trigger.

'No! Wait!' cried out Longman finally.

'Pause for a moment, Hershey,' advised McGruder. 'Yes, Longman, did you have something you wanted to tell us?'

'I don't know the name of the Judge who gave me the order but she was SJS, I could see the skull badge on her shoulder-pad, just make it out. I think she might have been black too,' effused Longman, desperate to avoid the suicide being arranged for himself.

'A black female SJS Judge? Can't be too many of those about, can there, Hershey?' smiled McGruder.

'No, Chief Judge,'

'No, Chief Judge. All right, Hershey, you can take the Lawgiver away from the prisoner's head now,' commanded the Chief Judge.

'You mean you're letting me go?' asked the bewildered Longman, his face lit up with hope.

'Letting you go?! Hahahahahahahahahahaha!' laughed McGruder. 'That's a good one, boy! Letting you go!' It took more than a minute for the grizzle-faced woman to stop chuckling. 'No, Longman, we're not letting you go. You're going to Titan for the next twenty years, to join all the other bad Judges. Since they're still rebuilding parts of the penal colony after that Grice incident, you can help them!'

Hershey nodded for two Judge-warders to come forward and return the disgraced undercover Judge to his holding cell, then followed the Chief Judge from the room.

'Thank Grud he talked, I thought you were never going to give the order for me to stop,' she told McGruder.

'Who said we were going to stop you?' asked the older woman and strode back to her office.

'You fool! This assassination attempt is the worst thing that could have happened! Who authorised it?'

The leader of the conspiracy was furious, screaming and ranting at one of his co-conspirators via a scrambled vid-phone channel.

'Well?'

'We're not sure, that's still being investigated,' replied the Judge at the other end of the line nervously. 'I agree it's unfortunate. I've been careful to eliminate any possible link back to us so – '

'Unfortunate!' spluttered the leader. 'This has set us back weeks, perhaps months. We've actually managed to create sympathy for McGruder among some of the Street Judges. I didn't think that was possible!'

At the other end of the line, the co-conspirator bit his tongue to avoid aggravating his superior further. Tek-Judge Freeman had already had message pods diverted, satellite signals altered, briefings changed and been forced to murder three members of his own division to disguise his part in the conspiracy. He could wash the blood from his hands, but he couldn't shift the guilt from his heart. He knew it was all necessary if McGruder was to be removed as Chief Judge, but he seemed to be doing all the dirty work. Now the conspiracy leader was blaming him for some half-cocked attempt on the Chief Judge's life. It just wasn't fair!

'Listen to me, Freeman. Find out who's responsible and make sure that Hershey finds out too. Then kill the stupid drokker! If Hershey and McGruder get a scapegoat, they'll think it's all over. Have you got that?' demanded the conspiracy leader.

'Yes, I understand.'

'Then do it – now!' The communication cut off abruptly, leaving the Tek-Judge to ponder his next move. He already knew who had set up the assassination – SJS Judge Clara Kitson. Freeman turned back to his vid-phone and activated the scrambler, before speaking into the voice-responsive dialing control.

'Get me SJS Judge Kitson.'

The Mount Rushmore National Memorial shares a special place in tourism history with London Bridge – both were moved from their original sites and resited elsewhere for tourism purposes.

The case of Mount Rushmore is perhaps the more notable for the bizarre circumstances surrounding its shift of location. In the early twenty-first century, as the cities along the eastern seaboard of North America continued their urban sprawl unchecked, their edges started to join together, creating the first of the Mega-Cities. It soon became obvious that tourists no longer wished to travel far for their holidays. So an ingenious scheme was hatched to raise the profile of the world-famous memorial, which depicts the faces of four famous American presidents, carved into the side of a mountain, hundreds of feet high.

The entire memorial would be transported – in one piece – to the Appalachian Mountains and given a new home. To make the shift even more special, the carving of a fifth president's face was commissioned, this time to be the face of one of the greatest presidents of the twentieth century, rather than another founding father of America, like the first four. The

president chosen to be immortalised in rock was none other than Jimmy Carter . . .

(Extract from 'Great Moments in World Tourism History', by J.R. Ffartleigh, 2100 AD)

'Grud on a greenie, look at that!'

The killdozer had been driving through the mountains for nearly an hour when it came to a sudden stop at the crest of a hill, tracks locking together. Tupolua and Brighton were taking their rotation in the cockpit, with the Tek-Judge driving the mighty vehicle.

Before them was the Mount Rushmore National Memorial, towering over the valley below, six faces looking down at the settlement nestled there. Brighton was not amazed to see the monumental memorial itself – it had been among the geographical landmarks mentioned on his briefing. The five faces of the past presidents were all in their usual order. It was the sixth face at the far end of the memorial that was capturing the young Judge's attention.

'The sixth face – it's the face of Judge Dredd!' exclaimed Brighton, pointing up at the gigantic cliff-face carving. He was absolutely correct: hewn into the rock was a perfect replica of the face of Mega-City One's most famous Street Judge, nearly a hundred times larger than life. The discovery was reported to Miller, who came forward to view for herself.

'It's Dredd all right,' she commented eventually. 'What do the scanners tell us about that settlement, Tupolua?'

'Estimate four, five hundred life signs – and they're rapidly approaching our position. Looks like they've spotted us. Oh, and something else – the computer says this is mutie country,' added the Tek-Judge.

Miller blew some of her pure white hair away from her face and pondered for a moment. 'Better break out a couple of war-droids, in case the locals ain't too friendly. But I don't want anybody to start shooting unless I give the order, is that clear?'

'Oh Reverend, thank Grud you've come! It was terrible!'

The thin man stood beside an open grave, a plain wooden coffin open by his side. Tears ran down the pale, drawn face as the trembling mourner explained what had happened.

'We were just laying my dear wife, Esther, in the ground to rest until the day of judgement, when she rose up from the box! I tried to talk to her but she ignored me, as if she were listening to the commands of some other, ungrudly force. Then the other dead, they got out of their graves too and just walked away . . .' The thin man broke down sobbing. 'What am I gonna do? I've lost my Esther twice in three days now.'

The Missionary Man remained silent, so Resurrection Joe decided to ask a question. 'Did ya see which way they wuz headed?'

By now the mourning man could no longer speak, tears flooding his features. Instead he pointed a bony finger directly north. Resurrection Joe nodded to himself.

'Straight towards the north, just like all the others,' he noted, looking to his superior for guidance. But Reverend Cain just turned his red-eyed steed to one side and began to ride slowly away. The thin man called after them as the marshal and his deputy moved off.

'What about my Esther?'

The two lawkeepers rode silently for a way, before Joe finally plucked up courage to ask his firebrand leader a question. 'Well what are we gonna do? Seems all the monsters, maniacs, killers, corpses and gila-munja are going north.'

'Good riddance. Less vermin for us to cleanse from the promised land,' replied the marshal.

'Ain't we gonna do somethin'? It don't seem right . . .'

'I'll tell you what's right and what's wrong, deputy!' spat out Reverend Cain. 'You remember the last time we went north of the territories, helping out those Judges. Did we get any thanks? No, all we got was abuse. Let 'em rot, that's what I say!'

Another pause, then Joe tried again. 'But what about the souls of those poor folk, pulled from their graves by some evil up there, like pins to a magnet?'

Reverend Cain stopped and pulled a copy of the Bible from one of the pouches in his saddle. He laid his hands upon the good book and closed his eyes, muttering a prayer.

'Lord, if it is your will that we should aid the Grud-forsaken Yankees in the north, give us a sign!'

For a moment there was silence, then a great billowing wind blew up as close by a black stormcloud transformed itself into a twister, touching down a few miles in front of the pair. It seemed to hover on the spot, then swept away, heading directly north. Cain sat for a moment, watching the tornado disappear over the horizon, then looked to his deputy.

'Looks like we're headin' north.'

* * *

'We are the Sons of Dredd! We are the Law! Show yourselves, that we may Judge you!'

The killdozer was surrounded by at least three hundred heavily armed mutants from the settlement of Keystone, in the shadow of the Mount Rushmore National Memorial. Tupolua, Brighton and Miller looked out at the angry mob around them from the safety of the bullet-proof cockpit. Nyder's voice crackled over the intercom.

'You want me to deploy the war-droids?'

'Not yet,' replied Miller. 'First, I want to try a hunch – I'm going outside to talk with their leader.'

'That's crazy! They'll tear you apart!' protested the Tek-Judge in the driver's chair.

'I don't think so. Something tells me this crowd are just a little, shall we say, misguided?' Miller turned and headed back to the centre of the killdozer, pausing only to grab a book from a shelf before climbing up a step-ladder set into one wall to reach the ceiling. There she drew back a service hatch and climbed onto the roof of the killdozer, looking down at the surrounding mutants. Activating her helmet mike, she patched it through the loud-hailer speakers built into the front and rear of the vehicle, amplifying her voice a dozen times over.

'I am Judge Lynn Miller, of the Mega-City One Justice Department, and I am here to take command of you all,' she announced.

Inside the killdozer, Brighton was bemused. 'What's she up to?' Tupolua motioned him to silence.

'Why should we listen to you? I am Joe Junior and I command here! What is your authority?' demanded the mutants' leader, his rank denoted by the justice eagle symbol which had been tattooed across his

180

entire face. For emphasis, he waved his third fist angrily at the interloper.

'This is my authority!' replied Miller, holding aloft the book she had grabbed before ascending. 'I hold in my hands the Word of Dredd!'

'Prove it!' shot back Joe Junior, not to be outdone, least of all by a woman. The crowd of mutants were murmuring their backing for him, and growing more impatient by the minute. Unless Miller acted soon, she knew she could end up on a cruciform of her own.

The young Judge opened the book randomly and began to read from a page. 'The Law is everything. It cannot be put aside, or bent, or twisted without perverting the course of true justice. The Law comes before all else, and all must obey the Law!' She flung the mighty volume down at the feet of the mutant leader, its title face up: THE COMPORTMENT OF A JUDGE AND THE IMPLICATIONS FOR LAWKEEPERS, VOLUME I. At the foot of the cover was emblazoned the author's name, JUDGE DREDD. 'That is the true Word of Dredd!' shouted Miller, fixing the mutant leader with a steely gaze.

Joe Junior picked up the hefty volume and opened the cover, running his fingers over the words inside. He flicked through the pages, looking at the words and images inside. Finally, when he looked up again, tears were forming in his eyes.

'Brothers! Sisters! The Word of Dredd has come to us at last!' he shouted. 'All hail the Word of Dredd!'

It was dawn the next day before the killdozer could leave, such was the enthusiasm of the mutants to learn more about the Word of Dredd. Miller talked with Joe Junior and the other mutant leaders for more than four hours, cajoling and persuading them that only by strict adherence to the Law – rather than ritual slaughter and crucifixion – could the sons of Dredd truly live up to the teachings of their idol. The mutants had some difficulty with the concept, but by sunrise the next day, Miller felt she was getting through to them.

Psi Judge Karyn had spent the time finding out more about how the people of Keystone came to name themselves the Sons of Dredd. It was an old woman called Shona who explained the genesis of this obsession to her.

'It was a dozen winters past, perhaps more, when He came from the east on his chariot of steel,' began the old mutant.

'Dredd, you mean?' interrupted Karyn and got a stern look for her impatience.

'He came and He saw the defilement of the monument and He was angry. The Lawkeeper punished the leader of our community, who had put up his own image on the mountain, placing himself amongst the gods of stone,' continued the elderly mutant.

She must mean the presidents, thought the Psi Judge, but kept her opinions to herself this time.

'Then He went away to the west to continue his mission of mercy, leaving us leaderless, without any guidance. But He did leave behind this,' and from a hiding place in her little hut, Shona produced five pages that had obviously been torn from a book. 'These are our sacred texts. These are the Word of Dredd!'

'And what were the pages?' Brighton asked Karyn

once they had restarted their journey the next morning.

'One of Dredd's volumes of law statutes, with his name handwritten on one of them. The mutants adopted this as their own credo and have been shaping themselves in the image of those pages ever since. They renamed themselves the Sons of Dredd and even used a laser-cutter to remodel the carving of their own leader into Dredd's face.'

'Amazing,' gasped Brighton. 'All that from just five pages? It's a good thing they didn't get hold of any Justice Department weapons!'

'Well, I don't know much about anthropology, but the hill-billies have been up in those mountains for centuries, virtually undisturbed by civilisation, so they're highly susceptible to suggestion. Hopefully now they'll have a more positive influence to work from,' said Karyn cheerfully.

'You know the last thing they said to me before we left?' confided Brighton. 'If we ever needed their help, we should just let them know! I sure wouldn't want them fighting against us.'

The body swung slowly from side to side, suspended from the neck by a stripped-down Judge's waist belt. The head was blue and purple, swollen, with eyes still open and the tongue pushed out between the lips.

'Some people will do anything to avoid telling the truth,' noted Judge Hershey grimly. She looked around the private quarters of SJS Judge Kitson for a moment, before motioning a Psi Judge forward. 'Cut her down, then give me a Psi probe. She's only been dead a few hours, there may still be some latent images.'

Once Kitson's body was on the floor, the Psi Judge placed both his hands to her temples and went into a deep trance, merging his psyche into hers, his eyes rolling back in his head as he spoke with the dead woman's voice.

'Not – suicide – murder – they didn't want – me – to talk – ' said Kitson, via the Psi Judge.

'Who didn't want you to talk?' demanded Hershey.

'Erebus – the child – must have – the child – it – was – Freeman – Freeman did this – to me – Erebus – sooooooooon – ' The Psi Judge stepped away from the corpse abruptly, shaking his head.

'Sorry, but I had to break the contact. She was trying to draw me into the death-rattle,' he explained. The death-rattle was Psi jargon for the moment of death. Psis attempting a post-mortem probe had to be careful not to be infected with it, lest they die themselves. Hershey waved him out of the room, then contacted McGruder on a private channel reserved for scrambled communications.

'This is Hershey. Seems it was Kitson who ordered the assassination attempt. Perhaps she jumped the gun. Seems to have angered the conspirators a little.'

'How can you tell?' crackled back the Chief Judge's stony voice.

'Well, they killed her and tried to make it look like suicide, for a start,' replied Hershey.

'Yep, we'd say that's a little angry. You get anything else out of her?'

'Three things: the name of her killer, Freeman – '

'Freeman! That's the little drokker in Tek Division. That explains the last-minute alteration to the Hotdog Run squad and how it was covered up, plus

184

the missing h-wagons. I've never trusted that little slimeball!' hissed McGruder venomously.

'And it explains why the message pod went astray, Freeman must have had it diverted,' added Hershey. 'There was also something about Erebus and "the child – must have – the child". Mean anything to you?'

McGruder pondered, leaving just static in Hershey's ear before finally replying. 'Erebus – that was an asylum we used to run out in the Cursed Earth, but that was shut down years ago. Nearly two decades ago! Jovus, I'd forgotten all about that place. . .'

'Maybe you were meant to,' commented Hershey.

'Perhaps, you better check it out. As for "the child" – nope, means nothing to me,' decided the Chief Judge. 'Like we said, you look up Erebus, and we'll look up our old friend Judge Freeman. We're overdue for a little chat.'

Tupolua, Nyder and Miller looked down at the blackened, grisly remains of the explosion.

'Looks like somebody went out in a blaze of glory – but who?' asked Miller rhetorically.

'Shouldn't that be "but whom?"', said Nyder sarcastically, but the team leader ignored him.

'Tupolua, you start an analysis of the remains. I want to know who died here, how and why – and when they died!' ordered the white-haired twenty-three year old.

'Roj that,' replied the Tek-Judge, breaking out her specialised sensing equipment. Miller left Nyder to stand guard over the site while she returned to the killdozer. Inside, Raimes was using the long-range scanners to assess their position, while Brighton and Karyn were comparing notes about their own Hotdog Runs.

'I've never run so fast in my whole life!' laughed Brighton, drawing a smile from the normally reserved Psi Judge. Miller went straight to the cockpit.

'Well, how are we doing for time?' she asked the designated driver and navigator.

'The time we save going straight over the Appalachians was wiped out – and a bit more – by staying with the Sons of Dredd.'

'Yeah, I know, but we could hardly let them slaughter anyone who had the misfortune to pass by, just because they whistle too loud on a Sunday. We've got our mission, but we must maintain the Law at all times, Raimes,' scolded Miller, dropping into Academy-speak, before relaxing again. 'So how far are we from the black spot?'

'About two hundred klicks – three to four hours if we go non-stop,' said the driver, checking his scanners to confirm his estimate.

'Only two hundred klicks?' Miller was perturbed. 'I would have thought at least another twenty or thirty. . .'

'Me too, that's what's worrying. The black spot is expanding outwards, and the spread is getting faster too. I think we can stop calling it a spot: by my estimate it's nearly forty klicks across in diameter.'

'Sweet Jovus,' whispered the team leader, trying to get the scale of it fixed in her mind. She looked out the front viewport to see Tupolua and Nyder returning from their assignments. 'Now we'll get some more answers to a few questions. Get everyone to gather in the systems section for a briefing.'

Quickly the six Judges were brought together in

186

the largest part of the killdozer and Tupolua announced her findings.

'There was a small explosion in the valley ahead, consistent with the use of a Lawmaster's auto-destruct. The area is strewn with remains, mostly those of gila-munja blown to pieces by the explosion. Most of the dead bodies have been picked clean by dog-vultures and other scavengers, but at the centre of the explosion I found enough genetic material fused with the metal remnants of the bike to make a DNA analysis,' explained the Tek-Judge.

'And? Who is it?' demanded Miller.

'I can say with at least ninety per cent probability that the human remains are those of Cadet Kate Jenks. This is confirmed by the chassis number on her Lawmaster and a few scraps of documentation in the area.'

'Jenks! She was the cadet Dredd failed, according to his personal log,' realised the team leader. 'She must have been making her way back to Mega-City One when she was attacked by a pack of gila-munja.'

'I concur,' added Tupolua. 'All the signs are that she was ambushed and used the auto-destruct to take out as many gila-munja as possible with her when she blew.'

There was silence while the six Judges absorbed this latest piece of the puzzle. Brighton got up and started pacing – not easy in such an enclosed area.

'So Zender and Agnew died in action, Jenks was failed and died trying to return to Mega-City One, the other three cadets are apparently held captive by this Soon creep, and we all know what happened to Chung. That just leaves one question – what happened to Judge Dredd?' he asked.

'That's what we've got to find out. It all comes

187

back to Dredd,' said Miller, before turning to look at the SJS Judge. 'Still think Dredd killed them all, Nyder?'

'Perhaps not the first three, but I've seen nothing yet to prove his innocence concerning what happened to Chung or the others,' grumbled Nyder.

'Nor anything to prove his guilt,' pointed out Brighton cheerfully. 'What next, ma'am?'

'I propose we skirt round Beakersville, where the two cadets died in action, and go straight on to the black zone. Everything seems to lead there. If necessary, we can confirm the identity of the two dead cadets in Beakersville on the way back, if we still require total proof.' Miller stood up and moved to the doorway before speaking again.

'I want us ready to roll in five minutes, if not sooner. We've had it pretty easy up to now, but I've got a feeling things are about to get tougher.'

And then he was running again, the demon close behind him, once more the inevitable fall, the limbs sprawling, the pain, the fear; the incredible, heart-bursting fear.

And the demon lurched over him, its breath fouler than anything imaginable, the teeth like tombstones, leering, jeering him towards them, towards death.

'Who are you?' demanded the hunted one.

'You should know me by now,' replied the demon, weapon in one hand, badge held aloft in the other. 'I'm DREDD!'

Jonah jerked away, gasping for breath, for relief, for reality. That nightmare again! But every time he had it, the demon got a little closer, the darkness crept a little nearer, like a dagger worming its way through his flesh, piercing him, ice through warmth, darkness into light.

Jonah clutched a hand to the bandages around his head, they were soaked with sweat and, yes, some drops of blood. His wounds were seeping again. 'Got to find the little girl,' he told himself, staggering to his feet. 'She can make me better again.'

He staggered in from the field where he had fallen – the nightmares were getting worse every day now, taking him into sleep where none had existed moments before. Soon, he doubted he could resist them at all.

The little girl was playing in the sunshine outside the main building in the centre of the corral when he found her at last. 'Please, help me. You've got to help meeeee – ' Jonah slurred before slumping to the ground, unconscious again, sprawling out like a corpse.

The little girl knelt beside him and started to unwrap the bloody bandages from around his skull. 'You must get better, you are the guardian! That's what the old women say. You are the guardian, Jonah!'

'They've past Beakersville and are heading directly towards the black zone now – we estimate their arrival time as three, maybe two hours from now.'

'Good,' nodded Tek-Judge Freeman, speaking to the vid-phone moulded into his desk. 'Are they aware of your presence in the area?'

'No, I don't think so. We've stayed well back, out of visual range, and our operative on the killdozer crew has "adjusted" the scanners so they won't be able to pick us up that way either.'

'Good. Any news on the child?'

'Nothing yet, sir, but everything seems to lead into the black zone, so the answer must be in there,' replied the Judge at the other end of the communication, his voice blurred with scrambler static. 'Our sensors are still unable to probe the zone or discover its origins.'

'All right, stay back and continue monitoring their progress. But be ready to move in at a moment's notice if you hear from our operative in the killdozer. Maintain radio silence from this moment, unless you find something.'

'That's a roj.'

'Freeman out,' concluded the Tek-Judge, deactivating the vid-phone. He nearly jumped out of his seat at the next voice he heard.

'Interesting conversation, Freeman.'

The Tek-Judge turned to find Chief Judge McGruder standing in the doorway, flanked by a dozen personal guards.

'Want to tell us about it?' she asked.

Freeman grabbed for his Lawgiver but his hand was pinned to his desk by a boot knife, flung by one of the guards. A second guard moved forward to hold down the Tek-Judge's other arm, while a third advanced, wielding a syringe full of the Justice Department's latest truth serum, squeezing it delicately to send a tiny spurt of liquid shooting from the tip of the needle.

'We didn't think you would,' said the Chief Judge wryly, 'so we took the precaution of bringing a few – shall we say – incentives?'

Freeman smashed his jaws together, shattering teeth, blood bubbling from his mouth. But in moments this was replaced with white foam, frothing outwards.

190

'Drokk! Suicide pill!' exclaimed one of the guards, trying to prise Freeman's mouth open.

'See you in hell, McGruder!' spat Freeman, and his head slumped forward. Then his body lay still, unmoving, quite dead. The Chief Judge stepped forward and pulled the face back upwards by the hair to look into the dead man's eyes.

'Not if we see you first, drokker,' she muttered darkly.

'Ma'm, should we arrange a post-mortem Psi scan?' asked one of the guard Judges.

'Forget it. Freeman's a past master at masking his thoughts. He'll tell us even less in death than he did alive,' said McGruder, stomping from the office.

In the Justice Department archives, Hershey was getting frustrated. Two hours of checking, cross-checking and counter-referencing had found no trace of Erebus in the files and compu-storage dumps.

'It's like the place has been erased from history,' she muttered, then stopped to listen to her own words. 'Erased . . . that's it!' As fast as she could manage, the senior Judge accessed the log for all systems deletions. The log noted every single file or document that had been purged from the system since it was first instituted more than thirty years before. Once accessed, Hershey began to scroll backwards through the thousands, the tens of thousands of deletions from the data-dumps.

She had barely begun when a name flashed before her eyes, triggering a jab at the pause control. 'Go to Anderson deletion, this file,' she commanded the voice-responder.

The system immediately threw up on screen the file that had caught her eye: ANDERSON, CAS-

SANDRA – PSI JUDGE. A deletion had been made from the file less than a month before. 'Go deeper,' Hershey commanded, her green eyes blazing at the screen.

What she discovered amazed her. Carefully memorising the contents of the relevant file note, she returned to her scrolling backwards through history. It was another hour before she stumbled across the first of more than a dozen deletions from the systems, all of files originally dated 2095AD.

'That's nearly thirty years ago,' she wondered aloud. Then she started reading what was inside the files. Hershey had only got two screens into the first one when she contacted the Chief Judge on their private channel.

'This is Hershey. I've discovered the Erebus files. And there's something else you should know – somebody's been hacking chunks out of Anderson's personal file too.'

'You better come see us,' was the grim reply. 'There's a few things you should know, too.'

CHAPTER FOUR

Karyn had been feeling progressively more and more uneasy as they approached the black zone. At first she put this down to her psychic encounter with the monster calling itself Soon, and the horrible fate of the three surviving cadets. But the unease continued to grow, until she could no longer ignore it. Finally she went to see Miller in the killdozer's rest area.

'I think I'm losing my Psi powers,' she said.

'What do you mean?'

'My Psi abilities – it's as if they're draining away, almost as if they're being sapped from my psyche,' explained the Psi Judge downheartedly.

'When did this start?' asked Miller.

'I've felt an unease ever since I was selected for this mission. Now, the closer we get to the black zone, the worse it gets,' said Karyn, a tear starting to form in her left eye. 'It's as if my very life were being slowly taken away piece by piece, like I was going blind. But it's not my eyes, it's my Psi talent that's fading!'

'What do you want to do about it? Should I send you back to Mega-City One? Leave you here with a war-droid for protection, at least until we return? What?'

'I don't know, I don't – ' Karyn was sobbing now, tears streaming down her face. 'It's Soon – he's stealing my mind, a piece at a time!'

Miller just hugged the Psi Judge for a minute, letting her regain some composure. 'I think the best thing we can do is to keep going forward. If we can find this Soon and defeat him, then perhaps your Psi abilities will return.'

'And if they don't?' said Karyn, brushing the tears from her face, embarrassed at her emotional display.

'Then I think you'll make a damn fine Street Judge, Psi talents or not.' Miller stood to go but Karyn called her back.

'There was something else. I've been getting brief Psi flashes, unlike any I've ever had before, incredibly powerful.'

'Soon?'

'No, it's something – or someone – else. But it's close, very close to the black zone, I'm sure of that,' ventured Karyn.

'Hmm,' pondered Miller. 'Another mystery to add to our collection. It's obvious – ' Before she could say any more, the intercom boomed into life.

'Miller, this is Raimes. I think you'd better get up here – now!'

'What do you know about Cassandra Anderson?'

Hershey paused to think before answering. 'A fine Psi Judge, quite eccentric and frequently flouts authority, but one of the best we've got. And I know that she sent her badge back after the Mars incident.'

'Yes, we've got it here,' replied McGruder, fingering the thin slice of metal. 'But do you know about her childhood, how she came to be a Judge?'

'No, I presumed she showed Psi talents at an early age and was inducted into the Psi School.'

'Not exactly like that. Perhaps you'd better sit

down,' suggested the Chief Judge. 'Cassandra Anderson was abused by her father while still an infant. Her first conscious Psi-act was to kill him. After that she was inducted in the Psi School, and given special treatments to hide these facts from her. Did you know that Anderson was placed in the psycho-cubes for a short period two years ago?'

Hershey just shook her head, speechless.

'After an incident in the Cursed Earth, she began to lash out at others, putting several good Judges in the medbays. Eventually she had to be cubed for her own safety,' said McGruder quietly.

'What happened?'

'She got better. According to Shenker she must have journeyed deep into her own psyche and confronted the monsters of the past. But since that day, her disenchantment with the Justice Department has grown more palpable. Just before Judgement Day she attacked another Judge during a routine interrogation. We sent her to Mars to cool off – it didn't work. Now she's sent back her badge.'

'Something happened to her out in the Cursed Earth,' deduced Hershey.

'Exactly,' agreed the Chief Judge. 'Shenker ordered a secret investigation – it was called Operation Hope.'

'That's the file that's gone missing!'

'Right again. So has the Psi Judge who was preparing it for Shenker. His body turned up at Resyk yesterday.' McGruder paused. 'There's a lot more to this conspiracy than meets the eye.'

'What was the report about?'

'Shenker had only received an interim update, but it seems that while in the Cursed Earth, Anderson encountered a new Psi talent of unimaginable proportions. While trying to protect its own identity, it unlocked the secrets hidden in Anderson's mind. . .'

'Hence the attacks on other Judges.'

The Chief Judge nodded. 'Those who stand against us know they don't have the numbers to stage any sort of coup. But if they could get Dredd out of the way, and find this Psi talent. . .'

'The child!' exclaimed Hershey. 'It all fits together.'

'That's what we've been afraid of,' agreed McGruder grimly. 'What have you found out about Erebus?'

Hershey was still reeling from all this new information. Putting that together with what she had gleaned from the thirty-year-old files. . .

'You ain't gonna like it.'

'What is it, Raimes?' demanded Miller, storming into the cockpit in answer to his summons.

'Look at the scanner.'

On a screen set into the control panel, the black zone had grown appreciably larger since Miller had last looked at it. Even more worrying, it seemed to be accelerating in its growth outwards.

'I'll put it on tri-D for you,' volunteered the driver. Light surged up from the console to create a three-dimensional hologram of the scanner's findings. Cut off in a cross-section, it showed the blackness surging over a tiny cube. 'That was the last building in Lazarus – the entire town has been absorbed into the black zone. It's speeding up, too. We'll be on top of it in minutes!'

Miller's brow furrowed as she examined the light projection. 'Hang on – what's happening over here?' she said, pointing to the right side of the display.

* * *

'The blackness – it's coming!'

One of the mutant farm-hands had burst through the door and was pointing behind him. The old women moved to look out of the nearest window. Beyond the corral, they could just see the edge of the farm's most western field. The creeping blackness was oozing towards the boundary. As one, the trio turned to look at the voice.

'We must flee now, the blackness is nearly here!' said the three old women as one. Beside them the farm-hand, Kimus, nodded his agreement. As leader of the farm-hands, the other men would follow his decision.

'No,' replied the voice. 'Watch.' A delicate finger pointed towards the boundary fence. There the darkness was about to reach it, to engulf when – it stopped! At either side the blackness surged onwards but whenever it reached a boundary, it was pushed sideways. 'The blackness cannot overwhelm this farm while I live here. This is our sanctuary. But it will also be a sanctuary for others. . .'

'That farm – the blackness doesn't seem to be penetrating its borders!' exclaimed Miller, looking to Raimes in the driver's seat. 'Can we reach the farm before the black zone engulfs us?'

'We don't even know what effect this black – '

'Can we make it?' demanded Miller.

'Just,' replied the driver.

'Do it – NOW!' bellowed Miller and was nearly toppled over backwards as the killdozer surged forward along the dirt track towards the property, heading straight for the rapidly advancing darkness.

The black zone was visible to them now; at least, its presence was discernible. The darkness itself seemed to creep forward like molten lava, but black and oily in appearance. Behind the leading edge visibility extended only a few feet, and beyond that an impenetrable black cloud seemed to hover, swallowing all light.

'We're not going to make it to the front gate,' realised Raimes. Before the killdozer, the blackness oozed forward besides the perimeter fence of the farm.

'Then we make our own entrance!' announced Miller, grabbing the steering wheel and swinging it wildly to the right. The mighty vehicle lurched sideways, then powered through the fence, smashing over rock and metal to get in. From beneath it came a terrible screaming of metal as the tracks were torn from their wheels. The killdozer stuttered on a few feet then shuddered to a halt, listing to the left as its substantial mass began to sink into the soft soil.

'Rear view!' commanded Miller, and the voice-responsive console computer projected the scene behind the killdozer onto its front viewport, as seen from tiny cameras set into the back of the vehicle.

The darkness had surged past their impromptu entranceway and flowed on down the dirt track, still skirting the edge of the property. 'East view,' requested the team leader, and now those in the cockpit saw the blackness continue its journey towards Mega-City One. A minute later, the darkness had rolled round from the northern and southern sides of the farm and the two parts of the blackness were amalgamated again into one.

The farm was completely surrounded by the black zone, cut off, totally isolated.

* * *

Inside the main building, the little girl had finished rebandaging Jonah's head and was gently shaking him.

'Jonah, it's time to wake up. We've got visitors.'

Deep inside the glasseen towers of Erebus, Soon was both furious and triumphant.

'The judges – they have escaped my darkness!' He hovered in a high-ceiled chamber, adjoined to the bone cathedral. Formerly a meeting place for therapy sessions, Soon had transformed it into a war room. Pride of place was given to the Map of Eyes, a hideous construct created from slices of eyeballs squeezed together between two sheets of glasseen. Jammed together, the organic matter merged into a grisly membrane activated by Soon's force of will. Onto this he mentally projected a light-map of Erebus, the surrounding black zone and settlements and townships beyond its boundaries.

The blackness continued to surge outwards in a satisfying fashion, but it was a tiny point of light on the screen which attracted Soon's attention. This dot represented the killdozer which he had been tracking since it came within a two-hundred klick radius of his domain. Soon had waited for it to encounter his all-conquering darkness, when it had suddenly turned aside. Now it was land-locked inside an oasis of pure white to the east of Erebus.

'What is this? Something resists my will? How can this be possible? Unless. . .' He thought, then snapped his fingers. In an instant, Novar appeared before him. 'Novar, you went to this farm, didn't you?'

'Yes, my lord,' replied the cowering lieutenant.

'What happened?'

'A man was there, my lord, a man unafraid. I tried to twist his mind, as you taught me, my lord, but his will was too strong,' trembled the servant, not daring to look at his dark master.

'Interesting. Did you see anything else?' enquired Soon sweetly.

'I thought I saw – saw a – a – '

'A what? Spit it out, or I shall feast upon your soul for my supper tonight!'

'A child, my lord, a little girl. But I wasn't sure – '

'WHAT?!' bellowed the twisted one. 'Why did you not speak of this, you fool!'

'Have mercy, my lord, she was but a little girl, barely more than an infant. You sent me searching for the greatest Psi of the century, you said. I thought – ' stammered Novar.

'You thought! If I wanted you to think I would have let you keep your intellect, fool!' stormed Soon, hovering menacingly over the abject Novar. The twisted genius's hands turned into fists, then knives, then a thousand razor-sharp needles as he comtemplated a suitable punishment for this dolt. Finally he settled on a fitting death, his left hand reshaping itself into a six-foot-long scimitar blade. Soon raised it behind his head, about to slash downwards, when he thought better.

'No. No, I shall not kill you yet. You will be my general on the field of blood we shall make of that farm. You shall be my eyes and ears, Novar. But to do that, to truly represent me, I must reshape you in my image,' projected Soon sinisterly. 'That is what gods do, I understand, and once I have the power of that child absorbed, I shall be like unto a god!'

Soon lowered himself to the ground before Novar,

mentally reshaping his hands into a hundred tiny scalpels extending from each wrist. With these he began to slash at Novar's face, hacking, tearing through flesh and bone and cartilage and sinew, gouging out one eyeball, slicing away the ears, dragging teeth out, root and all, viciously slashing, faster and faster and faster. Through all of this Novar screamed, just one long continuous terrible scream.

At last Soon's frenzy passed and the ends of his arms melted into a new form, this time gentle, soothing hands and fingers. These massaged the bloody, jagged mess of Novar's face, creating a new visage from the remnants of the old. Finally, Soon stepped back to admire his handiwork.

Novar's head was an exact replica of Soon, except he had a mouth of sorts. But instead of a normal mouth, this was like some obscene orifice, just a jagged circle, a flap of bloody skin hanging away from where the bottom lip should be.

'There! Not bad if I say so myself. Now, you shall gather my army so I can address you all before the battle.' With a thought, the lieutenant was gone again, and Soon turned back to his Map of Eyes, pondering the possibilities that lay ahead.

'It seems the black spot, when it first appeared as a navigational hazard, was situated on the exact centre-point of what had been the Justice Department's secret asylum, Erebus.'

Hershey was using the wall of tri-D screens in the Chief Judge's office to explain her discoveries to McGruder. 'Erebus was opened in the 70s, to house Judges mentally disturbed during the fighting in the Second Civil War. Later it became a dumping ground for psycho cases, mistakes made during

201

cloning and eugenics experiments, all sorts of sordid little secrets the department didn't want anyone to know about. After a diplomatic incident involving Texas City back in '95, Erebus was officially shut down. All remaining human Med-Judges and security guards were removed, and the entire place was turned over to full automation and purged from the files.'

'So far, so bad. What else?' asked McGruder.

'Although the place was officially shut down, none of the patients were removed or resited. They were simply left to rot, their physical needs and medication seen to by robo-docs and automatic systems. It was estimated all would be dead within ten years anyway. But this didn't take into account the very last set of patients, or more accurately inmates, sent to Erebus. They were six children, the by-product of illicit eugenics experiments by a Doctor Swale – '

'Sweet Jovus, the Swale monsters! We remember now!' exclaimed the Chief Judge, sitting bolt upright in her chair. 'We were a young SJS Judge, sent in to discover who had authorised the work. Those kids were monsters, all with wild Psi abilities. We put in our report that they should all be terminated, as soon as. . .'

'It didn't happen. They were sent to Erebus, the place closed down a week later, and they were forgotten. Ironically, Swale himself was a patient at Erebus. One of the last notations of the deleted files concerned his "mysterious" death, which seemed to coincide with the arrival of his creations at the asylum.'

'So what has all this got to do with the black zone?' asked McGruder impatiently. Hershey responded by having an image of the seven-year-old projected onto the multi-screens, the mouthless face unnerving, the eye malevolent.

'This child seems to have been the leader of the children. He called himself Soon. I ran some projections through the computers on what he would be like now, if he was still alive.'

Now the image on the tri-D screens was replaced with an older version of the same frightening features. Hershey stood before the screens for emphasis.

'All the children were heavily sedated with Psi-tranq when sent to Erebus. Chances are that the robo-docs will have continued administering the recommended dosages to all of the children. The computer estimates that after twenty years, all of the children would begin to develop resistance to the drug. If tended by Med-Judges, such a change would be noted and dosages or even the drugs used altered to compensate. But robo-docs can be pretty inflexible, and Psis are good at hiding their abilities, especially from machines.'

'What are you saying? The kids have now grown up and aren't affected by the drugs any more?' Hershey nodded. 'When would this have happened?'

'Any time in the last year. I checked some other records too. Seems Med Division has still been supplying drugs to the asylum for the past two decades, sending them out in automated h-wagons, despite it being officially closed. All contact was lost with the asylum three weeks ago. And it was about that time that the – '

'The black spot first appeared. Jovus,' muttered the Chief Judge. 'So the lunatics have taken over the asylum.'

'It's worse than that. Seems Soon's special ability was to twist and absorb the Psi talents of others.

Once he'd stolen the talents of the other experimental offspring, he probably started on the rest of the surviving inmates. Then the people in surrounding settlements. After that, passing aircraft. . .'

'The crashed h-wagons! The gunbird!'

'The computer projects that Soon – or whoever is behind all of this – probably has Psi powers to match fifty to a hundred of our best Psi Judges. Probably more,' said Hershey grimly. 'He seems to have been content to stay inside Erebus, use it as his power-base, almost a focus point. But now he's getting bored, expanding his grasp – hence the rapidly expanding black zone. Unless he's stopped soon, we might never get another chance.'

'Okay. How do we stop him?' asked McGruder, her hard, flinty eyes boring into Hershey's face.

'I don't know,' replied the younger woman resignedly. 'We can't bomb him, the black zone knocks out all approaching aircraft. Ground teams probably wouldn't even get close. That just leaves nuking Erebus from space, and we're not even sure that'll work. Plus, if we try to use our orbital weapons, he might discover their presence and turn them against us. Right now, our best weapon is his ignorance – and the fact that's he's probably a raving psycho.'

'Meaning?'

'He won't attack us logically, he'll make mistakes, he'll be vulnerable in some way. The difficulty is getting close enough to find that weakness and exploit it.'

'Good Grud! And we've sent a handful of Judges in a single killdozer to investigate!' realised McGruder. 'Any word from them?'

Hershey shook her head. 'Contact was lost an

hour ago. Their last reported heading was taking them directly into the black zone.'

The Chief Judge rubbed the stubble on her bony chin before deciding the next move. 'Looks like the nukes are our only chance. How long before they're ready?'

'At least twenty-four hours. The black zone is playing havoc with communications to all satellites,' explained Hershey. 'I'll get things started.' But before she could leave, the Chief Judge had a final question.

'Before we lost contact with the killdozer, did they have anything to say about Dredd or the Hotdog Run?'

'No, just that everything seemed to lead directly into the heart of the darkness.' Hershey strode out of the office, leaving the Chief Judge to her thoughts.

'Miller, it's amazing. My Psi abilities – they've returned!'

Karyn was standing in front of the killdozer, clutching a hand to her forehead, a look of mixed bewilderment and joy on her face. 'It's like the static in the background has been switched off!'

'What? Explain,' ordered the team leader, pulling off her own helmet to look at the Psi Judge, who had been so distraught just hours earlier. The killdozer crew had climbed out to survey the damage to their vehicle, with only Tupolua and Nyder left inside to unload stores and prepare the war-droids for any possible action.

'I can't!' said the delighted Psi Judge. 'It's just that since we came through the boundary fence, I've been able to think clearly, to use my abilities to probe for possible Psi flashes.'

'Interesting,' nodded Miller. 'Not only does this farm keep out the black zone, it seems to knock out the psychic interference that was draining your abilities. A real little oasis, this place! I think it's time we had a look around. Karyn, Brighton – you come with me. Raimes, you better stay here and see what repairs you can make to the killdozer.'

The designated driver didn't look very hopeful. 'I'm not sure I'll be able to make any. The half-tracks are torn apart, the hydraulics are shot – we may be stuck here until help arrives.'

'Well, that could be a long wait,' said Miller. 'Just do what you can, okay? Then help the others with the supplies and the war-droids.' Raimes nodded, then turned back to his beloved killdozer, a mournful look on his face. 'Right, let's start with those buildings in the centre of the farm, shall we?' Miller marched ahead, Karyn and Brighton running to keep up with her hefty strides.

No army like it had ever been seen before. At the front were the Soonites, inmates of Erebus and people from surrounding settlements that had been lured into or simply swallowed up by the black zone. Each had been brought before Soon and judged whether they were fit to serve in his army. The lucky ones were brutally, callously murdered on the spot. Those deemed worthy were 'converted' by Soon, their DNA rewritten to cause horrific mutations of the body, not unlike those that had transformed him into such a repulsive monster. But while his mutation had taken years, even decades, for these poor souls it took only hours, but hours of excruciating agony and torment.

Now they were simply replicas of their master,

brains wiped to create total, unswerving obedience in all things. These were to be the cannon-fodder, the meat to be thrown first before the dogs of war. They numbered just a few hundred in all.

Behind them were the zombies, pulled up from their graves and forced to march into the blackness, some journeying hundreds of klicks to reach Erebus. In body, they ranged from the freshly buried, like the unfortunate Esther, still clothed in her finest funeral attire, through to those that had long been rotting in the grave. Some were barely skeletons, just a handful of rad-maggots still crawling across what little putrefying flesh remained on their bones. Perhaps a thousand zombies were gathered. There would have been many more, millions perhaps, but the zombie war known as Judgement Day had seen the decimation of the numbers of undead still left intact in the Cursed Earth.

Finally, at the back lurked the gila-munja. Thousands of the ruthless chameleon-skinned monsters had been drawn to Erebus by the stench of evil and murder and death. More than three dozen different packs were present. Normally, if a single scout from one pack encountered gila-munja from another pack, the fighting would be brutal and deadly. But today they had put aside such tribal differences, in preparation for the slaughter to come.

So the gila-munja slithered and hissed and waited impatiently, a giant mass of almost translucent, murderous monsters, blending into the blood-stained background of the Cathedral of Bone.

And before them all floated Soon, his twisted arms poking sideways in a perverted attempt at messianic status. Robes of purest white hung about his warped body, and his pallid, clammy skin seemed to glow, almost radiant with light. At the rear of the cathedral, the gila-munja covered their eyes, shielding themselves from this vicious brightness.

'My children, my army, I have brought you all here, together, for a single purpose: conquest!' announced Soon telepathically, beaming his thoughts into each and every mind, no matter how small or animalistic.

'Tomorrow, at dawn, you shall attack an outpost, an oasis of all that is good and pure. And you shall destroy it. But not just destroy it, you shall leave it so no stone stands atop another, so that no trace lingers of their heinous affront to my beautiful empire. And all that live within this place shall be torn asunder so you may feed upon their organs, their brains, their hearts. You shall smash their bones and suck out the marrow. You shall feast upon human flesh!'

This brought a chorus of grunted approval from the gila-munja. Soon held up a hand to quell this feeding frenzy before it got out of hand.

'But there is one human that must be kept alive, brought to me for my infinite pleasure. Bring me the child!'

And he was running again, falling sprawling. The demon leered over him, flashing its badge.

'Who are you?' demanded the hunted one.

'Don't you recognise me? I'm hurt!' mocked the creature. 'I'm DREDD! I'm –'

Jonah jerked awake to find himself surrounded by the five farm-hands looking down at him anxiously. The little girl sat by his side, smiling at him.

'I'm sorry I had to wake you, Jonah, but the time of reckoning is come,' she said.

'What? What are you talking about?'

'Don't worry, you'll see soon.' She smiled, stood up and skipped from the room into the main chamber next door. Jonah struggled to his feet, his head spinning.

'What is it, Kimus? What's going on?'

The leader of the farm-hands looked terrified, sweat trickling down the side of his mutated face. 'The blackness, it come. It surround the farm.'

'What!' Jonah pushed away the wooden shutters from the windows to look outside. He could see the darkness at the perimeter of the property, almost as if it was lurking there, waiting for a chance to come inside. Glancing around the boundary, he saw a strange metal vehicle which seemed to have crashed through the fence and become bogged down in one of the outer ring of fields. Three people were climbing over the corral fence, seemingly having come from the vehicle close to the perimeter. They wore strange costumes he felt he half-recognised.

'Intruders! I've got to stop them!' Jonah ran from the room, into the main chamber. Kimus tried to stop him, but Jonah pushed the arm away.

'Jonah, you can't! They're Judges!' But Jonah didn't hear the mutant man's words.

Outside, Brighton was the last to clear the fence and climb down into the central corral. Suddenly Karyn doubled over, clutching her hands to her head.

'Grud on a greenie! Psi flash!' she cried out.

'What is it?' demanded Miller. If there was something hostile inside the farmhouse, they'd better be prepared for it. She nodded to Brighton and removed her own Lawgiver from its boot holster.

'Incredible! I just got a flash of a Psi so powerful. . .' explained Karyn, still recovering from the shock. 'I've never felt anything like it before. More powerful than someone using a Psi amplifier – and that increases your natural Psi abilities a thousand-fold!'

'Is it Soon?'

'No! No, this is far more powerful than him. But there's something else, something almost familiar. . .' Karyn shook her head, unable to explain any further.

'All right, get ready, we're going in – '

The farmhouse door burst open.

Close to the perimeter fence, Raimes was still labouring to assess the damage to the killdozer. Inside the vehicle, Nyder and Tupolua had unloaded all the stores and spare ammunition onto transportation hover-trollies. Now the pair were activating the war-droids.

Surreptitiously, while the other wasn't looking, one of the pair drew their Lawgiver and held it against the base of the other Judge's spine.

'Sorry about this, but needs must. Hope you understand,' smiled the traitor and fired at point-blank range. A tiny entrance wound appeared in the victim's back, but the exit wound was bigger than a fist, punching blood, bone and major intestine all over the interior wall of the killdozer. 'Now for Raimes,' muttered the murderer.

'We can't let you go out there, Jonah, it's too dangerous. They're Judges!'

'What do you mean, they're Judges? Who are the Judges?' demanded Jonah, his head swimming with pain and confusion.

'Bad people, who want to take our hope away,' said the eldest of the mutant eldsters.

'Then I'll stop them!' announced Jonah, looking around for a weapon, his eyes lighting on a knife on the meal table. He picked it up, assessing the weight in his hands, taking a few practice swings.

'No, you can't, they'll kill you! Then they'll kill us, and take the voice away!'

'What voice? What are you talking about, old woman?'

'The voice, that which guides us in all things. It is our talisman, our adviser, our entrustment. Without it we are nothing, without it we have no hope. The world will have no hope if the Judges take the voice away!'

'I don't fear death,' said Jonah. 'It can't be any worse than my nightmares. Anything worth as much as you say it is, is worth dying for!'

Pushing away the despairing grasp of the old women, Jonah ripped open the front door and burst out, knife held at the ready.

'All right, get ready, we're going in – ' said Miller, then the farmhouse door burst open and a madman came running out towards them, screaming and shouting with rage, knife pulled back in the air, ready to attack.

'Drokk! Fire!' yelled Miller and started shooting. Brighton too began firing, the pair of them pumping round after round into the charging attacker. The bullets ripped through his body, almost shredding

211

his torso, punching out through his back, stabbing through his arms and legs.

'NO! STOP!' yelled Karyn. 'You've got to stop!' She grabbed at Brighton and Miller, throwing off their aim. By the time they could adjust, the lone attacker had fallen to the ground, a few feet short of them, his body convulsing slightly, blood pouring from his many wounds.

'Jovus drokk, Karyn! What were you doing?' demanded Miller, spitting with rage.

'His face – I thought I recognised his face,' said the Psi Judge, moving closer to their attacker.

'Careful, he's still alive,' urged Brighton, his Lawgiver trained on the open doorway, ready for another attack at any moment.

Karyn stood beside the body, which jerked once more, then lay still. 'No, he's dead now.'

'Jonah! They've killed Jonah!' screamed the little girl, looking out at the window of the farmhouse at the carnage outside. 'They've killed Jonah!'

'Come away from the window, or they'll kill you,' said the tallest of the old women, pulling the little girl back.

Outside, Miller and Brighton had joined Karyn beside the corpse of their attacker. The Psi Judge crouched down and reached forward a hand to turn over the body, which was sprawled out on the orange soil, face down.

'Careful, he could be foxing you,' warned Miller.

'No, he's dead, I felt his spirit leave the body,' said Karyn firmly. She rolled the body over and gasped, quite speechless. The face was caked with blood and dust, the skull swathed in bandages, but the features were unmistakable. Miller looked down wide-eyed, amazed.

'It's Dredd! We've killed Judge Dredd!'

Part Three: Today

CHAPTER ONE

Judge Kevin Brighton was on sentry duty outside the farmhouse, scanning the perimeter of the farm with night-vision binoculars. He was glad of the chance to be alone. The events of the past six hours since discovering they had murdered the man they were searching for had left the young Judge reeling. It seemed that more had happened in that short time than during his fifteen years at the Academy.

No sooner had he and Miller realised their mistake in gunning down Dredd than a little girl in a white dress had burst out of the farmhouse, running to Dredd's body. She knelt by the corpse and cradled the dead man's bloody, bandaged head in her tiny arms.

'They didn't mean to hurt you, Jonah, wake up! They didn't mean to hurt you . . .' repeated the infant.

Karyn tried to pull the little girl away but she resisted. 'Come away now, he's dead. There's nothing you can do for him, nothing anyone can do for him.'

'You're wrong!' pouted the girl, pushing a blonde pigtail away from her face. She turned back to Dredd and closed her eyes, seeming to go into a trance.

* * *

*Dredd was running, sprawling again. The demon
leered over him, but this time it had no smile – it had
no mouth at all. Instead he could hear its voice inside
his head.*

*'Don't you recognise yourself? I'm Judge Dredd!'
mocked the voice, all cunning and cleverness.*

*'No! I'm Judge Dredd!' screamed back the hunted,
lashing out at the hunter. 'I'm Judge Dredd!'*

'I'm Judge Dredd!' shouted Dredd, sitting bolt
upright. All the blood had vanished from his body,
all the wounds had disappeared. Just a stabbing pain
in the head remained, like a nagging doubt.

'Sweet Jovus!' exclaimed Karyn, shocked and
stunned. Brighton and Miller were simply speechless, struck dumb by Dredd's apparent resurrection.

'I told you I could bring him back,' announced the
little girl triumphantly.

'Amazing, simply amazing,' stammered the Psi
Judge. Behind her, Miller had recovered from the
initial shock enough to take stock of the situation.

'Karyn, the girl. Is she?'

'The Psi power I sensed before? Seems so,' agreed
the young woman. 'I'd say she's probably what's
keeping the black zone outside the boundaries of
this property.'

'So if we stay in here we're safe?' asked Brighton
hopefully, before being distracted by the approaching figures of two killdozer crew members across the
fields.

'I wouldn't go that far. Something tells me Soon
might have other plans for us and the little girl,' said
Karyn, turning to the infant. 'What's your name?'

'Hope,' smiled the child. 'I am Hope.'

'Look, it's Raimes and Tupolua,' pointed out

Brighton. 'Hey guys, come over! We've found Dredd and something else – it's amazing!'

The two Judges from the killdozer clambered over the fence into the corral, Raimes in front. It was only when both of them had cleared the fence that the others realised Tupolua was pointing a Lawgiver at Raimes' back.

'Tupolua! What are you playing at?' demanded Miller.

'Just shut up,' replied the Tek-Judge curtly, motioning Raimes over to join the others while covering them all with her weapon. With her other hand Tupolua activated her helmet-com and began to speak into it. 'Tupolua to Gunbird, come in Gunbird. Come in!'

'Where's Nyder?' whispered Brighton to Raimes.

'Dead – murdered by Tupolua!'

'What!'

Dredd struggled to his feet and squinted at the Tek-Judge. 'She's a traitor – part of the conspiracy against the Chief Judge.'

'Very shrewd guesswork, Dredd,' said Tupolua sarcastically. 'Thank you for finding the child for us. She will make the toppling of that old fool quite simple. Then we can restore proper law enforcement to the streets of Mega-City One. No more will a half-crazed old woman dictate to us!'

'It'll never work. The vast majority of Judges will never support a *coup d'état*,' chipped in Miller, motioning with her eyes for Brighton to try and work his way around Tupolua while she did the same from the other side.

'I said shut your freakin' face!' shouted back the Tek-Judge and concentrated on trying to contact the Gunbird.

'How do you know about this conspiracy?' Karyn whispered to Dredd.

'When you've been on the streets as long as I have, you tend to hear about all the murmurings of dissent. This one's been festering since Necropolis.'

'Tupolua to Gunbird, come in!' bellowed the traitor into her helmet mike. A faint voice crackled back to her.

'This is Gunbird, what is your status?'

'I have the child. Come and get us. Home on this frequency,' smiled the traitor, and turned back to the others. 'Now we wait.'

Many miles up in the sky, beyond the atmosphere, a satellite altered its trajectory. Computer signals from Mega-City One activated systems unused since the horrors of Judgement Day, nearly eighteen months before. The sky defence system had been used then to nuke five mega-cities in different locations around the globe to prevent them becoming zombie factories for Sabbat the Necromagus. Two billion people had died that day, by order of the world council of Judges.

Now the deadly systems were slowly coming alive again, brought to life once more for another murderous task: destroying Erebus and everything within a two hundred klick radius of it, living or dead, good or evil. This weapon did not discriminate in any way.

In Mega-City One, Judge Hershey watched in the central despatch section as a Tek-Judge began the long process building up to firing the sky defence system.

'May Grud forgive us,' she prayed to herself, but was interrupted by a message relayed to her by a

218

monitoring Judge, somewhat archaically on a scrap of paper. It read:

'If you want to meet the leader of the conspiracy about the Chief Judge, come to SJS Interrogation Cell 101 at one hundred hours tomorrow. Sagassi.'

Hershey read the message, then had it sent on to McGruder. So the SJS judge was going to reveal himself as the traitor – this should be interesting!

The first hint anyone had of the Gunbird's approach was a sound like metal screaming, faint at first, but gradually building into a shrieking crescendo, until it became almost unbearable.

'Drokkin' hell, what's going on?' shouted Brighton.

'Something's wrong – it's coming in too low!' bellowed back Miller, pointing at the horizon. Soon everyone could see a silver blur racing towards them, barely skipping over the rocks and bumps in the ground. 'The black zone – it must be affecting their propulsion systems.'

Moments later the Gunbird clipped a rock formation and began to pinwheel through the air towards the farm. It bounced downwards again and this time one of the wings ripped away, fire starting to engulf the aircraft. Within moments it was just a fireball cart-wheeling towards them.

'Everybody down!' commanded Dredd and the group threw themselves to the dusty orange surface. Moments later the Gunbird zoomed overhead and finally plunged to earth at the western edge of the farm, the side closest to Erebus. A massive explosion rocked the ground.

Tupolua was shocked. What had happened, what had gone wrong? The plan had been perfect. Now she was alone with a group of hostile Judges. How could she maintain control of the situation now?

The problem was rapidly taken out of her hands. She looked up to find herself staring down the barrel of a Lawgiver held by Judge Lynn Miller.

'Show's over, Claire,' said the team leader. 'You've got some explaining to do.'

It was two hours before the first warning of the coming conflict was sounded.

'There is going to be a battle,' announced Hope. 'You must get ready, or else all will die.'

'Don't listen to her, she's evil, a witch! She made the Gunbird crash!' screamed Tupolua.

'Everyone hates a sore loser,' muttered Dredd and stuffed a rag into the captive traitor's mouth to shut her up. He turned back to the little girl, crouching to speak with her face to face. 'How long have we got?'

'The monsters won't come till the morrow, but they will be many – thousands perhaps,' said Hope, biting one lip with her upper teeth.

'Terrif,' grunted Dredd, standing up again. While the others had fruitlessly interrogated Tupolua, he had been to the killdozer and selected a new uniform – though the badge was blank, of course – and helmet, and drawn a new Lawgiver from the mini-armoury within the vehicle, taking care to have his palmprint 'signature' implanted into its memory chip first. Now he scanned the property, taking in the natural features and man-made additions.

'Miller, how much combat experience do you have?'

The white-haired Judge stepped to his side. 'Very little. I was going to suggest you take – '

'From this moment I'm taking command of the

situation. We've got less than ten hours until dawn, not much time to prepare. Not enough, dammit!' He slammed one gauntlet-clad fist into the other, thinking hard. 'You better tell me how much ammo and weaponry you've got in that killdozer – we're going to need every bullet we can get.'

Inside the main farm building, Karyn was talking to the old women. The farm-hands cowered at the far end of the long dining table, fearful of being in the same room as a Judge.

'Tell me about the child,' pleaded the Psi Judge.

'You remind us of another woman, a Judge like you. She came looking for the child but found much else,' said the tallest of the trio, who had introduced herself as Melva. 'She asked many questions too.'

'Where did Hope come from?' pressed Karyn.

'She is the pure, born of the unclean. One day, she could heal the world. Already she does incredible things.'

'I know, she brought Dredd back to life,' nodded the Psi Judge. Next to her the oldest of the women, Jana, waggled a finger sternly.

'That is just a fraction of what she could one day achieve. But to do that, she must be left alone. Hope will never become all that she must if you Judges take her away. You have to promise us she will not be taken away!' The other two old mutants nodded vigorously.

'I'm not the leader of this mission, I can't make that promise. But I will promise you that I'll try,' vowed Karyn.

'Then that is all we can ask of you,' said the third woman, the amiably round-faced Keeta.

* * *

221

The small team of Judges gathered in the corral to find Dredd scratching in the dusty soil with a stick. He ignored them initially, concentrating on his work, then finally stood back and began to speak.

'The situation is this: we're in deep stomm. This entire property is surrounded by the black zone, which knocks out all mechanical systems and even Psi abilities. So it looks like we're staying put. Unfortunately, we have an enemy called Soon, the master of Erebus and this blackness. It seems he plans to send an army against us, probably attacking at dawn. This army could number hundreds, thousands, perhaps tens of thousands.

'We can expect no help from outside. Even if the Big Meg knows our location, there's no way they can get help to us. We're on our own and we have a mission – we have to protect the child Hope. If what Karyn says about this Soon is right, if he captured the child the result would be terrible.'

'That's right,' agreed Karyn. 'Soon is a Psi parasite, from what I've experienced. He drains away the Psi talents of others, either directly or from a distance, then twists those powers for his own evil use. Hope is perhaps the greatest Psi ever born. If Soon should enslave her powers, he could conquer the world easily. He must be prevented from doing this, at any cost.'

'If the little girl's so powerful, why can't we use her to defeat this Soon creep, kill him outright?' asked Brighton. But Hope shook her head violently, and Karyn was just as negative.

'Hope's powers are for good, not for evil. She cannot kill, only create. Besides, it's taking nearly all her current abilities just to maintain the perimeter

222

line, keeping out the blackness. She is only a little girl, so she has only limited abilities as yet.'

'Like I said, we're on our own,' added Dredd. 'So, we better start making some rockcrete defence plans. Raimes – can the killdozer be moved?'

The driver considered for a moment. 'It will not travel much further, the tracks are shot to pieces, the – '

'I ain't looking to go for a vacation. Can it move?'

'Maybe half a klick, then it'll never move again,' replied Raimes. 'Why?'

'I want you to bring it down to the corral, use it to block off the gateway to the dirt track. It'll block that entranceway to the corral and we can use the on-board weapons systems for extra firepower, working direct off the batteries,' explained Dredd. 'Brighton, you worked with Tupolua on the war-droids. How many are functional?'

'All twelve of them, sir, fully armed with more than fifty thousand rounds loaded into each,' said the young Judge crisply.

'Okay, once the killdozer is in place, unload the war-droids and position them a hundred yards apart, spaced around the immediate inside of the corral, facing ouwards. We're going to make the corral our main line of defence, so it will need strengthening. Suggestions?' asked Dredd.

'This is a farm, there must be crops,' offered Miller.

'Good. Yes, there's dozens of bags of tainted grain in one of the outbuildings,' Dredd recalled from his days as Jonah the farm-worker. 'Bring them in and use them to block up any gaps in the corral wall. Put in some firing steps too. How much fuel left in the killdozer?'

'Well, the nuclear rods – ' began Raimes.

'No! Liquid fuel, petroleum for the back-up combustion engines,' corrected Dredd.

'Er, just the usual reserve tank – about one hundred gallons,' stammered the driver, struggling to recall. Fossil fuels had long since gone out of use as a primary motive source, but vehicles like the killdozer kept a reserve in case of emergencies.

'Right, I'll take charge of that – good to have something up our sleeves as a surprise for the enemy,' growled the veteran lawkeeper. 'Karyn, you've talked to the old women – will they let the farm-hands help us?'

'Hard to say. The men seem pretty scared of Judges. They may be persuaded . . .' she replied.

'You work on them. We need all the help we can get. That's it,' concluded Dredd. 'Everybody know what they're doing? Then get to it!'

Even that planning meeting seemed weeks ago to Kevin Brighton as he continued his perimeter patrol, but it had only been a few hours. Of course since then, there had been the incident with Tupolua and the farm-hands.

Karyn had persuaded the mutant men to come outside and take some instruction in how to fire a scattergun, drawn from the killdozer armoury. No one had noticed Tupolua desperately working the gag loose from her mouth where she lay, her arms and legs still firmly bound.

The leader of the mutant men, Kimus, had just fired a shot and been blown over backwards by the recoil when Tupolua began shouting at the top of her voice.

'Fools! Fools! You're all going to die! Do you hear

me? Die! The blackness shall engulf you and the monster shall tear your souls apart, piece by tiny piece – '

Then Dredd was standing next to the traitor, his Lawgiver drawn and held next to her face. 'Shut up or else, Tupolua.'

'Shoot me! You'll be doing me a favour, Dredd!' she spat back. Dredd's finger lingered at the trigger for a second but then he drew back the weapon and smashed it across her face, once, twice, three times, pistol-whipping her into unconsciousness.

The other Judges had come running but the damage had been done, the farm-hands were panicked. The excitement proved too much for Kimus, their leader.

'Let's get out of here!' he told the others and vaulted the corral fence, running towards the outside boundary. The rest of the farm-hands followed him towards the blackness waiting for them outside.

'No! Stop!' pleaded Karyn but they kept running and disappeared into the darkness, gone the moment they stepped into the black zone.

'Hmm. Looks like it's just us then,' was Dredd's only comment, but his face was like thunder.

'All quiet boy?'

A startled Brighton whirled round, Lawgiver at the ready, to find Dredd approaching. 'Er, yes sir, all quiet.'

'Good. I'm not expecting an attack before dawn, but the child could be wrong,' nodded Dredd. He stood beside the young Judge for a while, probing the night with his bionic eyes, searching for any signs of threat from outside the farm's boundaries. Brighton plucked up the courage to ask Dredd a question.

'Sir, what happened to you? I mean, how much do you remember of what happened to you?'

'Everything,' replied a voice heavy with weariness. 'Every moment. Especially what happened when we first entered the black zone.'

Brighton said nothing, afraid to press any further, but Dredd continued, answering the unasked question.

'There were five of us by the time we reached Lazarus – Judge Chung, Cadets Singh, Archer, Coster, and myself. We were lured into the blackness, tricked into it by Soon's lieutenant, Novar. I remember we rode around a corner and suddenly the darkness was upon us, overwhelming, total, like a cloudless night sky – like tonight,' added the senior Judge, looking at the firmament above them.

'Blows pummelled us, battering us, tearing us away from our bikes. I feigned unconsciousness, the others were knocked out, I think. We were taken into the heart of the asylum, the centre of Erebus, brought before Soon.' Dredd went quiet for a few moments, remembering. 'We were held captive for hours, days, it was hard to tell time because of the endless pain. I managed to conserve a little of my strength, hoping for a chance to attack. I remember Chung throwing herself at Soon, yelling for me to escape. I didn't want to leave the cadets but I had no choice, somebody had to get out, to warn others, to get help. Somehow I managed to stumble out, I think Soon was concentrating all his energies on punishing Chung.'

Brighton swallowed heavily. He knew Miller had related Chung's fate to Dredd earlier. The young Judge wondered how Dredd felt about her sacrifice, but again the senior Judge seemed to be thinking ahead of him.

'She was a good Judge. Brave,' muttered Dredd before resuming his story. 'Just before I broke out of the black zone, Soon must have remembered me. It was too late to stop me but he attacked my mind, stripping away the memories, everything he could steal from me. By the time I stumbled out into the light, there wasn't much left.'

Brighton took up the thread, filling in the missing fragments for Dredd. 'Hope told me she found you wandering, lost and blind, at the edge of the farm more than a week ago. She brought you here, has been looking after you ever since.'

Dredd nodded. 'Seems she knew I was coming. Precog's one of her many abilities.'

Brighton frowned. 'Sir, how do you think the battle will go? It's just that, well, I don't want to end up like the cadets did, just playthings for Soon . . .'

'Don't worry. If it comes to that, we'll take out as many of the enemy as possible when we go,' said Dredd grimly. 'Of course, we'll have to kill the little girl first – we can't allow Soon to have her. I'll pull the trigger myself if it comes to that.'

The senior Judge walked away, continuing his tour of the perimeter, leaving Brighton alone to contemplate his grim words.

'So why all the cloak and dagger, Sagassi?'

Hershey had arrived ten minutes early for her meeting with the SJS Judge, trying to grab the initiative. But as she stepped into the interrogation chamber numbered 101, Sagassi was already awaiting her arrival, with just one other person in the darkened room. The walls were the customary black of an SJS interrogation cell, designed to instil just the right sense of despair and hopelessness into a subject, blotting out all concepts of night and day or the passage of time, leaving just questions, always questions – and the brutal beatings, of course.

'Why Judge Hershey, you're early! How punctilious of you. But as you can see, I'm ready for your arrival.' Sagassi smiled, stepping aside and waving his arm like a showman to reveal the person strapped into an interrogation chair behind him. The figure was quite naked, with heavy lethereen belts binding it to the hard wooden seat. Massive cuts and welts festooned the torso, arms and legs. The head hung forward, blood dripping from the nose and chin. 'This is the leader of the conspiracy against Chief Judge McGruder!' Sagassi reached out and grabbed the hair of the captive, viciously jerking it upwards to show the bruised and bloody face beneath the single beam of light in the cell.

'Collins!' gasped Hershey involuntarily. 'There must be some mistake!' But the face of the captive looked towards her voice, puffy, bruised eyelids forcing him to squint to make her out. The head of Tek Division breathed for a few moments before speaking at last, his voice broken, almost weeping.

'No, Hershey, it's true. I'm the leader, I organised the movement, recruited my supporters, ordered Freeman to use those other Tek-Judges and then dispose of them. My fault, it's all my fault.' His voice stammered through swollen lips and chipped teeth.

Sagassi held up his handheld Birdie lie-detector smugly, its verdict obvious on the readout screen: TRUE.

'Test him yourself, if you want,' volunteered Sagassi.

'That won't be necessary,' spat back Hershey. 'It looks like you've "tested" him enough already!' She had been convinced Sagassi was the conspiracy leader, never suspecting Collins, yet her logic had been flawed. The altered briefing, the missing Tek-Judges, the intercepted message pod, Freeman's involvement – it had all pointed to Tek Division. Only the Wally Squad assassin and SJS Judge Kitson had indicated elsewhere. Perhaps they hadn't even been involved with the conspiracy, pondered Hershey. Still, she did have a few questions left for Sagassi.

'What put you on to Collins?' she asked.

'Everything seemed to point to Tek Division. I've been busy interrogating a few other Tek-Judges and they named Collins as the common factor. He kindly confessed – it only took three hours for him to admit his guilt.' Sagassi smiled triumphantly.

'What will happen to him now?'

'Well, usually a twenty-stretch to Titan, but knowing how some of the other Judge inmates are there, I doubt he'd survive long. Perhaps something else could be arranged – suicide, accidental death. Even shot while attempting to escape has a nice ring to it . . .'

'You sick drokker!' spat Hershey and strode angrily from the dark chamber. Collins' eyes followed her forlornly, then closed for the last time. He had already seen his post-mortem report: ACCIDENTAL DEATH FROM A FRACTURED NECK, SUSTAINED FROM FALLING DOWN STAIRS IN SJS HEADQUARTERS.

Once Hershey had gone, another figure stepped into the room, grim-faced, with a carefully sculpted goatee beard and slicked-back black hair. 'Well, did she buy it?' asked SJS Judge Eliphas.

'Of course. She had no choice,' replied Sagassi. 'But we'll have to lay low for a while. One whiff of conspiracy and she'll be down on us like a ton of rockcrete.'

Eliphas just smiled. 'Don't worry. This little folly of Collins' has cost us six months, perhaps a year. We won't be able to move against McGruder again until next summer at the earliest. But when we do act . . .'

'Hershey will be first in line?' asked his partner in the conspiracy.

'Quite. I can't wait to kill the bitch.'

Many miles above the Cursed Earth, the sky defence satellite began its long countdown to firing upon Erebus. Deep within the heart of the complex circuitry, a simple numerical readout stated the time remaining until firing.

'12.00.00; 11.59.59; 11.59.58; 11.59.57 . . .'

CHAPTER TWO

Karyn felt the approach of the enemy long before she saw them coming, sensing the dark surge of evil and death in her psyche before even Miller's bionic eyes spotted the first of the throng appear at the edge of the black, encircling horizon. It was as if a dark storm was clouding her soul, crushing her will to live, filling her with despair. She fought back the terrifying oppressiveness to warn the others.

'They're coming!'

'Where from?' demanded Dredd. It was nearly dawn and the five Judges had been preparing a few extra surprises for the enemy. Dredd clambered atop the killdozer to get a better look at their surroundings. 'Where are they coming from?'

Karyn looked up at him, her face gloomy, devoid of its normal cheerfulness. 'Everywhere,' she replied grimly. Miller climbed up beside Dredd and swept her gaze around them in a full circle.

'I can't see any – Jovus drokkin' Grud!' she exclaimed. Dredd turned quickly to follow the line of her pointing hand to the west, towards Erebus.

At the edge of the darkness, a menacing silhouette had appeared. Then two, one either side of it, then another one beside each one of them, and more and more and more. The ring of black zone warriors grew and grew, stretching ever wider. In less than a minute, the entire farm was surrounded by a ring of the enemy, each figure pulsing and surging on the spot, like figures pressed against a glasseen wall, dying to be let in.

'Maybe they can't penetrate Hope's barrier?' said Brighton hopefully, always the optimist. Dredd shook his head, watching the ranks of the enemy grow ever stronger. Soon they were standing two-deep at the boundary, then three deep, then four.

'No, I don't think so. They're just waiting for their orders to advance.' He jumped down to the ground, Miller following him. Dredd turned to each of the Judges, looking at their pale faces. 'Take your positions – and hold them!'

The small group scattered, Raimes climbing into the killdozer to operate its laser defence system; Miller heading for the western side of the corral, nearest to Erebus; Brighton staking out the north side as his territory to protect; Karyn standing at the east. Dredd pulled the gag from Tupolua's mouth and slapped her back to consciousness.

'You've got a choice – either fight with us or I shoot you here and now, so you don't get in our way. Up to you, creep,' he offered.

'You'd give me a Lawgiver?' spluttered Tupolua. 'What's to stop me shooting you in the back?'

'Nothing. But if you want to survive this battle, killing me won't improve your chances,' reasoned Dredd.

'True enough,' said Tupolua, getting to her feet. 'But when the battle's over . . .?'

'Worry about that if it happens, punk,' replied Dredd, dropping the traitor's Lawgiver on the ground before her and walking away. Tupolua picked up the weapon and held it before her, aiming it at Dredd's head.

'Dredd!' she shouted.

He stopped and turned, not bothering to raise his own weapon in self-defence. 'Yeah?'

Tupolua smiled, lowering the gun barrel. 'Where do you want me?'

'North wall, help Brighton.'

'That's a roj!'

In the Cathedral of Bones, Soon waited, floating in front of the huge blood-stained window that faced east. His mind was in communion with every single one of his warriors, holding them, commanding them, possessing them by sheer force of will.

A single beam of light hit the outside of the central glass tower, refracting through the bloody window, showering the twisted genius in crimson light, as the sun rose to the east. It was dawn.

'ATTACK!' commanded Soon.

The dark army surged over the perimeter line of the farm, pushing over the fences by sheer weight of numbers. Those who fell at the front were trampled by their fellow warriors, such was the eagerness to attack. The army swarmed across the orange and yellow fields, racing inwards, helter-skelter.

'Here they come!' bellowed Dredd, who had moved to the west wall of the corral to help reinforce Miller. 'Choose your targets, don't fire until they're half-way down to the wall!'

Around the corral the six Judges sighted down the telescopic sights of their Lawgivers, waiting, waiting . . .

'FIRE!' commanded Dredd.

The volley of shots tore into the front-runners of the enemy, slicing them down. But the dead were swallowed up in a moment as the dark army surged on.

'Rapid fire – fire at will!' bellowed Dredd, shouting to be heard above the pounding of thousands of feet as the massed foe raced towards them. At the north wall, Tupolua couldn't help suppressing a smile at the command.

'That's very kind of him,' she said, but her words were blotted out as Raimes activated the war-droids from inside the killdozer.

The mighty machines had yet to see the light of day on this mission so far, but that was common with forays into the Cursed Earth. War-droids were exactly what they sounded like, massive metallic robots designed for killing and combat. Research showed they often worked best as semi-fixed gun emplacements, blowing seven shades of stomm out of the enemy if it attacked in waves.

Each war-droid was fitted with its own sensing equipment to first identify the enemy, verify the identity, then target the vulnerable parts of its anatomy, and finally fire. Here the war-droid truly came into its own, able to fire more than two hundred rounds per minute from its massive revolving multi-barrelled 'arms'. These resembled vintage Gatling guns, but were far more efficient and deadly. The only drawback was the noise these fearsome fighters made, and their lack of mobility or quick manoeuvrability. But in a stand-up shoot-out, there was no better warrior while its ammunition lasted.

The war-droids started firing, and quickly outgunned the Judges. Line after line of warriors were mown down in moments, the corpses themselves creating another obstacle for the attackers to clamber over in their frantic advance.

'They just keep running at us, no pattern, no planning!' Miller shouted to Dredd.

'One-dimensional thinking – be glad Soon isn't a good tactician, he's making the fight easier for us,' replied Dredd, screaming to be heard above the thundering war-droids.

Still the enemy surged forwards, getting closer and closer to the wall, but its lines of attack were growing thinner. At the east wall, Karyn was the first to see darkness through their lines.

'Nearly there, nearly there . . .' she muttered to herself, slamming another clip into her Lawgiver and blasting away at the advancing enemy. The attackers were only a few yards away when suddenly they seemed to falter, their twisted, ugly faces filled with fear and indecision for a second. Then, incredibly, they turned and ran, sprinting back to the safety of the black zone.

Still the war-droids blasted away, reducing the retreating force by nearly half before the warriors disappeared back into the darkness. As soon as the attackers stepped into the darkness they disappeared, as if stepping into night itself, all-encompassing, all-enfolding.

'Cease fire!' commanded Dredd. The war-droids had automatically stopped once the enemy had vanished into the black surroundings, but some of the other Judges were still blasting away. Brighton in particular was nearly dancing with joy as he shot another clip into the darkness before finally resting his weapon.

'We did it! We did it! We beat them!' he yelled to the sky, his voice jubilant and triumphant. A few feet to his side, Tupolua was not interested in rejoicing yet.

'Shut up, Brighton. It's not over yet – look!' She pointed to the boundaries where the silhouettes of thousands of warriors remained. 'That was just a first stab, assessing our firepower, you fool!'

'Oh!' exclaimed the young Judge.

Dredd's voice crackled through the helmet-coms of each of the defenders, now audible with the war-droids standing silent, awaiting the next attack.

'Everybody reload and stand fast at your posts. Raimes, how are the war-droids holding?' he asked urgently.

Inside the killdozer, Raimes punched up status displays for each of the metal machines on his console, quickly assessing death counts and ammunition levels.

'We logged more than a thousand kills, and a similar number of woundings. Ammo holding up well for now, too,' he reported.

'Good, because here they come again – everybody get ready!' said Dredd. Around the corral boundary, the six Judges tensed, ready for another attack.

'Interesting, very interesting,' nodded Soon. 'Rather than come out and take our attack, they stayed back, absorbing it. Casualties?'

Before him the Map of Eyes had become a battle-map, with a constant stream of data from his mind being sourced through it to show statistics of the dead and dying.

'More than twelve hundred killed outright, the wounded – well, they hardly matter. I'll keep them fighting while they still crawl, they have no choice!' he gloated. 'They barely scratched us. Time to send in the Soonites, I believe. Yes, definitely the Soonites . . .'

* * *

The second attack wave was bizarre; not running, not attacking, more a lurching, staggering parade of atrocities, obscenities of the human body wrought by Soon's genetic tampering. The thousands of unfortunates he had reshaped in his own, warped image dragged themselves into battle on misshapen legs, pulling their brittle-boned bodies towards oblivion, relentlessly moving forward into the firing line.

The war-droids sensed the attack and opened fire, but the slowness of the attackers was deceptive, forcing the war-droids to fire far too fast, wasting valuable ammunition shooting at enemies already dead but too slow-witted to realise it yet.

At the east wall, Karyn was sickened by this advancing wall of human misery, gross deformities thrust at them like some grotesque human shield. The Psi Judge felt the bile rise in her gut but swallowed hard and controlled it, closing her eyes, letting her Lawgiver do the slaughtering for her.

Yet still the enemy came, relentless, remorseless and unstoppable. Standard-issue bullets simply blew chunks off the ambling attackers, but Soon's force of will kept the living obscenities moving forward. Even those who had their legs blown off kept coming, crawling over the corpse-strewn ground to try and reach the corral wall.

'They won't drop! The drokkers won't drop!' yelled Miller to Dredd, who nodded grimly, his trigger finger pumping all the while. His spare hand slipped up to activate his helmet mike, trying to shout his orders to the others.

'Switch to hi-ex! Blow these drokkers apart!'

Around the corral, the six Judges altered the bullet selecter on their weapons and began firing again. While the war-droids slowly riddled the foe with shells, the Judges started blowing them apart with the explosive rounds, one by one, like some morbid, grotesque shooting gallery.

It took more than half an hour to put down the last of the advancing Soonites so they would stay down. Even once the last figure was blown apart by Raimes with the killdozer's laser defence beams, a few body parts still twitched on the outlying fields, holding some degree of animation.

As the last volleys died away, Karyn could hold back no longer, retching uncontrollably, vomiting again and again, sagging to her knees, drained of all feeling, just numb, numb, numb.

'Here comes another wave!' called Miller.

The young Psi Judge pulled herself back up to her feet and reloaded, preparing to choose her target. She had never been a party to such carnage before, and she prayed to Grud she never would be again.

Inside the main building of the farm, the three old women were gathered around Hope, who sat with her eyes closed in the centre of the room. The child was concentrating, watching the war outside in her mind.

'The guardians are fighting well, but they cannot win. They need help,' she said, opening her eyes to look at the old women.

'What can we do?' protested Jana, the oldest. 'We can barely fend for ourselves, let alone join a battle!'

'Not you! There are others – some are already coming, more will be needed. I must gather them,' announced Hope. Her body sagged to the floor.

Keeta caught the child in her pudgy arms, looking down with concern at the pale face. 'What's happened?'

'She's left her own body, she's on the astral plane,' said Melva. 'She will appear to these others she spoke of, bringing them to the battle.'

Jana stood by the window, holding one of the wooden shutters open a crack to look outside. 'We'll need it, judging by what's happening out there.'

The third wave of attackers were a mixture of mutants and zombies, running low, hard and fast towards the corral wall, hugging the ground, making themselves into smaller targets for the targeting weaponry of the war-droids. The Judges were having to use grenades now, simply to stop the warriors advancing closer, such was the weight of numbers coming towards them from the blackness.

In the killdozer, Raimes looked with concern at the energy levels within the battery storage banks, which had already dropped below fifty per cent. Once these batteries' reserves were gone, the laser weapons on board would be useless and the war-droids would have to be turned over to full automatic control, without anything to monitor their progress or ammunition levels.

At the north wall, Brighton reached for another clip of ammunition as his trigger clicked uselessly, but found the pouches around his belt empty.

'I'm out!' he shouted to Tupolua, and started to hoist frag grenades into the ranks of the enemy.

'I'm down to my last clip too – you'd better do an ammo run!' she commanded. Brighton nodded and turned to run, only to find a mutant climbing over the wall to his left, where one of the war-droids had jammed its weapons and was standing stymied. Several more mutants were starting to climb over – in moments the corral would be invaded!

'Breach in the wall!' shouted Brighton and flung himself at the first mutant, drawing his boot knife from its holster and slashing down at the intruder, adrenalin giving the young Judge strength beyond his years. He hacked at the attacker, stabbing, slashing, until the limbless corpse lay twitching at his feet. But another mutant was atop the wall by now and threw itself down onto him. The pair tumbled to the ground, Brighton screaming as the mutant lunged forward to sink its rotted black teeth into the flesh of his face.

Suddenly blood clotted Brighton's helmet visor as the mutant's head exploded. The young Judge threw the body to one side and looked up to see Tupolua smiling down at him. The Tek-Judge shoved another mutant back over the wall and lobbed a grenade over to join it.

'Fire in the hole!' she yelled and threw herself to the ground as the explosion rocked the other side of the wall, clearing away the mutant incursion.

'You okay?' Tupolua asked as the pair clambered back to their feet.

'Yeah,' stammered Brighton, nervously.

'Then go and get the ammo, boy!' replied the Tek-Judge as she returned to the wall, Lawgiver ready for another onslaught.

Preacher Cain and Resurrection Joe had been riding north, following the trail of the zombies for more than a day. Every settlement they reached had a similar story – the dead getting out of their graves and heading north, joining an ever-swelling rank of the undead shuffling slowly towards the centre of the Cursed Earth.

Now the pair of lawkeepers were close to reaching

the edge of the black zone, having stopped atop a nearby hill to look down on the scene before them. To the east and west lay the normal orange dusty terrain, but directly ahead was a vast black circle, seeming to almost ooze out towards them over whatever lay in its path.

'It don't look good, reverend, if ya don't mind my sayin' so,' ventured Joe.

'Hmmm,' was Cain's only reply, scratching a single match against the length of his saddle to ignite it, then using the flame to light the stub of cheroot clamped in the corner of his slit of a mouth.

'Perhaps we ought ta get some help with this, maybe 'lert somebodys?'

'Hmmm.'

'Course, we could always just ride away, real quiet like – ' began Joe, but a piercing look from his superior soon silenced that notion.

'I say we should – ' began the reverend, but he never finished the sentence. Something had appeared in front of them, like an angel of the Lord, like a vision.

She glowed white, a light so blinding and pure that his eyes could barely look at her, even clenched in their tightest of squints. She floated above the ground like a true angel was supposed to. And she spoke in a voice so simple and pure, it was almost like singing, its tones soothing and touching to the very soul.

'I am Hope and I need your help,' said the angelic vision to Preacher Cain. Joe sat dumbstruck on his mutant mule, not believing what was before his eyes. The Missionary Man had seen a vision like this once before, so he knew what to expect, but he still lowered his eyes in supplication before the angel called Hope.

'There is a war going on and I need you to join it.'

'A holy war?' asked Cain, hope in his voice.

'A war between darkness and light, between good and evil, a war that must be won by the just. Will you join us in this fight, the good fight?' asked the vision.

'Show us the way,' was all Cain could say.

The vision hovered, then shrank, becoming a point of light like the tiniest of stars, but staying exactly ten feet above the ground. Below it, the earth was cleansed of its waste, turning from the radioactive orange dust into clean soil, full of life and energy.

'Follow me,' spoke a voice in Cain's head, like the singing of the angels themselves.

'I will,' he murmured to himself and jabbed his spurs into his black steed. The horse trotted after the point of light, leaving a bewildered Joe behind it.

'What was all that about?' he wondered aloud, before realising his master was disappearing over the horizon, heading straight for the black zone ahead of them. 'Reverend Cain! Reverend Cain! Where are we going?'

To the east, more than three hundred klicks away, Joe Junior was leading a justice squad across the wastelands to the west of the Appalachian Mountains, practising the new Word of Dredd that the killdozer crew had introduced them to just a few days earlier.

Suddenly, a glowing apparition appeared before

them, nearly a hundred foot tall, lanky, foreboding, grim – it could only be one man.

'Judge Dredd! Mighty one!' gasped Joe Junior.

'Sons of Dredd, I have need of you! A mighty battle is being fought between myself and my disciples in justice against the forces of the Lawless. Will you stand beside us and fight?' demanded the towering, glowering figure.

The Sons of Dredd had flung themselves to the ground as the vision appeared, prostrating themselves before their own godhead. Joe Junior sneaked a peek up at this mighty presence.

'We shall,' he whispered.

'Good!' boomed the vision. 'Then follow the sun across the sky – it shall lead you to battle. Fight well, my sons!' Then the vision was gone and the Sons of Dredd were left cowering on the dusty ground. Joe Junior stood up and looked around at his warriors, nearly three hundred strong, armed with guns and knives and anything else they could lay their hands on.

'You have heard the Word of Dredd – charge!' he bellowed and with a mighty scream ran into the west, his warriors following him.

'Reverend, I got a bad feeling about this, ain't you?'

'Did you not see the vision, deputy?' asked the missionary man, his stubble-clad face set hard and fast as he advanced into the blackness that lay before them.

'Well, yes, I saw somethi – ' muttered Joe.

'Then have faith in the Lord,' replied Preacher Cain. 'He will show us the pathway of righteousness!'

'Good,' said Joe sarcastically. 'Funny how these

paths of righteousness always seems to lead us into mortal danger,' he added under his breath.

Ahead of the pair, the point of light hovered for a moment, then went forward, above the edge of the black zone. Beneath it, the darkness seemed to fall away at each side, creating a path of safe ground on which to ride their steeds forward.

'See?' shouted Cain. 'The Way of the Lord is shown!' Urging his horse forward, the reverend rode onto the path through the darkness as it continued to divide before him. Reluctantly Joe followed along behind.

'Well, I hopes he keeps showing his path – I don't want to be stuck out here in the middle of all this,' muttered the hunchback, his mutant mule whinnying in agreement.

The war-droid nearest to the killdozer stuttered as its gun emplacements coughed out death one last time, then went silent.

'Raimes to Dredd – we've lost the first of the war-droids, it's out of ammo!' bellowed the driver/navigator from inside the killdozer.

Dredd could barely hear this communication above the turmoil, but was able to pick up the gist of it. 'What about the others?' he bellowed back.

'Three more are running low, two of them on the east side with Karyn,' came the reply amidst squeals of static.

'Terrif. When this attack ends, reposition the remaining war-droids so they're evenly spaced around the wall again. But keep back the three that are low on ammo.'

'Why?'

'I'll explain later! Dredd out!' shouted the stone-faced Judge. He had better things to do than talk with Raimes. The heaviest concentration of attackers had been coming more and more frequently at the west wall, where he and Miller were facing directly towards Erebus. Despite the efforts of the war-droids in this sector to turn the fields beyond the corral into an abbatoir, the attackers were surging ever closer to the wall, almost upon it now.

'Time to get a little closer to the action,' said Dredd and vaulted up onto the top of the structure, bracing himself backwards against a pole sticking up into the air from the base of the wall. 'Ricochet!' he shouted and his Lawgiver responded with a hail of rubber-tipped bullets that tore into the enemy, then bounced out to hit another and another. He followed this up with a volley of armour-piercing rounds, shooting through several attackers with a single shot. By this point the dark warriors nearest the wall were starting to clutch at his boots.

'Back off!' he commanded and followed it up with several powerful kicks into the heads of his foes, one of the blows smashing right through the brittle skull, splattering those behind it with blood and brains. It did not slow them down.

In the killdozer, Raimes was directing the laser defence system across all of the southern sector of the battle, able to take out dozens of the enemy in moments with this, the most powerful weapon in their arsenal. But despite its ferocity, the overwhelming numbers meant some of the mutant and Soonite attackers were still getting through. They thrust themselves against the front of the all-terrain vehicle, hands clawing desperately at the windscreen, bloody fingers scrabbling for a grip. In a flash of inspiration, Raimes flicked on the windscreen wipers, brushing several of the foe aside with the harmless blades. But a sudden dimming of the lights within the vehicle soon wiped the smile off his face.

'Drokk! Batteries are going!' He glanced down desperately at the display readouts but they confirmed his worst fears – only a minute or two of energy was left to the systems. It was time to get out, but he already had his orders should this occur.

'Initiate auto-destruct sequence alpha beta gamma, code zero zero niner zero,' Raimes commanded. 'Fireball front and centre compartments,' he added as a final flourish, then flung himself out of the back of the vehicle, grabbing his scattergun as he abandoned the vehicle.

Tumbling from the back, he was amazed to see the attackers had already hauled themselves to the top of the killdozer and were staggering down the roof of the vehicle towards the interior of the compound.

'Oh no, you don't!' he muttered and blew three of them backwards with the powerful discharge from his scattergun, riddling the trio with bullets. Then he flung himself to the ground as the killdozer's auto-destruct systems channelled the last of the energy in the vehicle, turning it into a flaming obstacle.

A massive explosion ripped the front out of the vehicle, shrapnel shredding hundreds of attackers standing directly in front of it. Then came the fireball, burning away those still standing around it. The interior of the killdozer kept burning, turning it into an impassable blockade of fire and molten metal.

* * *

Dredd had spotted the explosion – it had been hard to miss, shaking the ground so hard he had fallen backwards off the wall, inside the compound again – and quickly barked new instructions to Raimes via the helmet radios.

'Go to the west wall, Karyn's in trouble!'

'Roj that!' replied Raimes, pausing only to grab an ammunition case from one of the piles set around the exterior of the central farm building.

The explosion nearly shook Resurrection Joe from his saddle and it brought even Preacher Cain to a standstill for a moment, watching as the fireball rose to the sky.

'Come, deputy! We must ride like the wind!' commanded Cain and galloped ahead, charging towards the source of the explosion.

Joe was less eager, especially being surrounded by thousands of gila-munja lurking either side of their special pathway. He couldn't see them, of course, no human eyes could. But he could sense them deep in his gut, their presence, evil and heavy, with a brooding menace unlike any other, and that trade-mark hissing and the slight haziness they brought to the surroundings with their chameleon skin. For a gila-munja tracker like Joe, to be surrounded by thousands of these devils was like dropping someone afraid of slithering things into a snakepit. The pathway might be safe, but Joe desperately wanted to be somewhere else.

He too dug his heels into the sides of his steed and trotted after his master, getting up a fair turn of speed. 'Wait for me, reverend,' his voice wailed as they galloped towards the oasis of light head.

* * *

Above all of this, the sky defence satellite's count-down to firing continued unabated.

'05.23.19; 05.23.18; 05.23.17 . . .'

'Another one's gone!' shouted Karyn into her helmet mike, as the war-droid to her left spluttered and died, its last ammunition fired into the attacking throng. 'That's the third one out and the drokkers are still coming!'

'Hang in there,' shouted back Dredd. 'The attack's faltering, they'll pull back in a minute.'

'We haven't got a minute over here!' screamed back Karyn. There was a sudden surge and then mutants were pouring over the walls around her and Raimes, one, three, five, ten, more all the time. 'Raimes – to me!' she shouted and the other Judge managed to burst through the invaders to join her. Then the pair stood back to back, Karyn with her Lawgiver, Raimes armed with his scattergun.

'Ready?' she asked as the mutants gathered, pre-paring to tear the two of them apart.

'Ready,' confirmed Raimes, gritting his teeth. 'Rapid fire,' he commanded his weapon, which responded to the vocal command and altered its velocity setting to pump out rounds at twice the normal speed.

'Let's do it!' screamed Karyn and the pair began firing, great sweeping screaming scythes of bullets spitting from their weapons, tearing apart the enemy, cutting them down like paper targets, blow-ing them apart, exploding them in balls of flame, splattering the walls, the ground, themselves in blood and viscera.

In one minute of absolute blood-frenzy, the pair wiped out more than thirty mutants, the last of the attackers. When the final foe was blown apart the pair were left standing back to back, panting, gasping for breath, wiping the blood and gore from their faces, arms heavy, fingers cramping, hearts thumping, legs barely able to support them. As one, Karyn and Raimes sank to the ground.

After a moment, they turned to look at each other. Karyn started to speak, but found she couldn't. She had no breath left to speak with. Raimes just nodded.

'I know, I know. Thank you too.'

Karyn smiled weakly.

In front of them a huge black horse leapt over the wall.

CHAPTER THREE

'You again! What are you doing here?' demanded Dredd.

'Saving your hide again, it seems, yankee!' retorted Preacher Cain. He and his deputy had ridden through the lines of the enemy, protected by Hope, and then jumped the corral wall to enter the compound. But they were not receiving the warmest of welcomes from Dredd.

'Yeah?' spat Dredd.

'Yeah!'

'Yeah?'

Before the arguing could descend into pantomime, Miller dragged Dredd away to one side. 'Look, I don't care what little machismo games you guys have got going, but right now we need all the help we can get!'

'Hmph!' fumed Dredd, but eventually returned to face Reverend Cain for a serving of humble pie. 'We do need all the help we can get – even from you, amateur!'

'So I can see – yankee!' spat back Cain. In the background, Miller and Joe rolled their eyes at each other conspiratorially and smiled.

The arrival of the two new recruits had signalled a lull in hostilities, giving the Judges time to regroup and rearm. Four of the war-droids had now run out of ammunition, with no way to reload them after the

250

loss of the killdozer. Raimes repositioned the remaining eight at even spacings around the corral before turning the others over to Dredd. 'What are you going to do with them?'

'The war-droids are only out of ammo, right? They can still transport themselves?' asked the stone-faced Judge.

'Yes, not fast, but they will walk,' replied Raimes.

'Send them out beyond the wall. When the next big attack comes, they can light the way.' Raimes nodded, understanding. While he set of to accomplish this task, Dredd surveyed the others. The battle had raged for more than four hours now, and all were looking exhausted, shocked by the ferocity of the conflict and the seemingly endless wave after wave of enemy surges at them.

'They just keep coming and coming and coming,' mumbled Brighton, shaking his head. 'It's like they're not human.'

'They're not, really,' explained Dredd. 'It's Soon. His will is keeping them going, even when they're already dead or mortally wounded. Human soldiers stop fighting when they're dead. Zombies, mutants and those other creatures, Soon keeps them going no matter what.'

'Then how do we beat them?' asked Brighton, almost despairing for the first time in his life.

'Never give up. We fight to the last bullet, the last breath, the last person standing,' maintained Dredd.

'And then?'

'And then we die,' interrupted Tupolua cheerfully, getting a baleful stare from Dredd for her comment.

'Then we keep fighting, no matter what!' was his

final word on the subject. Defeat was not a word used by Judge Dredd.

Off to one side, the little mutant Joe was chatting with Psi Judge Karyn. 'So you read the future?' he asked.

'Not so much read, more feel it, sense what's coming – but only sometimes,' she explained. 'Precognition is hardly precise.'

'So what's going to happen here today?' the hunchback asked, a little fearful of the answer.

'I don't know really. The blackness blots out a lot of the signals I usually receive, but the little girl, Hope, she doesn't seem too worried. And she's a far greater Psi than I'll ever be.'

'Yeah, that girl, she guided us here. Convinced the reverend she was some kind of angel,' chuckled Joe, who didn't place as high a value on religious matters as his master.

'She is in a way,' mused Karyn. 'An angel in need of our protection. If Soon should ever take her, the world would be plunged into a darkness that would make this battle seem like summertime in paradise.'

'That bad, huh?'

Karyn nodded.

'Well,' said Joe, 'always good to know yer fightin' in a good cause, dyin' fer one if needs be.'

'Here comes the next wave!' went up the cry and everyone rushed to their positions, steeling themselves for another attack from the endless stream of dark warriors.

'The zombies, I think. Yes, definitely the zombies this time,' decided Soon, and with a thought sent a thousand reanimated corpses against the firepower of the few warriors sheltering inside the corral.

On his Map of Eyes, a dark ring separated itself from the black circle and began to move inwards, advancing on the white spot in the centre. He did not notice the clump of light approaching from the east, outside the edge of his dark domain.

The Sons of Dredd had been barrelling across the radioactive countryside for hours in their ragtag fleet of battered vehicles, chasing towards the towering vision of Dredd that always remained just in front of them.

Then, at last, they reached the top of a hillside and found themselves facing a vast army of swarming gila-munja. Joe Junior brought the convoy to an abrupt halt and stood atop his hovercar to address the others.

'These are the Lawless, we are the Lawkeepers, the Sons of Dredd. Let battle commence and pray to our Lord, Dredd, that we may fight well for the Way of Justice. Charge!' he bellowed and launched his vehicle at the nearest clump of mutant monsters.

'What's this? Someone else has joined our little conflict?' smiled Soon inwardly. 'How wonderful! I do so love to make a killing, but two in one day!'

He assessed the situation for the moment before unleashing his predatorial pets upon the new arrivals to the conflict. Soon had been holding the gila-munja back, but had sensed their growing impatience. This little battle should keep them happy until their presence was needed on the front line.

'Destroy them,' he commanded. 'Total destruction!'

* * *

Inside the corral, Dredd watched the advance of the latest wave carefully, standing ready to bark his orders to the other Judges. Out in the fields, the mutant and zombie hordes swept forward, just drawing level with the four war-droids positioned beyond the corral wall, at the four points of the compass.

'Now – armour piercing!' commanded Dredd, firing his own weapon. Brighton, Karyn and Miller did the same, each blowing a hole in the war-droid nearest them in the field. 'Incendiary!' Dredd and the others followed it up with a round of fire-starter, turning the exploding war-droids into metal infernos, huge beacons.

From the war-droids the fire sprung out and surged across the ground, igniting the gallons of liquid fuel Dredd had spread earlier in a series of rings, creating three circular walls of fire around the corral.

Still this did not deter the advancing foe, who stepped through the flames, many catching alight themselves but moving resolutely ahead, urged on by their master.

'Jovus, don't these creeps stop for anything?' exclaimed Miller, full of exasperation.

'Seems not,' replied Resurrection Joe cheerfully. He had joined her on the west wall, while Dredd and Preacher Cain were either side of the killdozer wreckage, facing south. Tupolua and Brighton were at their posts to the north, while Raimes and Karyn did their best to hold the eastern wall, a task made slightly easier, unknown to them, by the second front created by the Sons of Dredd.

So the gunfire began again, the war-droids shooting thousands of rounds at the advancing enemy, tearing them to pieces, the Judges content to bridge the gaps in their defence. Combined with the fire, they were able to hold the attackers about twenty yards out while the ammunition lasted, but for every enemy blown apart, another two stepped forward to replace it.

After ten minutes, the war-droid to Dredd's right ground to a halt and the foe advanced closer to the corral in that sector. Then the next war-droid along, between Dredd and Miller suddenly died as well and the dark warriors were at the wall, climbing it, over it, invading the compound – dozens of them!

'Ahhh,' cooed Soon, 'now we're getting some-where!' On his Map of Eyes, the blackness had stabbed into the heart of the white oasis. Victory could not be far away now . . .

'Q-Bike – to me!' screamed Dredd into his helmet radio, still spraying the invaders with bullets. To the side of the main building, an engine roared into life and then a Quasar Lawmaster bike burst out of the small lean-to shack that until recently had been home to Jonah. The bike roared to Dredd's side and the Judge quickly slipped astride it, checking with a glance that all systems were fully functional.

'Bike cannon!' he commanded and drove the Lawmaster straight at the invaders, mowing them down with the twin barrels mounted either side of the front and rear tyres. In seconds the intruders were cut down from dozens to a handful and these Dredd quickly mopped up using the scattergun mounted in a chassis holster.

Having dealt with the intruders, he rode his bike around to the shack, where the other five Q bikes stood ready for action. Turning to face the corral wall, he blasted a six-foot wide hole through it with the bike cannons, allowing entry for the attacking monsters. But before they could surge inside, Dredd had already barked a new command to the other Lawmasters.

'Bikes to auto – seek out and destroy hostiles!'

The five Lawmasters leaped forwards, burning through the gap in the defence wall, their own cannons blazing away at the enemy. The on-board computers were programmed to identify all mutant and non-human life as hostile, unless given data to the contrary. It was just as well the mutant Joe was at the west wall with Miller, Dredd thought, or he could have become a potential target himself.

The others cheered as the Lawmasters careered around outside the corral wall, cutting the enemy ranks to pieces with their powerful weaponry. In less than three minutes, the latest attack wave had been more than halved, with the remaining foe demoralised and fleeing for the safety of the black zone. Unfortunately for the Judges, the Lawmasters followed them into the darkness and disappeared from sight, swallowed up as if taken into a tar pit. Seconds later there were a handful of muffled explosions, then silence reigned.

'Well, that's our last surprise gone,' announced Dredd.

Nearly a thousand klicks to the east, in Mega-City One, Hershey watched as the countdown continued in Control, deep inside the Halls of Justice.

'01.49.09; 01.49.08; 01.49.07 . . .'

'Less than two hours until the sky defence system starts nuking Erebus,' she told McGruder via a vidphone link.

'Good. The sooner the better. If this Soon is half as powerful as Psi Division is now projecting, we may only get one shot at him – if that.'

'Roj that. Hershey out.' She stepped away from the vid-phone to ask one of the deep-probe monitoring Judges a question. 'Anything from the area of the black zone?'

A shake of the head was the only answer.

At the eastern edge of the blackness, the leader of the gila-munja pack was licking his lips, as he surveyed the carnage around him. The Sons of Dredd had been routed, torn apart by a vastly bigger force of ruthless killers.

The pack leader cracked open the skull in his hands, that of the unfortunate Joe Junior, head of the Sons of Dredd. Human brains were considered a special delicacy for gila-munja warriors, to be savoured above all else.

'Enough!' announced Soon, examining this corner of the conflict on his Map of Eyes. 'No more Mister Nice Psycho, I think. Time to send in the gila-munja, finish off this little amusement!'

The twisted genius moved his mind from the few hundred remaining mutants, zombies and Soonites to the hordes of mutant assassins, thronging in their thousands at the edges of the blackness. 'Move in and destroy – but leave the child alive! She is mine, and mine alone.'

'Have you noticed? With each attack, the number coming against us is getting gradually smaller. I think we're whittling them down,' said Miller, allowing herself a little smile of satisfaction for the first time in hours.

'Maybe,' grumbled Joe. 'I ain't so sure. When me and the reverend rode in here, we passed enough gila-munja to keep me in hunting work for fifty lifetimes. But we ain't seen nothing of those monsters yet. I reckon we's got a long way to go yet.'

'Oh,' said a deflated Miller. 'Dredd, you hear that?'

'Hmmm,' came the less than loquacious reply via helmet radio. Dredd was considering their next move, but options were becoming more and more limited with each attack.

Now just three war-droids were left functioning, and Raimes doubted that any had more than enough ammunition to last another attack. Frag grenades were all gone, the rings of fire were burning down, all but one of the Lawmasters were lost, the killdozer was a burnt-out wreck and their general ammunition was down to the last few boxes. Barring outside intervention, the battle had less than an hour to run, depending on when the next attack came and how strong the enemy numbered this time.

After due consideration, Dredd gave his orders. 'If you cannot hold your perimeters, prepare to retreat into the main farm building on my command. The walls are solid. If we use the shuttered windows and barracade the door, we should buy a bit more time.'

Time for what, Brighton wondered. They were as good as dead already, with no help coming and no way to replace their lost ammo. He had never liked the words 'suicide mission' and if someone had told him this would become one, he might not have been so eager to come.

'Here they come,' announced Karyn, first to spy the next attack-wave forming around the boundary line. But rather than surge in, these attackers waited until they had formed a giant, encircling ring, just like the first wave had done several hours before. Letting the Judges know just how many they were up against, striking fear and despair further into their hearts.

Then, when it seemed all were assembled, the enemy stepped forward and revealed themselves, an unusual tactic for gila-munja who normally preferred to retain their chameleon invisibility. This, this was almost a taunt, a display of arrogance, saying 'Look at us! We need not hide from you, we need not fear you!'

Raimes was still trying to count the number of gila-munja when the crescent-shaped claw slashed across his face, drawing blood and injecting its deadly poison into his body. 'It's a trick, they're already here!' he shouted before collapsing, dead as he hit the ground.

'Sweet Jovus!' screamed Karyn and opened fire, blazing away all around herself, downing half a dozen gila-munja in seconds. Then she started running for the farmhouse door, blasting away in front of herself, praying to make it safely to the sanctuary inside.

At the north wall, Brighton and Tupolua quickly adopted a back-to-back formation, the better to protect themselves. Shooting from the hip they slowly, carefully picked their way backwards to the northern entrance to the farmhouse, Tupolua kicking at the door with her leg to summon one of the mutant women to open it.

'Open the door, you drokkers, let us in!' she

screamed. The door opened a fraction and Tupolua shoved the younger Judge through first, turning to fire off a last couple of rounds before retreating inside. The decision was fatal as a claw clamped around her leg, biting through the reinforced leathereen uniform, deep into the flesh of her calf muscle. 'Drokk you!' she screamed and flung herself at the beast which had already killed her, shoving the barrel of her Lawgiver down its throat and clutching at the trigger with the last of her strength.

'Hi-ex!' she shouted and the gun exploded, killing the monster and herself instantly.

At the west wall, Joe and Miller had the benefit of Raimes' warning to make their retreat, the valiant deputy dragging his master away down off the wall and into the farmhouse with them. Last through the door was Dredd, who stood stock-still in the open doorway for a full minute, blasting off a clip into the attackers until his Lawgiver at last clicked empty, before diving inside. Miller slammed the door shut behind him and began building the barricade. Immediately the gila-munja started flinging themselves at the door but it was well made and heavy, giving those inside a few extra seconds to blockade themselves securely behind it.

All the wooden-shuttered windows had long since been nailed shut from inside, a few barrel-holes drilled through the walls the only remaining access point in or out of the farmhouse. Or so it seemed.

'Miller, how much ammo we got left?' demanded Dredd.

The white-haired Judge quickly assessed their small stock. 'Not enough – whatever everyone is carrying and these two boxes. I've got three grenades left, the war-droids have all finished outside and there's at least two or three thousand gila-munja queuing up to have us for lunch. We've had it, basically.'

'Have faith, the Lord will show us a way out,' announced Preacher Cain grandly, clutching a Bible in his hand. 'Let me read a passage from the good book – '

Dredd slapped the Bible out of his hand, sending it flying across the room. 'Save us the sermons, padre, we ain't got the time!'

As if to emphasise the point, the two doors into the building began to shake and jolt, as hordes of gila-munja flung themselves at them from outside. Dredd drew his Lawgiver and advanced towards the three old mutant women, who were sheltering Hope between them.

'I said if it came to this, I'd do it. Well, now we have no choice.' Dredd looked at the old women. 'Stand aside, I have no wish to harm you – it's the girl who must be dealt with.'

'What are you going to do?' asked Karyn, becoming increasingly concerned at Dredd's behaviour. He seemed to be willing to sacifice himself and all of them just to match his code of behaviour, no matter how they felt about it. Now it seemed he wanted to execute an innocent four-year-old girl.

'You said it yourself – Hope is the most powerful Psi born this century. If Soon gets her, he will be unstoppable. Now, it seems there's only one way to prevent that – kill the girl. Stand aside, crones!'

'Chung said you were a murderer – she was right! You're no better than Soon if you murder the girl. And that's what it will be – murder!' shouted Karyn, struggling to be heard against the hammering of the beasts outside, trying to get in.

261

'I never said I was better than Soon, but you know I'm right!' Dredd levelled his Lawgiver at Hope's head, aiming directly between her eyes, and squeezed the trigger.

CHAPTER FOUR

'There's another way to resolve this.'

Dredd eased his finger back from the trigger. 'How?'

'I cannot use my power for evil, to kill. I must use it for good,' continued Hope. 'If we went to Soon, confronted him, perhaps he could be defeated.'

Dredd looked to Karyn. 'Feasible?'

'There seem few limits to what Hope can do for good. It's worth a try. Worst comes to worst, you can just resort to your original plan,' she said bitterly.

'True,' nodded Dredd. 'Contact Soon, tell him we're coming. Tell him to call off his pets outside.' Karyn concentrated, putting all her energy into breaking through the black zone outside to contact Soon. Once she had broken through, she quickly passed on the message and broke the trance.

'It's done – he's waiting for you.'

Brighton had eased open one of the shutters a fraction to peer outside. 'She's right – the gila-munja, they're retreating!' he exclaimed.

Dredd stepped forward to take Hope by the hand. Still the old women stood between him and the little girl, but this time it was Hope who spoke to them.

'Don't worry, it'll be all right. Dredd is the guardian, remember?' she said. As one the trio chanted back in unison:

263

'The Voice has spoken, it shall be so.' They all stepped aside. Dredd scooped the little girl up into his arms and walked to the door, where Joe and Miller were pulling away the barricade.

'May the Lord walk with you,' offered Preacher Cain, as they stepped outside.

Soon spun and soared about the Cathedral of Bones, jubilant. 'At last, the child shall be mine! All things shall be mine, for ever and ever!'

Slowly he allowed himself to drift back down towards floor level, pausing in front of the Map of Eyes to watch the progress of Dredd and Hope across the dark wasteland to his domain. With a thought, he summoned his general on the battlefield to his side, Novar appearing a moment later, a mirror-image of his twisted master.

'Let them get clear of the farmhouse,' said Soon.

'Yes, my Lord . . .?'

'Then tear the place apart!'

Dredd strode through the gaping hole in the corral wall left by his Lawmaster, and stepped out onto the fields, now stained with the blood of the fallen, littered with hundreds, perhaps thousands of corpses.

'Which way?' he asked the little girl and Hope pointed to her right, to the west. 'To Erebus, of course,' muttered Dredd and walked on, still holding the child in his arms. Soon they reached the edge of the black zone but it parted before them, creating a safe path. 'Your doing?' he asked but Hope just shook her head.

* * *

Inside the farmhouse, Preacher Cain was quoting from the Bible as Dredd and Hope disappeared into the darkness outside.

'Yeah, though I walk through the valley of the shadow, I shall fear no evil,' he pronounced, misquoting again.

'Yeah, well I wouldn't speak too soon if I were you,' remarked Miller, watching the blackness gather again on the outskirts of the farm. 'Now that Dredd and the girl have gone, I think we're just cannon-fodder for the gila-munja out there.'

'Better get that barricade rebuilt then,' said Joe sensibly and started the task, assisted by Brighton and Karyn.

As he walked through the darklands towards Erebus, Dredd was hit by flashes of memory, reminding him of his last journey through this desolation two weeks before. The ground was still black and sickly, except along the narrow path he walked, clutching Hope to his chest, but now hideous new relics and fragments had been added to the landscape.

To one side lay a veritable aircraft graveyard with the fused remains of the two lost h-wagons fused into the soil, metal strewn over a wide stretch, like a scar on the ground. To the right were piled the bones and decomposing bodies of more than a hundred victims of Soon's reign of terror, perhaps the inhabitants of Lazarus who had not heeded the warnings of those two crazy bikers.

Then, as he drew closer to the screaming spires of Erebus, Dredd was confronted with an all-too grisly set of constructions, moving slowly, listlessly in the breezeless air.

They were windmills, but not just any windmills. The gantries and scaffolding were not made of metal but human bones, fused together at the ends to make spindly legs and cross-beams. So too were the spokes made of bone, some still with scraps of flesh hanging off them, a reminder of their origins. But worst of all was the material creating the 'sails' – dried, stretched human skin, pulled taut over the bone frames, just like the skin pulled taut over Soon's jaws, where his mouth should be. Hope buried her head in Dredd's chest, not wishing to look, and the Judge didn't blame her at all.

Finally, there was Erebus itself. Part of the glasseen protective dome was still visible, but up around its sides new walls of bone had been formed, some reaching up into spires, stretching towards the sky like the fingers of a skeleton.

The air above Erebus shimmered and a giant image of Soon's face formed, its lone eye glaring down at the lonely pair. A voice boomed into their heads: 'Welcome to my domain! Please, do come inside.' Then the face was gone and a massive doorway appeared directly ahead.

Dredd started striding towards it but just before he entered the figure of Hope began to shimmer and fade away.

'I'm sorry, the others need my help right now,' she said and smiled. Dredd tried to grab at her but she was already gone, leaving him clutching at thin air.

'Terrif,' muttered Dredd and continued inside.

High over them all, the sky defence system countdown was drawing to its conclusion.

'00.57.27; 00.57.26; 00.57.25 . . .'

* * *

In the farmhouse, the situation was desperate. Hundreds of gila-munja were flinging themselves at the two doorways while the Judges, Preacher Cain and Joe fired out through the shooting holes. Then the sound of scrabbling could be heard from above and Brighton looked up to see the roof tiles being ripped away by crescent-shaped claws.

'Sweet Jovus, they're coming through the roof!' he shouted and started firing up into the air.

Gila-munja began dropping into the building, some dead, some very much alive, their claws clacking shut and open, their mouths drooling at the prospect of this final vicious slaughterfest.

Then a light appeared in the centre of the room, hardly noticeable at first, but growing ever brighter until the whole room was ablaze with its glory.

'Ahh, Judge Dredd – we meet again!' said Soon into the Judge's mind. The twisted genius floated high over him, rejoicing in victory in the Cathedral of Bones, his inner sanctum. To one side the Map of Eyes lay shattered, discarded, abused and abandoned. Soon had no need for it. Everything was his now that he had the child.

'The child – where is she?' he asked.

'I don't know,' replied Dredd.

'What!' stormed Soon in rage.

'We were entering the asylum when she disappeared – '

'This is not an asylum! This is my domain!' thundered Soon. 'Now, where is the child? Tell me, or I shall be forced to do to you what I did to your precious cadets.' He waved a hand and the altar appeared from above, hovering before Dredd.

'Would you like to see them whole again, restored to full health?'

'Yes,' admitted Dredd, horrified by the twisted construction the mutant held before his eyes.

'Then it shall be so,' replied Soon and raised a hand. The altar shot up to the ceiling of the cathedral. Soon snapped his fingers and it began to fall, accelerating towards the ground below, smashing into it and exploding into tens of thousands of tiny fragments. 'Oops,' said Soon. 'Slipped!'

Dredd lunged down for his Lawgiver but Soon plucked it from its boot holster in a moment, letting it float just in front of Dredd, out of the Judge's grasp. 'What an interesting little weapon – I wonder how it would work on you?'

The trigger twitched backwards and a bullet blasted from the barrel, shooting through Dredd's upraised right hand and embedding itself in his stomach. The Judge sagged with pain, clutching at his wounds, but Soon would not let him fall to the ground.

'My, they do go off so easily – a person could get hurt, couldn't they?' taunted the mutant.

The weapon fired again, blasting through Dredd's left kneepad and shattering his knee. His whole leg went numb but still his body hung just a whisker above the ground, like some grotesque human-sized puppet. The Lawgiver fired again and again and again, hitting Dredd in the shoulder, the arm, the chest. Blood was pouring from his wounds, his whole body was leaking its lifeblood onto the floor below him and there wasn't a thing he could do about it.

Miller threw up a hand to shield her face from the blazing lightstorm in the centre of the farmhouse.

'What the drokk is it?' she shouted.

'It's the girl!' yelled Karyn, pointing into the centre of the brightness.

Miller's bionic eyes adjusted moment by moment to the increasing glare. Squinting, she could just make out Hope's silhouette, floating above the ground angelically. The Judge looked around her to see the gila-munja attackers cowering before this visitation.

'She's stopping them!'

At that moment the lightstorm exploded outwards, engulfing the room in pure white.

'Now, where is the child? I can keep this up all day, or for years at a time, if you like, if you enjoy pain. Are you a masochist, Judge Dredd?' Now the Lawgiver floated towards Dredd and, twisting, lashed its heavy handle across his face. Then it lashed back the other way, backwards and forwards, pistol-whipping him to the edge of unconsciousness but always there was Soon, jerking at his mind to keep Dredd awake, keeping him aware.

'Oh no, no passing out! That would spoil all my fun!' smirked Soon, his eye glowing with passion. 'I haven't had this much fun since I shredded your little friend Judge Chung and sent her back to Mega-City One in a bodybag!'

Dredd's head snapped up at this, his eyes blazing with pure hatred at his captor.

'Touched a nerve have I? I must tell you, I particularly enjoyed the moment where I made her say that you had killed all the cadets on the Hotdog Run – and they believed her, too, the fools!'

* * *

269

And above, as the torture dragged on, the seconds ticked away.

'00.22.46; 00.22.45; 00.22.44 . . .'

Dredd's body was at the point of total collapse, just one leg tapering down to touch the ground below him, the rest held upright by Soon's sadism. The Judge's head lolled forward helplessly, unable to support itself any longer. Soon floated down to get a closer look at his victim.

'Not dead already, are we? I would hate to have to resurrect you, you're such a tiring conversationalist!'

Behind him a tiny white dot of light appeared and began to grow.

Soon reached out a hand, plucking at Dredd's helmet. 'I wonder what you look like under there. I forgot to take a look last time . . .'

The tiny dot kept growing, becoming larger, a circle of light, then elongating itself behind Soon.

The mutant Psi paused to scratch the back of his smooth, hairless head, feeling a tingling sensation at the nape of his neck, then lent forward, grasping both hands around the helmet of Judge Dredd, starting to pull it up and away from the head of the beaten, bloody, broken-bodied, barely conscious figure hanging in the air before him.

Suddenly Dredd's head jerked upwards and he stared straight into Soon's single eye. 'Hands off, creep!' he spat and head-butted the god-like figure across the bridge of his twisted nose, smashing it with a satisfying crack. A gush of blood began to pour from each nostril. 'Now!' shouted Dredd, over Soon's shoulder.

The injured monster turned round, clutching at

his broken face. A single finger reached out and touched his forehead.

Psi Judge Karyn opened her eyes to find herself staring up at the blue sky. 'What the drokk?' she wondered aloud and sat up. Around her the others were also waking up; Miller, Brighton, Cain, Joe and the three old women. Of the gila-munja there was no sign. 'We're alive?'

Miller looked out the window. 'The black zone – it's gone! All the gila-munja, they've disappeared!'

In Control headquarters, Hershey was in the last few minutes of the countdown when a monitoring Judge rushed over. 'You've got to see this, ma'am!'

She went to the tri-D display and looked down to find it clear, no sign of the black zone which had threatened to engulf all the Cursed Earth and soon Mega-City One itself. 'Have you checked the instruments? What happened?'

'All systems are fine, triple-checked. The darkness – it just disappeared!'

Hershey wondered for a minute what might have happened, then remembered why she was in Control in the first place. 'Stand down the sky defence!' she screamed across the huge room.

Up above the atmosphere, the countdown slowed, then halted.

'00.05.19; 00.05.18 and holding, holding, countdown erased. Countdown erased. Clock now stands at 12.00.00 and holding . . .'

'What happened?' asked Dredd from the floor where he lay, bleeding to death.

'I took his evil away. Now Soon is just a child like me, in age at least,' said Hope, now fully formed again.

'Here, let me help you.' She held a hand over Dredd's face and within a moment his injuries were gone, as if they had never existed. Dredd sat upright, looking around him.

'And the others?'

'They are safe – I froze them in time. That was why I had to leave you,' smiled the little girl. 'Come on, it's time to go home.'

'Soon – should we leave him here?'

'He can do no harm. He will remain like a four-year-old forever now. And the asylum is as good a home for him as any,' said the child, showing wisdom beyond her years. As they walked out of Erebus, the bones and blood and flesh began fading away, leaving the original glasseen towers and dome, clean and pristine again.

EPILOGUE

Tomorrow

'Time for us to leave. The Lord still has much work for us to do!' announced the reverend, grasping the reins of his steed. Both it and the mutant mule had been sheltered in the side-room of the farmhouse during the conflict, but now they were outside again in their natural habitat.

Preacher Cain hoisted himself up into the saddle and began to slowly trot away, heading south. Behind him, Joe was saying his last farewells to them all.

Hope laid a hand on his hump. 'I could take away your infirmity,' she offered.

'Oh no, I like my hump, reminds me I'm no better than anyone else and they're no better than me!' replied Joe, and soon he too was gone.

Brighton looked toward Hope. He already knew what had happened to Nita and the two other cadets, but no one had explained Soon's fate. 'What about the monster behind all of this? What happens to him?' he asked.

'He's a child again, trapped in an adult's body, a prisoner in his own fortress. Soon will never harm anyone again,' smiled the little girl, speaking with wisdom beyond her years.

'What about the asylum?'

'Look! Soon's handiwork is disappearing!'

The young Judge glanced up at the glass towers and could indeed see their bone cladding crumbling away from them already. He turned to Miller. 'I hate to ask a question I'll regret hearing the answer to, but how are we getting back to Mega-City One?'

'No killdozer, no Lawmasters – I guess we walk!' she replied, eliciting a groan of dismay from the young Judge. 'Don't worry, I'm sure an h-wagon will be out to investigate and should pick us up quite soon.'

Karyn winced. 'Don't say that word. I never want to hear it again!' With a smile she turned to say farewell to the old mutant women, but it vanished from her face. Dredd was standing next to Hope with his Lawgiver pointed at her head, one arm clutched tightly around the little girl.

'We're taking the girl with us,' he announced curtly.

'Dredd, what are you talking about? We saved her from Soon. He's no longer a threat, you said so yourself. Why do we have to take the girl?' demanded Karyn.

'She's too dangerous to leave out here with just three old crocks for protection. You forget, the conspirators were trying to snatch her too, to use against the Chief Judge. She's too dangerous for us to leave here.'

'So what do you suggest we do?' asked Miller.

'Take her back with us, have her enrolled in the Psi School at the Academy. She'll make a fine Psi Judge one day,' maintained Dredd.

'That's madness!' exclaimed Karyn. 'She wasn't born to enforce the Law, she's meant for a higher purpose than that. You know she is!'

'Well, either she comes back with us, or I kill her here and now – take no chances,' said Dredd bluntly.

The three old women, their expressions horrified, tried to intercede. 'No, please, kill us if you must, but leave the girl alive. She is the only hope for the planet . . .' one of them pleaded.

Dredd was unmoved. 'Nobody has to die but if anyone tries to stop me I kill them first, then the child.'

Karyn was about to step forward and put herself before the challenge, when she heard a voice in her head.

'It's all right, Karyn. Listen to me . . .'

There was silence, then Hope stepped away from Dredd and turned to face him. 'You must kill me, it's the only way to be sure.'

'What are you talking about? Hope, have you gone crazy?' protested the old women. To one side stood Miller and Brighton, not speaking, watching impassively, trying to control their own feelings.

'No, Judge Dredd is right, I must die – here, now. I could never become a Psi Judge and I'm too dangerous to leave alive. Kill me, Judge Dredd,' she implored him.

Dredd stepped forward and pressed the barrel of his Lawgiver against her small forehead.

'I forgive you,' she said in a small voice.

Karyn and Brighton turned away, not wanting to watch. Miller looked away. The old women sobbed quietly.

Judge Dredd pulled the trigger and Hope died.

EPILOGUE TWO

Two Hours Later

The funeral was a simple affair, just a little box constructed from the wood of the farmhouse's window shutters. Brighton and Miller had dug the shallow grave and the old mutant women laid the coffin inside it, all the time staring at Dredd who stood away to one side, keeping his thoughts to himself.

Karyn said a few words but they seemed hollow after all that had happened. Eventually, the four Judges gathered together and began the long walk back towards Mega-City One, numbed into silence. As they walked away, they didn't even notice the area had been cleansed of radiation.

A tiny voice appeared in Karyn's head for the last time.

'Thank you for your silence, Karyn. We had to convince Dredd and the others that he'd killed me, or the Judges would come searching for me again someday, sooner or later.'

'Where will you go?' asked Karyn.

'We're moving over again, I can't tell you where, it's better that you don't know. In fact – '

'I know. You have to take away my memories of you, let me believe that Dredd killed you like the others do.'

276

'Yes. I'm sorry, but it's necessary.'

'That's all right,' said Karyn softly. 'It's worth it, to give the world back its hope. Goodbye.'

'Goodbye, Karyn.' And the memory faded, leaving just a bitter taste in the Psi Judge's recollection of the last few hours, yet still some faint, unexplainable peace too.

Back on the abandoned farm, a single white daisy appeared in the field, sprouting up from where Hope had been buried.

In minutes it had opened, blossoming, soaking up the sunshine. Around it, hundreds, thousands more blooms were springing up. This ground was the Cursed Earth no longer, if only in one small place.

And deep inside Erebus, the curled up figure of Soon rocked slowly backwards and forwards, backwards and forwards, the eyes serene and untroubled. But deep inside the child-like mind, in one tiny corner, a little voice was still shouting.

'Kill you! Kill you all – forever! Especially you, Judge Joe Dredd!'